BLACKBIRD

LISA SHELBY

LISA SHELBY BOOKS, LLC

Blackbird

ISBN: 9781794064195

Cover Design: Bite Me Graphic Design

Editor: Ellie McLove at My Brother's Editor

S,

As always, this is for you.
Thank you for sharing your dreams with me.
Thank you for going on this crazy ride with me.
Thank you for being my home.

L

1

Huck ~ Now

"Sorry, little buddy, but I don't understand sign language."

To say the little boy sitting in the waiting room chair across from me is cute would be the understatement of the year. With his little round glasses, his perfectly spiked blond hair and his chubby little hands and cheeks, he's a welcome distraction. The beige waiting room, complete with standard issue fish tank and magazine racks covered in celebrities and royals has me feeling itchy, but he's brought a smile to my face and to do that here, in this place, is saying something.

His mom; blonde, attractive and undeniably exhausted, signs my reply back to him and without hesitation, he slides off his chair and is rubbing his little fingers over the intricate details of the tattoo spanning the length of my forearm. The tattoo that represents who I used to be. Who I'll never be again.

I glance up at his mom who shyly apologizes for his excitement, but I wave her off and let her know it's okay.

His little fingers stop tickling the bird on my arm when he looks up at me with the sweetest smile I have ever seen.

I'm not sure what it is about him, but this kid makes me all warm and fuzzy inside. I don't do warm and fuzzy. Not anymore.

"Do you like birds, little man?" I can't help but want to hang with this little nugget. I mean, he's wearing a Hulk Smash shirt, the Hulk is practically my spirit-animal.

He looks to his mom who signs my question and he signs something back. She doesn't get to translate for me though. Their attention is taken when the waiting room door opens. My new friend takes off in a flash to run toward the foot holding the door open. I can't take my eyes off him as I follow him across the waiting room marveling at his exuberance. If only I could muster his level of excitement to be here.

His mom waves goodbye, still shy and when I look back at little mister exuberance my heart stops and my entire body throbs like one big pounding pulse as my heart beats so hard and fast it takes over my body. The owner of the foot has come into view bringing my life to a screeching halt. The little boy plows into her and wraps his arms around her legs.

This cannot be happening.

Her mouth falls open and her eyes, still the bright color of emerald gemstones, are huge with shock and glistening with tears, a smile slowly forming on her perfect lips.

Flashes of the moonlight dancing across her tan skin, giggles floating on the salt air and the memories of us mixed with the sand, surf and sun play like a montage through my brain.

Before she has a chance to speak or engage me in any way, the option of flight or fight kicks in. I choose flight.

It's all too much.

I never called.

Two years and I never fucking called.

Pretending I don't see her, like the coward I am, I make a hasty escape out of the waiting room, begging myself not to look back. The risk that comes with real eye contact with her is too great. How do I explain where I've been or not want to kill myself when I see the inevitable pity in her eyes?

Seeing her in person is an all-consuming combination of each and every one of my dreams coming true only to crash head first into my worst nightmares.

I dream of her every night.

Her face. Those freckles. That giggle of hers.

But those dreams usually turn into nightmares when her soft sweet features change to pity and sadness as she realizes I'm no longer the man she met two years ago. More often than not, I wake up screaming...begging for her forgiveness. Forgiveness she doesn't owe me. No matter how hard I try to latch on to the dreams full of paradise, the nightmares seem to leave a deeper mark.

I feel her rushing after me catching a flash of her dark blue clothes out of my peripheral as I all but sprinted out of the office, you know, like a man who doesn't have the balls to face up to his broken promises. Not looking back, I've made my escape and in seconds I'm slamming through the door at the end of the hall leading to the stairs. The thought of standing in place waiting for the elevator seems inconceivable at the moment.

Keep moving. I need to keep moving.

Flying down four flights of stairs at a fast clip I bust out of the stairwell door landing in the parking garage heaving with anger, just like the image on the little boy's t-shirt. Storming to my bike, throwing on my helmet and bringing the engine to life, my bike is the relief I'm looking for. She vibrates all the way through my body, rattling my bones. Providing the calm I need.

The clouds above hang low, threatening rain. I could care less. I plan on riding until I run out of gas.

Running away from the pain and the loss are what I seem to do best these days. My bike and my rum are the only things getting me through.

2

Huck ~ Then

"Thanks for the hookup, man. I'll see you tonight." Nico and I do our bro-shake, the one we created several years back on a drunken night here in Bali and somehow never forgot.

I've been coming to Bali for years. It's my respite from the intensity of my job and my home away from home. Nico was one of the first people I met way back when. Preferring watering holes where the locals spend their time and not frequenting the louder places tourists tend to flock to, I met Nico and his brother, Marcus, in a bar down a dark alley years ago. We drank, we talked, we sang songs on the beach. It was an instant friendship.

"I'll be there and I'm bringing Marcus. It's been too long since we all hung out."

"Truer words have never been spoken, my man. I'll see you guys tonight."

"Sounds good, dude. Oh hey, don't forget…"

I don't hear another syllable coming out of Nico's mouth

because my ears are filled with the sweetest sound I have ever heard.

Her giggle is floating on the breeze atop the sound of the crashing waves just feet away. Turning toward the sound, my heart nearly stops when I take in a sight unlike anything my eyes have ever seen.

Sitting under an umbrella relaxing on a lounger, is simply put...perfection. Long dark hair and even longer legs peek out of her short black cover-up. Freckles dance across the bridge of her perfect button nose and her tan skin would allude to the fact she's been here all week, but there's no way I could have missed her if she had been within a hundred-mile radius. She's laughing with reckless abandon while applying balm to her full pink lips. Laughs out loud as though she doesn't have a care in the world.

She radiates pure joy and natural beauty.

Nico's grabbing my shoulder attempting to stop me as I gravitate toward her but what happens next is out of my control. It's like my body has been taken over by some sort of alien-like creature focused solely on her and the rest of the world fades away.

I've only taken a few steps when I'm stopped in my tracks. She's picked up what looks to be what's left of a pina colada and she's trying her damnedest to take a drink but try as she might, she can't get the straw in her mouth. Her tongue keeps popping out of her perfect lips but cannot seem to find the damn straw. She must be reading something good because I swear, she wouldn't take her eyes off the page if her lounger burst into flames. Completely engrossed in her book, she hasn't even noticed me standing a few feet away gawking at her.

The book in her hand has a bold cover and I can easily see it's called *44 Chapters About Four Men.* I'd give my left nut to know what these four men have that have her so transfixed. I may have to jump online and order myself a copy and educate myself.

She turns the page while continuing to giggle but this go

around, she bites down on the straw keeping it in place so she can suck down the sugary goodness she had so desperately been in search of.

Fuck me if that straw between her teeth while she smiles at her book, isn't the hottest thing I've seen.

The slurping sound from her straw indicates she's clearly run out of her drink, but she swirls the glass and tries again hoping to get more out of it. I take this as my cue and take advantage of the opportunity.

"Looks like you're out. Can I get you another one?" I ask, approaching her chair without thinking, getting an even better glimpse of her.

Still not looking up from her book she replies. "Sure, that would be great. No rush though. Just on your next time around."

Ha! She thinks I work here.

I must chuckle out loud because she finally looks up from her book.

"Oh, my gosh. I am so sorry. I thought you were Nico." She leans to the side looking around me where he's spying a few feet back and gives him a wave.

"Sorry about my friend, Miss Keaton, he was just leaving. I'll bring you another one right away."

"Please, for the tenth time today, call me Harper, Nico, and take your time. No rush at all. I have a bottle of water in my bag," she says sweetly. The voice of a goddamned angel.

"You'd have to put down your book to open a bottle of water. You sure you're up for that?"

"Excuse me?" My audacity has her lifting her sunglasses up to the top of her head to get a better look at the stranger hovering over her. I'm a goner when her bright emerald greens stare me down with a look that says, *Who the hell are you?*

Her eyes aren't just green. They fucking sparkle.

I'm a grown ass man, but there is no other way to describe

them. I swear they're filled with a million tiny crystals that make her eyes shine or better yet, fucking sparkle.

"Cat got your tongue?"

Shit. How long have I been gawking at her? *Smooth, Finnegan. Real smooth.* She's still waiting for an answer so I clear my throat and will myself not to make an even bigger ass of myself. Something I don't usually have to worry about, but this woman already has me feeling off balance. I like it.

"Uh, yeah. I saw you struggling to wrangle your straw. My guess is with a bottle of water you'll need two hands to get the lid off and from the look of things, you're way too into your book to put it down."

"Yeah?"

Never taking her eyes off me, she puts down her empty glass, reaches into her bag, pulls out her bottle of water and places it between her thighs. Her thighs are tan and toned, but there is no way I'm looking at them while she's keeping her gaze on me. Besides, I already have them memorized. The vision of her sitting under her umbrella was etched into my memory the moment I saw her.

With the bottle between her legs, she squeezes them together and holds tight so it isn't going anywhere and then with her book in one hand she twists the cap with the other. As much as I want to look down at the bottle between her legs, there is no way I'm taking my eyes off hers. As long as her eyes are set on me, I'm not moving a muscle. She casually sets the cap down on the table and takes a long slow drink.

Her eyes never leave mine.

Her confidence is sexy as hell.

I'm not sure how I'm still on my feet because this woman has fucking hit me like a truck.

"I stand corrected," I say, admitting defeat. Defeat that is oh, so worth conceding.

"Never underestimate a stranger. You never know what you might get."

"I promise never to make that mistake again." I take two more steps closing the space between us and offer my hand. "Huck. Nice to meet you."

Her head tilts to the side as if she's contemplating whether or not to take my outstretched offering. Luckily, her contemplation leads her in my direction, and she shakes my hand. Firmly. Confidently.

"Harper."

"It's nice to meet you, Harper," I say without letting go of her.

"Huck, huh?" she questions with her hand still in mine, making no effort to release it.

"Benjamin James Finnegan at your service, but my friends call me Huck."

"Ah, because of your last name. Huck Finn. I get it."

"I'm impressed. You're clearly more than just your water bottle opening skills."

"Damn straight, Mr. Finnegan."

She tries to release my hand, but when I give her a tiny squeeze, she stops her efforts.

"Aw, come on. I thought we were friends. Call me Huck."

"Friends, huh?" she says, sliding her hand from mine and leaving me wanting much more of her touch.

"Oh, I would definitely say we were friends."

"Okay, Romeo…time for you to go and leave Miss Keaton to her vacation," Nico says, walking behind her lounger and mouthing *GET OUT* as he drags his fingers across his throat illustrating how he's gonna kill me if I don't get to stepping, but I continue to ignore him, never truly taking my attention from her.

"Harper," we both say without looking at Nico correcting him when he calls her Miss Keaton again. Neither of us can stop the grins that grace our lips.

"It's okay, Nico. If he's a friend of yours, he can't be that bad, right?"

"Exactly," I confirm. "So, please, Harper, call me Huck."

"Huck…" Nico warns.

"Listen, I don't want to get my friend in trouble so, I'm gonna get out of here."

Swinging one final blow, she pulls her sunglasses down and devastatingly takes her eyes away from view. She picks up her book and it's clear she thinks our conversation is over.

Oh, honey. We are so far from done.

"Well, it was nice to meet you, Huck." She opens her book and looks away thinking she can dismiss me.

She's not getting rid of me so easily. And if she's honest with herself, she doesn't want to either. I can see it in her eyes. Hell, I can feel it in the static electricity in the air.

"Harper, I'd really like to see you again."

Nico's now jumping up and down in the sand behind her signaling for me to abort the mission, but again, I ignore him.

"Is that so?" she asks her book.

"I think you know it is."

"Wow, you always so sure of yourself, *Huck*?" she asks, finally looking away from her book and making an exaggerated point to call me Huck.

"I just think we could be really good friends."

"Friends, huh?"

"Great friends."

Shit! Could you sound creepier, Finnegan? Now she probably thinks you're some kind of sicko stalker or something.

"Sorry, that sounded a little creepy didn't it?"

She lifts a brow in reply.

"What I meant to say is, I would really like to see you again."

Her giggle, the one that stopped me in my tracks minutes ago, takes center stage again and even though she's laughing at me, I know I'm right. I have to see her again. "Listen, I'm going to be back here later tonight, meet me here, over by the bonfire. If it makes you feel better, Nico and his brother, Marcus, will be here too."

"*Sundays*? Meet you here at the beach club? This place is a first come first served sort of place and impossible to get a spot at night. I was only gonna stay about another hour before I head back to my room. I'm not sure I'll be able to get back early enough to get a spot. Maybe next time."

"Nice try, but I've got it handled. I work here from time to time and I'll be sure to save you a spot. So, you go do what you were gonna do and meet me back here tonight. It'll be fun. Say yes."

"Hmm…thank you for the offer but—"

"Don't say no!" I blurt out. It's clear by the satisfied look on her face my desperation to see her again has been exposed, and that's fine by me. "Think about it. I'll save you a place either way. Show up any time after seven and if it makes you more comfortable feel free to bring someone with you."

"You mean, like another *friend* like you?"

"Oh, Harper," I say, giving her my best attempt at a charming grin while gritting my teeth at the prospect of her bringing another *friend*. "You don't have any other friends like me."

Shit, of course a woman like her is probably taken. Please, God, let her be single.

"Do you have a *friend* to bring?"

"Not at the moment, but the day is young."

"How about a boyfriend back home?"

"Don't have one of those either."

Thank you, Jesus!

"Then it's settled. I'll save you a spot with a good view. You'll know it when you see it." I know I'm grinning like an idiot, but I can't help it. "I'll see you tonight."

I walk backward in the sand not wanting to take my eyes off her. She continues to watch me from behind her glasses and it's clear…

She feels it too.

A few steps later, Nico cuts off my line of sight and turns me by my shoulders, escorting me away from his guest.

"Dude, are you trying to get me fired?"

"Nah, man. She's cool. You aren't gonna get fired," I say, looking over my shoulder for one last glance only to find her still watching.

I knew it!

"Bro, you know my boss cannot see my friend showing up here on the property accosting guests."

"Give me a break. We talked for two minutes. Besides, technically, I'm an employee too."

"She's out of your league, Huck."

"Nico, that woman isn't just out of my league, she's a damn game changer."

"Shit, Huck! Please don't…"

"Dude, there isn't a damn thing I can do about it. It's out of my control."

3

Harper ~ Now

My heart's racing and I'm pretty sure time just stopped.

I can't breathe.

It can't be.

Was Huck really just standing in front of me?

It all happened so fast.

By the time the shock of seeing him had settled in, the disappointment crushed me. Anger and sadness crossed his features the moment he saw me and the hurt hit me like a bus. Before I had a chance to react, he was rushing out of the office without a backward glance.

I let go of Tyler and rushed after him, but once I hit the hallway and saw the door to the stairwell slam shut, I had to remind myself that I was at work and I couldn't just abandon my next appointment because the love of my life showed up out of the blue.

Besides, he was already long gone.

"Harper?"

Our receptionist, Penny, tries to get my attention as I drag myself back into the office. She's worried. She should be. I think I'm seeing things because if he was just here, why would he have run away from me?

Unless he wasn't here for me.

"I'm fine, Penny." I turn my attention to Molly and Tyler who are still waiting by the door to go back for our weekly appointment. "I am so sorry about that."

"No need to be sorry. Are you okay, Harper?"

Good question.

"Molly, did you just see a ridiculously handsome man rush out of the office?"

She chuckles. "I did. He caught Tyler's attention too. It would be impossible not to notice him, if I'm being honest."

"So, you saw him? He wasn't a figment of my imagination?"

"Sweetie, he was here. I talked to him. He was really patient with Tyler and let him touch his tattoo."

"Blackbird."

"Yeah, I'm pretty sure it was a bird or something like that?"

Unprepared for such a detailed confirmation that my beautiful, sweet Huck was just here, I start to shake inside and out, and the first tear falls.

Shit! Not here. Pull yourself together, Harper. Just get through the day.

Molly's rubbing my back and Tyler pulls on my hand looking concerned. "Sorry, guys. Let's head back."

"You sure?"

"I'm more than sure. Besides, only getting to see this handsome little man once a week is never enough! How is it possible he gets cuter every time I see him?"

I squat down and give Tyler a hug letting him know I'm okay. He pulls back and puts his chubby little hands on my cheeks and poignantly looks me in the eye. This magical little boy doesn't need to say a word. His sweet touch and the sincere concern in his eyes says he sees me, he's worried about me and he doesn't want me to be sad. How could his father have ever left him? He has no idea what love and joy he is missing out on.

I let Tyler know I'm fine and had seen an old friend that brought back lots of happy memories. Of course, he didn't believe me. This little man is wise beyond his years.

It wasn't all a lie. There were happy memories, but there were also memories of heartbreak, fear, and wondering where exactly he had been these past two years. My hand goes to the tattoo on the inside of my left wrist and my thumb ghosts over the memento that reminds me of him every time I touch it. I don't have time for memory lane though. I have a little boy and his mom waiting on me.

"Okay, Tyler let's go. You're always my favorite part of the week," I say, squeezing his cheeks. "And just what I need right now."

Molly gives me a knowing look. She can tell I'd rather be anywhere but here and she's sorry. But there's no need for her to be sorry. It was more than obvious Huck wasn't here to see me. In fact, he couldn't get away from me fast enough.

I spend the rest of the day distracting myself with work. I'll fall apart when I get home tonight.

4

Harper ~ Then

I can't believe I'm doing this, but then again, I can't believe I opened a bottle of water with the assistance of my thighs this afternoon just to prove a point to a stranger. It's not like I flashed him or anything, but I still have no idea what came over me. Maybe it was his undeniable charm or the itty-bitty fact that he is without a doubt the hottest man I've ever met in the flesh. Whatever it was about him brought out the flirty side of me. I mean it's not like I don't know how to flirt, but it's been a while. I should have been intimidated by a man like him…but instead he brought out a confidence I didn't even know I had.

Now, here I am, in a foreign country, wandering around the beach looking for a saved spot he said I wouldn't be able to miss. However, the big blue puffy chairs, or *puffs* as they call them, all seem to be full of people who were smart enough to get here early, because it's the only way to get a spot on the beach by the fire.

Harper, you are so stupid. This Huck guy was full of crap and you fell for it hook, line, and sinker.

I'm not the kind of girl who falls for a lazy smile or gets distracted by the gold flecks that pop out of hazel eyes. Hazel eyes I was lost in the moment he reached out to shake my hand. Or maybe it was the handshake and the shock of adrenaline that pulsed through me every second our hands were connected. Then there was his voice. Rich and smooth. It could have been the smile or the arms on full display in his tank. Hell, I'm not sure what it was, but he's certainly done something to me.

First, I flirt with him like a professional working her corner and now, here I am, regretting the fact that I didn't follow my gut instinct not to show up here alone.

About to leave, because it's clear he's stood me up, I see one lone puff along the edges of all the others that surround the fire. Only this puff is off on its own a little closer to the restaurant and bar.

Dying inside, I do my best to casually saunter to the empty bean bag chair. This is the moment that will…well, I'm not sure what it will mean. If it's not saved for me, it will be a nice little slap in the face and a reminder not to succumb to the charms of a man with the charisma and looks of Ben Finnegan. If it is saved for me, well…I'm not quite sure what exactly it will mean, but it scares me more than the first prospect.

Approaching the one and only empty spot on the beach, I keep looking over my shoulder to see if I can spot him, or maybe the camera crew filming the practical joke being played on me, but nothing seems out of the ordinary. There's a note on the empty puff, but because the sun has already set, I need my phone to light the paper. I silently thank God it's dark out here because I can feel the blush rush up my neck and straight to my face and set my ears on fire.

Freckles,
Yes, that means you, Harper.
Your pina colada is on its way.
Sit back, relax and enjoy the show.
I'll see you after.
Huck

Whoa.

What did I say about his charisma?

This guy knows what he's doing…he's already given me a nickname.

Yes, he is oh, so very charming.

I fold up the note, tucking it into the pocket of my cut-off jean shorts and take my seat on the overstuffed bean bag shaped like a chair. I know it's a piece of paper and light as a feather but it feels like I've just dropped a ten-pound dumbbell in my pocket. The weight of emotions from those few simple lines is unexpectedly heavy.

I've been sitting down for no longer than thirty-seconds when a sweet Balinese woman with a bright smile hands me a tall frothy pina colada just like Huck promised.

She's beautiful. There is no escaping her effortless beauty. Her black hair cascades down her back and her skin glows without a stitch of makeup on, because she doesn't need it. But it's her smile, the one that says she knows something I don't, lighting her up.

"Mr. Finnegan says he hopes you enjoy the show and he looks forward to seeing you after," she says, all too pleased with herself.

"What do you mean? He isn't meeting me here?"

I am so confused.

Her smile turns coy and she points in the direction of the

stage. "He's here, Miss Keaton. Let me know if you need anything else." With that, she's gone and once again I'm left wondering what exactly is going on here tonight and how does she know my name?

Luckily, I don't have to wait long to find out.

Sitting down on a stool and resting an acoustic guitar on his lap is a tall, tan, sandy-haired man dressed in blue and white board shorts, a simple white t-shirt and flip-flops. He looks like he was born to live the life of surf and sand.

He finds me the moment his butt hits his stool, grabs the microphone in front of him with one hand while his other hand rests easily atop his instrument. He looks like he's about to say something but nothing comes out. Instead, he holds my gaze like we're the only two people on the beach.

I can't help it, I start to giggle at his blatant staring and the corner of his mouth lifts, and he finally comes to his senses.

"Good evening, everyone. How about some music?" he asks the crowd with a crooked smile.

The moment his fingers strum the strings on his guitar and the beginning chords of a song I've known and loved for years hits my ears, I'm instantly turned on.

When he opens his mouth and starts singing my favorite Jason Mraz song, I melt on the spot. A mere puddle of the woman I was when I got here. If I thought I was turned on a few seconds ago with just his guitar playing…I was seriously mistaken. Pressing my thighs together I try to suppress the ache developing deep within my core, but it's no use.

He's charming, handsome, *and* he's talented! Not to mention, we spoke for about two minutes earlier today and he knows my drink of choice and has already given me a nickname.

You don't stand a chance against this guy, Harper.

He's not playing fair. What woman can resist a man with looks and talent! It's a deadly combination.

Most of the patrons are roasting marshmallows, talking, drinking and doing their own thing so there's no clapping when he finishes his first song. He jumps to the next in his swoon-worthy line up of campfire songs unfazed and plays for the next hour. Rarely taking his eyes off me, he keeps me pinned to the spot.

At some point, Nico came by to check on me and introduce me to his older brother, Marcus. It was sweet of him yet annoyed me at the same time. It meant I was missing part of Huck's performance. I didn't want to miss a note. I think it was pretty clear to Nico I didn't feel like chatting. He left quickly, but not before he made sure I knew where he was in case I needed him.

For some reason as Nico walked away, I did come to my senses long enough to ask. "Nico, he's a good guy, right?"

"Miss Keaton, he's one of the best." He smiled and walked away before I could remind him to call me by my first name.

That's what I thought.

I'm screwed.

By the time his set is done, I've had two pina coladas and my original nerves have waned. This doesn't mean I don't start freaking out again when he takes his guitar from around his neck and gently places it in its case, closing up shop for the night. It's one thing to watch him from afar and another to actually talk to him again.

I swear my nerves are worse than when I first got here. After listening to him play and sing, I know he's going to be hard to resist. It's as if I am his prey just sitting here in this puffy blue bean bag chair waiting to be eaten.

He disappears from view but not before giving me another glance and heart stopping smile that says *don't go anywhere.* I couldn't go anywhere if I tried, these chairs are not easy to get out of. Maybe that was all a part of his master plan?

Just when I think my nerves may get the best of me and my

insides are knotted up with fear, excitement and the giddiness of a teenager, he comes bounding down the stairs from the restaurant above us. He's calm and casual when I am as far from those two things as I could be.

A few seconds later he's standing in front of me and all hope of this evening ending without having a serious crush, at the very least, is lost. Something about the way he looks me in the eyes and doesn't waver, has a way of hypnotizing me. I've never experienced anything so intense.

"Hey, Freckles. Glad you came."

"Me too. You were great." He uses my new nickname again and I'd be lying if I said I didn't kinda love it.

"Thanks. Let me grab one of these, be right back," he says referring to the puff I'm sitting in.

I wiggle my way out of my chair and stretch. There are even more people here than when I originally sat down, but I was so captivated by Huck I clearly had no idea what was happening around me. There are a lot of people who have abandoned their bean bags and are sitting in the sand. Huck talks to a couple and after their short conversation, they are both grinning ear to ear and he leaves them with his own puff to sit in, in his hands.

He plops his chair down and then spins mine around so it's touching his and we'll be facing the fire. Holding his hand out he gestures toward my chair and once I take my seat, he takes his, like a gentleman.

"Hi," he says quietly and sincerely turning in his chair, giving me his full attention.

"Hi," I reply back shyly, pretending not to feel the butterflies performing a full ballet in my stomach.

"So, tell me everything."

"Tell you everything? I don't even know you."

I don't mean to sound as shrill as I do, but seriously, he's a stranger to me. Albeit, a hot stranger, but a stranger none the less.

"Well, I'm hoping to change that. Let's make it easy. How about a game of twenty questions? Or more. We've got all night."

"Don't get ahead of yourself, Mr. Finnegan."

His reply is a toothy grin.

"Fine, we'll play, but me first."

"Shoot."

"Are you here on vacation? It seems as though everyone in Bali knows who you are, but you don't look like a native." I gesture to his floppy dirty blond hair, so he gets what I mean.

"Well, I have a job that's pretty all-consuming but also gives me long breaks in-between…projects and this is where I come to decompress. I hope to be here for another month, but if I get the call, I'll have to go."

"Wow, sounds interesting. What do you do for a living?"

"Nice try, Freckles. One question and then it's my turn. Them are the rules, little lady."

"You mean, those are your rules. Whatever. I'm patient. I can wait."

"A patient woman? What are you?" He leans in like he has a secret. "Some kind of unicorn?"

"Ha, ha. Very funny. Is that your question?"

"Nope, more of a statement." Oh man, he's good because my heart just dropped to my stomach when he leaned in and whispered his joke about me being a unicorn. I can barely breathe. "So, who are you here with?"

"I'm here with family and some family friends. My dad's getting married on Saturday. He flew a small group out and rented a villa for all of us here at The Ungasan. My turn. What do you do for a living?"

"I can't answer that."

"What? No way. That's not an answer!"

"If I told you, I'd have to kill you."

"Oh, please. You mean..." He nods his head before I finish the rest of my sentence. "You're serious."

"Well, I wouldn't have to kill you but let's just say I can't really talk about it."

"Is whatever you do, legal? Oh, please God tell me you aren't a freaking drug lord or something like that. I knew you were too good to be true."

When he grins ear to ear, I realize my mistake. Word vomit. It's a thing. And it's what I just did. I am such an idiot and here's hoping the firelight doesn't betray me and show my blush.

"First, that's two questions, but I'll give you this one. Yes, it's legal. Second, I'm not too good to be true, far from it, but I like where your head's at."

"Your turn," I huff, embarrassed.

"Okay, moving on. What do you do for a living or do you live off of your daddy? He must be doing okay if he can afford to rent out a villa for family and friends."

Excuse me? Did he really just say that?

"No, I do not live off of my *daddy* and I have to say that it pisses me off you would assume so." His eyes go wide and he opens his mouth but I cut him off. "Also, my dad worked his ass off to get to where he is. He owns his own electrical contracting company and started from the very bottom to finally owning his own company and having a ton of hard-earned success in California. We haven't always lived this lifestyle and I would never mooch off my father's hard work."

"Harper, I didn't mean to offend you. I was really just kidding."

I ignore his apology, but I can tell it was sincere. I go ahead and answer his initial question. "What do I do for a living? Well, I'd love to tell you but then I'd have to kill you and we're trying to get to know each other so, that seems counterproductive."

"Touché."

"Does your tattoo represent anything special?"

"Tattoo?"

"I'm thinking you know what I'm referring to."

I point to his arm even though it's not necessary.

"Oh, you mean the bird." He's playing stupid knowing I'm referring to the giant blackbird on his arm. The bird's body takes up most of his forearm and its outstretched wings wrap around his toned biceps. With the exception of the red tuft of feathers on its chest it's all black and pretty hard to miss.

"Yes, the bird." I roll my eyes and he smiles looking oh, so coy.

"Well, there was a time when I was a little obsessed with *The Beatles,* particularly the song "Blackbird." My grandmother was sick and the song really resonated with me. Not only did I walk around singing it day and night, but I would also spend all my free time teaching myself how to play it on my guitar. The guys at work had to endure my singing and playing for weeks and in the end, they dubbed me Blackbird. That's been my call sign ever since."

Call sign?

He's dragging his forefinger along the intricate feathers adorning the bird on his arm and seems lost in thought.

"It's beautiful."

He clears his throat and grins ever so slightly. "I got it after losing my grandma."

"I'm so sorry for your loss."

"Thanks for that, but she was pretty tired and had fought a long hard battle for a really long time. It was for the best but we all still miss her. She was the rock of the family and all I can hope is that I make her proud."

"I'm sure you do."

He claps his hands together as if to break the slightly sullen mood he's fallen into. "So, how about you? Any tattoos?"

"Nope. My turn."

"Bring it."

"How many other unsuspecting tourists have you lured here to listen to you sing? My guess is it's worked for you in the past."

"Jealous already, I like it." He gives me an all-knowing wink. I know his arrogance should turn me off but all it does is pull me in deeper. "No need to lure anyone here, but if I'm being honest?"

"Always."

"Well, there is a lot of self-promotion that goes into doing a show here so, I have invited quite a few people." He can tell by the look on my face that I'm not falling for this lame non-answer and the smirk on his face gets bigger. "No, Harper. I don't make it a habit of hooking up with tourists. You're the first person I've invited to watch me play with the intention of getting to know them better."

"Your turn," I reply, trying not to let on that his answer is exactly what I wanted to hear.

"Do you often accept invitations from total strangers?"

I drop my face in my hands in total humiliation and my laughter bubbles to the surface. "No!" I'm laughing really loud now but the sound is swallowed up by the noise of people talking, the crackling of the fire and the crashing of the waves. "This is so not me! I don't flirt poolside and I don't meet up with random strangers."

"So, what you're saying is I have some kind of effect on you?"

There's no stopping the eye roll that follows his arrogant comment. "That's two questions."

"It's okay. I get it. You're not ready to admit there's something here. You'll get there."

Again, with the cocky attitude.

"You are a very confident man, aren't you?"

"Kind of like the effect I have on you…you are having quite

an impact on me too. I heard you before I saw you and I knew in that split second you were a game changer."

I'm sorry, what? Did he really just say that?

"Wow, you really are something, aren't you?"

I can act like his boldness bothers me but it's all a front. I know exactly what he means but I'd never admit it to him. Not in a million years.

5

Huck ~ Now

I've been running for an hour when I slap the STOP button on the treadmill and step off the machine, my legs feeling like a pair of limp noodles. I wipe a towel over my face to try to get rid of some of the sweat raining down on me. When I bring the towel down, I catch a glimpse of myself in the mirror.

I see a man who, on the outside, looks whole and capable but the truth is, I'm broken. My dog tags rest on the olive drab t-shirt with the word DELTA in all caps across the front and I can't help but wonder if I still deserve to wear it.

Am I still a part of the team? Technically, yes. But being stuck here at Fort Hunter Liggett training real soldiers to do the job I did proudly for so many years is not exactly my version of being part of the team.

"Fucking pogue," I say, taking a disgusted glance at myself before I head to the stacks. Pogues are paper pushers. They aren't grunts or operators out there on the front lines. Operators don't wear regulation haircuts. Reg cuts are for boots and paper pushers when it comes to those of us in Special Forces. After finally getting through all my rehab, I work out more now than I ever did and I'm bigger and stronger than I've ever been.

Not that it matters.

Seeing her yesterday sent me into a tailspin that meant going way too fast on my bike only to go home and spend the evening with my old friend Jack. I can't believe I was out of rum on a night when I needed it the most. My sleep consisted of dreams full of green eyes, freckles and ocean waves that would twist and turn into nightmares over and over again. The only reason I slept at all was most certainly due to the empty bottle I tripped over when I stumbled to the bathroom this morning.

I was still feeling shitty when I got to work but when I opened my email the day just got shittier. My Master Sergeant wanted a recap of how my first appointment had gone. He knows, as well as I do, these appointments aren't a requirement of the job but we've worked together for years and he's my family. He only asks because he cares. He knows that I need something to get me out of the downward spiral I can't seem to pull my way out of.

As much as I hate to admit it, I do need help.

It's not easy for a man like me to admit I need this kind of help, but if I am going to do this, I won't do it with her there. She's a reminder of what I used to be, and it hurts too damn bad to think of what I could have been.

What *we* could have been.

I know it makes me a pussy, but I'm not sure I have what it takes to come face to face with her again.

Not now.

Maybe not ever.

How could I ever express to her how sorry I am? Would she ever believe me when I tell her I thought I was doing us both a favor by leaving the way I did? The thought of seeing the hurt in her eyes caused by me leaves me sick to my stomach. I could have stayed in Bali with her forever, but we don't always get what we want.

I tighten my grip on the metal of the barbell at my feet, lift it carefully to my waist and in one quick move push it above my head, all with perfect form. The poster I use as my focal point mocks me telling me to suck it the fuck up.

YOU MUST HURT IN ORDER TO KNOW
FALL IN ORDER TO GROW
LOSE IN ORDER TO GAIN
BECAUSE LIFE'S GREATEST LESSONS
ARE LEARNED THROUGH PAIN

Until yesterday these words were what I was doing my best to live by, but after seeing her, the pain it wants me to learn from is more prevalent than ever and all I want to do is run away.

Away from her.

Away from Top and his concerns about my well-being.

Away from this job that isn't what I ever wanted…or at least not until I was on old-timer nearing retirement.

I drop the two hundred and twenty-five pounds from above my head to the mat below and feel the weights rattle from my feet to my chest.

I love that feeling.

I stare at the poster and repeat the lift over and over until I'm afraid I may not be able to do it again. Each time I drop the weights back to the ground the pounding of them hitting the floor reverberates through me making me want to push harder.

This is why I spend so much time in here. There may be sweat stains on the walls, it's hot as fucking balls and smells like a goddamned dirty jock strap but this dank room is the only place I feel whole.

The yellowing clock on the wall that I'm pretty sure has been here since this army base was built back in 1941, tells me my time is up and it's time to hit the shower and get back to work. I have a new class starting next week and I have to finish all my prep work before leaving for the weekend.

~

I think today has been the longest Friday on record. Next week's class is ready to go and I can't wait to get out from behind this desk. Every minute my ass sits in this government issue chair, behind this ugly metal desk, feels like prison.

My very own solitary confinement.

Monterey is beautiful. Fort Hunter Liggett is unlike any other Army base I've ever been on. With its Hispanic architecture and wild elk roaming the hills, there are worse places to be. But every day I spend in the recycled air of this drab beige office I feel myself decaying slowly but surely.

If only I had finished a couple of minutes earlier I wouldn't have to end this shitty day with a guilty IM exchange from my boss and best friend.

Thomas Bradford: Stop ignoring me, asshole.

Benjamin Finnegan: Not ignoring. Been busy.

. . .

Thomas Bradford: So, how was the appointment?

Benjamin Finnegan: Something came up.

Thomas Bradford: Huck. Man, not again.

Benjamin Finnegan: I don't need a lecture.

Thomas Bradford: Just looking out for you, brother. You know you need to do this.

Benjamin Finnegan: Duly noted, Top. Listen, gotta go. Talk to you Monday.

The moving bubbles at the bottom of our exchange tell me he's writing me back, but I log off before he can hit Send. I've had enough for one day.

There aren't many people left in the building, but I can feel their stares when I pass by. I'd like to think it's for all of the reasons my presence used to gather their attention. There was a time two short years ago when I felt like a man at the top of his game. A member of the elite First Special Forces Operational Detachment Delta, better known to most as Delta Force. We're the ones they call to deal with international hostage rescues, counter-terrorism missions and special reconnaissance.

They say I'm still a member of the team and what I'm doing

now, teaching the men and women who have taken my place everything I know, is just as important. I call bullshit. Now my job consists of teaching and helping prepare my old team for their missions while I stay behind.

Top had me stationed here in Monterey not only because it's his home base, but because he knew it was near the best treatment for my rehab and with all the telecommunication options we have there's no real reason I have to teach or update the team in person. Some of the Delta members have come out to Monterey here and there and they do their best to try and make me feel whole and a true member of the brotherhood that had been such a huge part of who I am. If only I actually felt that way.

Nope, all my fucking dreams have come true. I'm a goddamned pogue. My existence is working behind a desk or in a classroom, riding my bike just a little too fast around the curves of Monterey County, drinking more than I should and then working out harder than ever the next morning to make up for the self-inflicted abuse from the night before.

But, it's Friday night. No work, and no gym in the morning. Relieved as I am to leave the dreary insides of the base behind me, I should be relishing the blue skies and perfect weather, but I don't. I rarely enjoy anything anymore. But, there is always Betty. My beloved Indian Chief Dark Horse. Her throaty growl sings a beautiful song that surges through me and hits me right in the chest the moment I start her up. She is pure and simple…sex on wheels. Every square inch of her is matte black. Pure power between my legs. I may get shit from the Harley riders and crotch rocket boys, but I also catch them staring at my beauty every time they walk by her.

I'm not in the mood for a helmet tonight, so it's just the cool dusk night air and my Oakleys. The wind in my face is what I need.

Tonight, I'll ride and ride until I finally end up with my ass in the sand in front of the beach cottage I'm staying in while stationed here. It's a small place I'm renting from a family friend of Bradford's while they spend a year overseas, but it's just what I need. If only the proximity to the ocean didn't remind me of Bali.

Of her.

6

Huck ~ Then

"Oh, my goodness, you are so stupid! It's *cool* beans! Not *sure* beans!"

That laugh of hers fills the air of the beachside bar we moved to after Sundays closed, and I swear it's a drug of the most addictive kind. Once you hear it the first time, you'll do anything to hear it again. Over and over and over again.

"I'm sorry you make my mind go a little haywire and my mouth didn't know if it wanted to say '*sure*' in answer to your question or make fun of the fact that you still say *cool beans*. I mean, cool beans is *so* eighth grade," I kid her and she rolls her eyes in reply. Her eyes roll at my comments every few minutes and I swear my heartbeat picks up every time she does. "Hey, it's not my fault you aren't cool like me and didn't just invent a new saying like *sure beans*. It's gonna be a thing. You wait and see."

"Oh, I think I'll be waiting awhile for that to happen."

"You're wrong, just wait. Besides, didn't your parents ever teach you it isn't nice to call people stupid?"

"Oh, they did. However…"

"Excuse me, would you like to dance?"

Who the fuck does this guy think he is?

Just as I'm about to jump off my bar stool in a jealous rage, Harper seals our fate when she links her fingers with mine.

"Thank you, but I'm taken," she replies over her shoulder without even giving him a backward glance.

The guy is swaying in a drunken stupor and blanketed in a sunburn he's sure to feel when he wakes up from his hangover from hell, sometime tomorrow.

"This is your guy?" he asks as if the idea is too far-fetched for him to comprehend.

Ignoring the mess of a drunk over her shoulder her sparkling emeralds dance with a shimmer of excitement when she confirms his question. "Yep, this is my guy."

Hell yes, I am!

With those five simple words, along with the smile on her freckled face and the mischief in her eyes my heart swells, my dick hardens and my ego feels like…well, just picture King Kong, the one with Naomi Watts, beating on his chest on top of that mountain. Yep, that's me.

"Hmpf…" Drunk dude stumbles away and I signal the bartender, who I've known for years, to keep an eye on him. He'll be asked to leave in the next couple of minutes I'm sure.

"Your guy, huh?"

"I was just trying to get rid of him," she says, attempting to slide her hand out of mine unsuccessfully.

"October nineteenth."

"What?"

"Today's date."

"What about it?"

"I just think it's a date we're both going to remember for a long time."

Her blush is my reward and if I didn't think this could be

more than just a vacation fling, I would rush her to my place and give her a damn good reason to remember today's date. But, I do have a feeling there is something here and I'm not going to rush things and take the chance of ruining what might be.

"Huck…" she whispers but doesn't finish. She's getting shy and this is the last thing I want right now, no matter how sweet and appealing it is.

"So, if I'm 'your guy' I should know your full name, Miss Keaton."

"Oh, dear Lord! I've given you every opportunity to guess my middle name. We've spent the last thirty minutes playing this game. It's not my fault you're coming up with things like Gertrude, Helga, and Pocahontas."

"Fine, how about another mangorita?"

"Are you trying to get me drunk and take advantage of me, Mr. Finnegan?"

"Oh, Freckles. I won't ever have to take advantage of you because when this"—I wag a finger from my hand not holding hers between the two of us—"happens, I won't need to. Besides, you'll be begging for it."

She opens her mouth to interject, but I cover it with my hand before she gets the chance. I may as well have struck a match and lit myself on fire.

"When you do beg for it…when this does happen…you will be stone cold sober. Neither one of us is going to want to forget a moment because we are going to burn so hot, we won't be able to put each other out." I feel her gasp and when she lets out the breath she was holding the heat from her release scorches my palm. A mere glimpse of what's yet to come.

Her lips are parted when I remove my hand for her reaction and the vision before me is like fucking kindling to the fire she hasn't stopped stoking all night. Her chestnut waves cascade over one shoulder and her t-shirt hangs off the other.

"I take that back. I think you're drunk." She's trying to dismiss what she knows is true.

"Darlin', you wish I was drunk. It would be easier that way, wouldn't it?"

"What would be easier?"

"To pretend what we're feeling isn't the real deal."

"Confident, much?"

"I feel what I feel, Freckles. There isn't a damn thing I can do about it. Neither can you."

"Does this work for you often?"

"What's that?"

"Getting tourists drunk and pretending you've met your soulmate?"

"Ooh…I like that. Soulmate." She smacks me on the arm and I know I'm going to enjoy years to come getting under her skin and I love that I know it already. "I answered this question, or one pretty close to it earlier in the evening. But I'll say it again if it makes you feel better."

"It will," she whispers.

Shy again.

"This is not my standard method of operation. You're different, Harper."

"You've only known me a matter of hours, how could you be so certain?"

"I knew when I walked away from you today on the beach. I knew then and there you were different than the rest. What did you think?"

"What? What do you mean, what did I think?"

"I told you what I was thinking, now it's your turn."

"Honestly?"

"Always."

She smiles knowingly. "I was thinking to myself, 'Did you

really just flirt with a perfect stranger? Did that really just happen?' And last but not least… 'Where did he come from?'"

"But you knew the instant I asked you to meet me at Sundays, didn't you? You knew your answer was going to be yes."

"Actually, no. I had convinced myself you were a serial killer until Nico came back to apologize for you bothering me. It was Nico who convinced me to show up. He vouched for you and even though I only know him from the last trip we took here and the day and a half we've been here this trip, I trust him. Call me naïve. I think what really sold me was when he told me you help him build houses for those in need while you're here on vacation." She shrugs her shoulders.

Now that's a wing man. I owe that man a drink!

"Well, if I were anyone else, I would tell you what you did was a little naive, maybe even foolish and unsafe, but since you'll be spending the rest of your trip with me, you won't have to worry about making that same mistake again."

There's her laugh again. I swear it's like heroin to my ears.

"Is that so?" She chuckles, coming down from her side-splitting laughter.

"You know it is. You can stop pretending now. We're too many shots in to keep up the facade any longer. Besides we aren't strangers anymore. We both agree the day doesn't start without coffee, your favorite color is blue and mine is grey. I don't drink soda unless it's mixed with rum and if you had your way you would mainline Diet Coke on the daily, but I'm going to do my best to change that. See, your naivety worked out this time and now you have a new friend."

She's leaning forward on the table and her leg is bouncing. I may not know her well, but I would have to say this little kitty is feeling frisky…and a little tipsy. "So, what are we going to do with our time together, *friend*?"

"Well…"

"Wait! Do you hear that? It's my song! I've been singing it all night!"

I can't help but chuckle at her enthusiasm. "I do hear it."

"Dance with me, Huck?"

I could never refuse you anything. All you have to do is ask.

"Nah, I only know how to do the running man!" I play with her.

"No way, prove it!"

"I'm not sure you can handle my moves, Freckles."

Standing she says, "It's okay if you're scared. I'll just go find someone else to dance with me."

She starts to take her first step away from me when I grab her hand and stand to meet her. "I don't think so, Harper. You came with me, you dance with me." I look around the bar. "The only problem is there isn't a dance floor."

"See, where I come from you don't need a dance floor. If you feel it, all you have to do is move."

With those words the chorus starts to play, and she starts to jump up and down to the music in pure abandon. I worry about her and the tall wedge looking shoes she's wearing and stay at the ready in case I need to catch her. Her hair is wild all around her, but in one quick move she throws her head back and takes her hair in her hands holding it to the top of her head to cool herself off.

I couldn't do anything with myself. I simply stood back, a foot away and stared in awe at her. Sure, she's drunk, but it is still the most adorable thing to ever happen in this bar. She's also sexy as hell with her long slender neck begging me to taste her. It takes every bit of strength I have to resist doing just that. I swear it's harder than half the shit I have to do at work.

Truthfully, being a gentleman with her isn't really all that hard. She's the real deal and I have no intention of fucking this up. If it means I keep my hands to myself and my lips off her neck, so be it.

The song comes to an end and an avalanche of chocolate hair is released tumbling into a perfect mess framing her freckled features.

"You didn't dance. You were scared, weren't you?" Her nose scrunches up moving her freckles along with it.

Nope, just couldn't take my eyes off you.

"Sweetheart, you don't know what you're asking for."

"I'm willing to take the risk." She points up to the thatch ceiling when Drake comes on. "Oh, now this is something anybody should be able to make work. I mean, you have seen Drake's dance moves, right? I think this song was made for you. Come on big guy, show—"

Before she can finish her thought I'm already moving. Her eyes grow large as does her smile. Bending my knees, I do my famous body rolls (okay, maybe not so famous) and walk myself as close to her as I can get without touching her. I don't think *Magic Mike* is what she was expecting, but I can't help myself. She's blushing and all it does is encourage me. This is why I turn my back to her and twerk my heart out. When I look over my shoulder, her mouth is hanging open and she's holding her hands up beside her head like she's trying not to touch the merchandise.

"That's right! You better keep your hands to yourself! Keep 'em where I can see 'em, little lady," I say, facing her again.

Her gaze is heated and it's clear she's turned on but because I am a gentleman and she's had too much to drink I keep my hands to myself and instead of rubbing my body all over her I bust out into The Running Man.

Throwing her head back she howls at the moon with laughter.

"The Running Man, as promised." I take a bow, she takes a breath and offers me a high five.

"It seems there is no end to your talents. You're actually a stripper, aren't you? You're just too embarrassed to admit it so, you eluded your job was all top secret and important." She hasn't let go of my hand since our high five. "Looks like I've got your number."

"Not yet. Give me your phone."

"Oh. My. Gosh. I didn't mean it literally, you dork."

It's not every day you get called a dork by a woman of her caliber. I'm just going to take it as a compliment. Especially, since she hands me her phone.

"Here, give me your thumb."

She moves in front of me, her back to my front. I hold the phone in front of us forcing me to wrap my arms around her. I'm doing my very best not to touch her but it's becoming impossible.

She lifts her thumb to her phone unlocking it for me. Her screensaver lights up revealing a picture of Harper and a pretty blonde. I would ask her who it is, but her proximity has taken all the air from my lungs. Keeping the phone held out in front of her, I save my name and number into her phone.

Sliding the phone into the back pocket she pulled it from I notice something I hadn't earlier in the evening. No purse. Yet another thing about her that makes her different. She isn't checking her makeup or reapplying her lipstick every five minutes. She doesn't need any of that shit anyway.

I expect her to turn around facing me to put distance between us again, but she doesn't. Instead, she presses her back to my front and my arms instinctually wrap around her waist lending me the opportunity to bury my nose in her hair. She lightly drags her fingers over my forearms while the scent of mangos infiltrate my brain, turning it to mush while my skin is electrified with her touch.

"Are you smelling my hair?"

"Yes, ma'am."

She giggles but doesn't ask me to stop.

Reaching her left hand up she ever so seductively caresses my neck and runs her fingers through my hair. If she had even an inkling of what she was doing to me would she stop or would she keep up her antics?

"Whatcha doin' there, Freckles?" I whisper in her ear.

Turning her head to gaze up at me the lust in her emerald green eyes is undeniable. "Huck…" She doesn't finish her sentence, but she does turn in my arms, our gaze never breaking. With both hands behind my neck, she lifts up on her toes ever so gently kissing me. It's soft. It's sexy. I feel it all the way to my cock.

"Shit," she curses under her breath. Acknowledging how spectacular that one barely-there moment felt.

I tuck her hair behind her ear. "You got that right."

She lifts up on her toes again, this time I take her face in my hands taking the lead. Keeping it soft and slow it's Harper who opens up for more filling my senses with mangos. The taste of the mangoritas she's been drinking along with the smell of her hair and I have a new favorite fruit.

I've been dying to taste her all night and this first nibble was more than worth the wait. She whimpers and the sound reverberates in my eardrums. My scalp is tingling from the feel of her fingers gripping my hair tighter with each swirl of our tongues, all the while she's looking up at me as if I hung the moon.

My senses may be overwhelmed but my heart…my heart is about to pound out of my chest. It's not often you can stand in a moment and know that your entire world has changed. Your future has been set in motion.

That's what this moment is.

The future.

Slowing things down, I place light kisses to the corners of her mouth. I want her attention and I want her to hear me.

To remember this night.

"You're so gonna marry me one day." I punctuate my statement with another soft kiss.

"You're *so* incredibly drunk right now," she whispers against my lips.

"Maybe so, but it doesn't mean it isn't true."

She drags a finger over my bottom lip. "Shut up and kiss me, Huck."

7

Harper ~ Then

"I cannot believe you convinced me to go cliff diving!" I yelp with a little spring in my step.

The adrenaline from my first jump this morning still coursing through my body. We had watched the sunset at Devil's Tears the night before. The reflections of the setting sun off the tide pools were insanely romantic. Absolutely breathtaking. Screaming as we took our first jump hand in hand was exhilarating yet romantic in an entirely different way. The calmness of the night before was moving and meaningful but experiencing something outside my comfort zone with his hand in mine was just as meaningful.

"It was amazing, Huck! Thank you so much!"

He lifts my hand and kisses the back of it. "Glad you had fun, baby."

"Baby, huh?"

"You don't like that name?"

"It's not that," I say, suddenly shy, kicking at the shallow water we've been walking in, walking along the waves as we have the last three nights. I'm not sure why I'm feeling unsure of myself or how one four-letter word could bring on my first real moment of trepidation.

"Harper, talk to me."

"I don't know, maybe it's because we've only known each other a short time. It just surprised me is all."

He has to know what I'm saying is true. Except for the few hours of sleep I get at my villa each morning and one dinner with my family, we've spent nearly every waking moment together the last three days and it has been amazing. Huck's adventurous side has me bounding out of my reserved shell and I've loved every exhilarating moment. But my favorite moments are the quiet ones. Sitting on the beach, or talking over a meal or a drink. Getting to know him has been the best time of my life.

He's unlike any man I've ever known or could have dreamt into existence. He's smart, talented, funny…simply holding his hand is so much sexier than it should be. Who knew the effect hand holding could have on a person. Even when we're deep in conversation, I couldn't be more aware of his touch.

And his kisses…well, his kisses are next level, even if, much to my dismay he has been more than a gentleman. He drops me off at the resort every night…well, every morning and he hasn't tried to take anything further than kissing. I mean, he did tell me I was going to marry him, but still, he's been a perfect gentleman.

"I didn't know there was a time frame in which a person had to wait to use the expression. Duly noted."

I stop our progress down the beach so I can look him in the eyes. My feet feel like they're sinking in the sand just like my heart is sinking into the pit of my stomach from fear I'm going to be left heartbroken when this trip is over. Better to get things out in the open now before they go too far.

"Stop being funny, Huck. I'm only here another week and a half. You could be called for your secret spy job and have to leave at any minute. What are we doing here?" He tries to speak, but I'm rambling as I do when I get anxious. Seriously, once I get started, I can come up with a really bad case of word vomit if I'm not careful. "I mean this is quite an adventure we've been on the last few days and I'm having a blast with you…"

"But…"

"But…what happens when vacation is over, and reality comes calling?"

His hands cup my face.

"Don't worry, Harper. I'll always find you." *How does he always know the right thing to say? Damn, he's good.* "Besides, we have time to figure all that out. For tonight, let's just be in the moment. Let's enjoy being with each other and we'll figure the rest out as it comes."

He tugs on my hand and guides us to dry sand. Pulling me down so I land between his legs with my back to his front.

We sit with only the sound of the crashing waves in front of us and the occasional cry from a lone bird watching the sky change colors and the sun set for the day. What's left of the sun ripples off the water like gold twisting into the glass waves. We're both transfixed and have been for some time when I feel his lips on the side of my neck. Of course, I tilt my head to the side giving him more access.

"Hmm…that's nice," I sigh into the ocean breeze.

He buries his nose in my hair. I know what he's doing before he says a word. He's infatuated with the smell of my hair.

"Mangos are my new favorite fruit. You have to tell me what brand of shampoo you use so I can buy cases of it so you'll never run out."

The warmth of his breath on my skin and his words that tell me he wants what we have here to last have me so hot and bothered I can't see straight. I know there's a beachfront restaurant not too far from us and yes, there's a chance we could be seen, but I have to take his touches farther.

I need more.

Turning in his lap, I push him back in the sand, crawling up his body until I'm straddling him, kissing him senseless.

Where I'm frantic and out of breath with lust Huck is slow and steady. If I wasn't dry humping him like a virgin in the back seat of a Kia and couldn't feel his growing erection, I would think he was nowhere near wanting me like I want him.

"Baby, I think we should take this indoors, don't ya think?" His husky voice suggests, motioning his head toward the beach-front restaurant that's only a hundred yards away, if that.

"Ugh," I sigh, rolling off him, dramatically flopping myself into the sand next to him.

I know he's right. I know we can't take it any further, but this is as far as we always get. Frankly, I'm frustrated. And confused.

He rolls onto his side and out of the corner of my eye I can see he's holding his head up with his fist watching me. He's finding his Balinese sexual torture tactics amusing.

"Entertained?"

"Are you pouting, Freckles?"

"Shut up."

"What's wrong?"

"Honestly?"

"Always."

"You have me so sexually frustrated I don't know what to do with myself! Well, I know what to do with myself but I would rather it be you who takes care of the ache that's been consuming me since I first heard you open your mouth at Sundays."

"So, this is about my singing?"

Is he kidding me?! What is his problem?

I sit up, putting my weight on my hands behind me. "Are you serious, right now? You say you're into me. In fact, I believe we're getting married someday. But you don't want me. I'm so confused."

"Harper." His hand snakes around my neck, into my hair gently pulling me down on my side so we're facing each other. Eye to eye. "I've never wanted anything or anyone more than I want you." With this bold confession, he places the gentlest kiss on my lips, his hand comes from around my neck and across my chest ultimately resting over my heart.

"Then what is it?"

"Harper, this *is* moving fast, but I'm serious when I say I'm all in. There's something real happening here, and it would kill me to think you thought I was only after one thing. You've mentioned more than once that we only have two short weeks… and well, as much as I want you and I don't want to waste a second of our time together not touching you, I also don't want to rush you."

"I know it's fast and trust me, Huck, this isn't normal for me. But like you said, this feels real to me and I don't want to wait. Please?" I bat my eyelashes at him, trying my best to change his mind and assure him I want more.

"See, I told you I'd have you begging for it the first time!" he says, reminding me of his smart-ass comment from the first night we met. In a flash, he's on his feet and has me slung over his shoulder.

"Oh! My! God! You played me!" I squeal from my upside-down perch.

"Freckles, I didn't play you, but I was right. I knew you'd beg for it and now that you have, I'm about to take you to my place and play the hell out of you!"

The short ride from the beach to Huck's place is awkwardly quiet.

There may not be a roof or doors on the Jeep Huck is casually maneuvering through the small village roads, but I swear the vehicle is closing in around me. I'm trying like crazy to think about what in the world to say to break the silence; to not sound as ridiculous as I feel when, as per usual, the beautiful sandy-haired beach boy next to me saves the day.

Or night as it may be.

"Nothing like awkward silences to keep things hot and sexy, yeah?"

I giggle with relief.

He really is perfect.

"What is wrong with us? We never stop talking when we're around each other. Why did we have to get all quiet? Gah!"

The Jeep is a manual and I didn't realize how much I missed his touch until he lets go of the stick shift to reach over and rest his hand on my leg. With his thumb lazily rubbing back and forth in a soothing motion he solidifies his *too good to be true* persona.

"I wanted to give you some time to yourself. I need to know you're one hundred percent ready for this because, Harper…I'm not sure there's any turning back after I take you in my bed. So, please do not take my silence as a lack of interest or to mean that I've changed my mind."

"No turning back, huh?"

"Yep. Don't say I didn't warn you, Freckles. I know how it feels to kiss you and I know how important you are to me already. Once I have you, I'm afraid I may never let you go again."

"What if I don't want you to?"

"That's my girl. I knew we were on the same page." His face lights up and his eyes promise pleasure, mischief and so much more.

He pulls the car to the side of the road. "Here we are."

"Here?"

I'm confused. Is he homeless? Does he sleep on the beach itself? He did say he had a bed a second ago, right?

He's around the front of the Jeep before my seatbelt is off my lap. I'm about to hop out when he fills the space where a door should be attached, leaning in to kiss me.

This kiss is different than the others we've shared over these last few kiss-filled days. This one feels serious. As though he's trying to tell me how important tonight is to him. It's working. I feel it all the way to my core. Pulsing, wet and waiting.

"Come on," he whispers, taking my hand.

We hold hands down a small trail that leads to the beach and when the first granules of sand find their way into my flip-flops, I freeze.

"What's wrong? Why are we stopping?"

I shake my head hoping it will help bring me back to reality, but it doesn't work.

"Huck…do you live in one of those bungalows over the water?"

"Would it be a problem if I did?"

"Well, no…as long as it doesn't have a glass floor. I've seen those on TV and just the thought of it freaks me out. Does it have a glass floor?"

He throws his head back, a full guttural belly laugh explodes from him. "No, babe. No glass floors. Are you afraid of the fishies, Freckles?"

"Not if I can't see them! I cannot believe *this* is your place," I say, pinching him.

"Ouch! What was that for?"

"Just making sure you're real."

"Oh, I'm very real and if you'd start walking, I could show you just how real I am."

At the promise of an evening in paradise with this living breathing dream man, I casually slip out of my flip-flops before I break out into a run in the direction of the walkway that leads to ten or maybe twelve thatched bungalows sitting on top of what I can only imagine to be crystal clear turquoise water during the day but tonight, with the recent sunset, the water is a deep violet. Even with dusk almost faded completely to the dark of night, it's breathtaking.

I hear his feet sliding across the sand behind me. This is the only hint that he's close when his arm wraps around my waist and he pulls me off my feet. "What's your rush?" he teases. "You looking forward to something?"

"Why, are you trying to delay things? Worried you won't be able to live up to all the fantasies you've been putting in my head all night?"

"You have no idea what you've just done, sweetheart. Hold on tight. You're about to go on the ride of your life."

Before I get to come back at him with a smart-ass comment, he's once again thrown me over his shoulder.

"Brut!"

He smacks my ass. "Admit it, you love this caveman shit."

"In your dreams, Hu…" My words are halted a few feet after his feet hit wooden planks. Beneath us is the dark beauty of the ocean. Tranquil but full of life. "Oh, my goodness, it's beautiful."

He puts me on my feet barely missing a beat pulling me to the very end of the wooden walk way to the hut at the very end of the dock.

"Of course, you'd have the one with the best view. Is everything about you perfect?"

His head hangs between his shoulders for the briefest moment.

The starlight from the sky and the shimmer of the ocean below shine bright pulling the gold flecks from his eyes that are heated yet sincere.

"I'm not perfect, Harper, but I am going to make you come all night long and you're going to beg for more each time you do, but I'm not perfect. Far from it."

I press up on the tip of my toes so I can whisper against his lips. "Open the door and let me in, Huck."

He does just this, only once I've crossed the threshold he rushes past me. He's running around picking up his dirty clothes and fixing the pillows on the bed where his guitar is laying. He leans the sexy instrument against the wall in the corner taking a look around with his hands behind his head making sure he got everything. It's cute as hell to see him cleaning up his room like a teenage boy who's brought a girl home for the first time.

"I see that grin. I told you. I'm far from perfect."

"If this is the worst of it, you don't have me running for the hills just yet."

"Good to know," he says seductively, slipping off his shoes, walking ever so slowly in my direction.

I follow his lead and step out of my flip-flops leaving them behind meeting him in the middle of the room.

Uncharacteristically, I take the lead reaching for the hem of his shirt. My fingers don't shake or fumble while getting the white cotton t-shirt over his head. I've never felt more confident. Huck is pure Adonis and I should feel insecure and shy. His confidence must be rubbing off on me.

Unabashedly, I take a detailed inspection of what I've uncovered. God, his body is a piece of sculpted art the way his broad shoulders taper to his narrow waist leading to that perfect V. I've seen him without his shirt during our daytime adventures and was more than impressed, but tonight, with the low light in the room and the shadows and flickers of light accentuating all of the peaks and valleys of his chest and abs, I see him for the masterpiece he is. The light lapping of the water beneath us simply adds to the atmosphere causing my body temperature to rise steadily.

I need him.

He lifts my hand and places it over his heart covering it with his own hand. He keeps it there a beat staring into my eyes saying so much without saying a word. Lifting the palm of my hand to his lips his eyes close and it's clear this is going to be a slow seduction when all I want is for him to rip my clothes from my body and take me.

"Come here," he says, releasing my hand and tugging on the belt loop of my cut-offs. We're so close now my hands land on his chest with nowhere else to go. I'm placing small kisses across his pecs when I feel his hands on the hem of my shirt.

"My turn."

With those two words, my shirt is over my head laying on the floor with his. He reaches behind me unclasping my bra with deft fingers while I pull at the drawstring of his board shorts. His shorts fall as the straps of my bra slide down my arms and the collection of clothes on the wood floor multiplies.

Stepping back a couple of feet, I shimmy out of my shorts letting my eyes take a tour of the naked body before me making a detailed appraisal.

Slightly bent over with my shorts around my calves I nearly choke on the breath that catches in my throat when my eyes take all of him in. Because there is *a lot* of him to take in. In the blink of an eye, my confidence shrivels up and dies a quick death.

Trying my best to keep my composure, I step out of my shorts sliding our pile of clothes out of the way with my foot.

Closing the distance between us, he steps close enough for me to feel his breath on my face when he pushes my hair behind my ear. "Fucking beautiful, Harper. That's what you are. You know that, right?"

"Huge. That's what you are, Huck. Fucking huge. You know that, right?"

"Maybe just a little above average," he says in all seriousness and not a hint of humor.

His lips are on mine without another word and he's kissing me like a man starved.

Apparently, our conversation is over.

His tongue seeks permission to enter and it's instantly granted. Before long he kisses his way down my neck over my sternum, finally pulling my nipple into his mouth with his big hands sprawled across my back to hold me in place.

My hands are in his hair and my mind has one singular focus. Pleasure. His tongue swirling around my tight nipple is like fuel to the fire that is already a flame so hot I'm not sure it will ever burn out. I whimper when his mouth releases my breast only to pant 'yes' when he finds the other and my grip in his hair tightens.

After taking me to the edge with only the feel of his lips and tongue, I'm not ready for the full force of what his touch has the capability of doing to me when his fingers journey over my hip bone to find me more than ready for him. His thumb expertly circles my clit as his mouth crashes into mine again. My leg lifts wrapping around his waist granting him better access.

It's clear he notices me offering myself up to him when I feel him smile against my parted lips. "You want more, baby?"

"Yes, please."

His hand stops the moment I ask for more. He doesn't leave me at a loss for long as he slides his fingers between my folds and enters one of his fingers inside.

"So wet, Harper."

"More," I whimper and moan simultaneously. Who knew that was even possible.

"You want more?"

"Yes."

Not stopping the motion of his finger, he ravages my lips with a fierce kiss and slides a second finger in. This time curving them inside finding the magic spot that sends me reeling and grinding myself against his hand.

"Oh, my God. Huck. Yes! Yes!" I exclaim.

My head rolling back between my shoulders in ecstasy. With my lips out of range, his tongue scorches its way from my ear down to my collarbone while he continues building me up and up, getting me closer and closer to my climax when he stops.

At an excruciatingly languid pace, he leaves a trail from his fingers up my stomach to the middle of my breasts leaving my skin sizzling from his touch. Finished with his leisurely tour of my torso his hands find their way to my backside and he lifts me off the ground carrying me to his bed. With him holding me this way, my arms wrap around his neck giving me the opportunity to leave my kisses along his traps and up his neck until my tongue is tracing the shape of his ear. We're pressed together, skin to skin in the most intimate way.

This first feel of my breasts held tight against his chest is a moment I hope I never forget. Our hearts beating, one against the other, in perfect harmony. My body achieving a level of lustful want I've never come close to feeling before.

He lays me on my back hovering over me. "You have no idea how bad I've wanted to taste you." His tongue darts out to follow the wet trail his fingers left. He laps up the taste of me and is halfway down my stomach when he speaks again, his voice laden with lust. "Delicious."

"Huck, where do you think you're going?"

"Oh, I think you know exactly where I'm going, Freckles."

"Huck…"

He continues to kiss and suck and lick down the path he made on my body and has been sliding his way down the bed until he's between my thighs.

"Fuck."

This is all he says as he gently pushes on my legs urging my thighs farther apart, slipping his hands under my butt so my hips are tipped back at the tiniest angle.

I'm completely enthralled with watching the most perfect man I have ever met that it startles me and my breath hitches when his eyes find mine just as his tongue takes its first taste. The combination of watching him along with the sensation of his tongue against me and my entire body is pulsating in anticipation.

Huck's eyes leave mine when he takes his efforts to the next level and his fingers are inside me again. The combination of the heat from his breath, tongue on my bundle of nerves and the feel of his fingers inside me has me clawing at the sheets. The sounds of my ragged breaths are all I hear as I tighten and pulse around his fingers. At the height of my ecstasy my legs straighten, and my body stiffens before going limp.

He doesn't give me time to recover though. Instead, he removes his fingers while his tongue continues its assault and the climax I thought I had ridden to the end is back in one last earth-shattering orgasm.

After he kisses his way back up my body, he reaches for something on the little table next to the bed bringing a foil packet to his mouth and using his teeth to open it. He's on his knees between my legs taking the condom out of its wrapper. Just the slightest movements cause his taut muscles to twitch and flex and my lust for him to push into overdrive.

As much as I long to touch him, I don't. Instead, I sit back and examine every square inch of him. From his broad shoulders, strong arms and rippled abs. His thighs are thick and what's between them is more man than I ever thought possible. Watching him roll the condom on his long length brings me back to the here and now.

"Uh, Huck…"

"Shhh…don't worry, I'll go slow."

"I'm sorry, but I don't see how all of that is going to fit."

Just as I say the words, his body covers mine, with most of his weight resting on his forearms his fingers move the hair from my face so he can peck a soft kiss to my forehead at the same time I feel him nudge my entrance. Instinctually, my legs spread wider for him so he can slowly press his length into me. He takes his time and with every inch that enters me, I feel more and more full. He pulls back and then pushes in, this time going a little farther.

"Hey, breathe for me," he coaches.

I release the breath I didn't realize I was holding and my body relaxes allowing him to slide in even farther.

"There you go. Just breathe, baby." He kisses me with gentle nibbles to my lips, giving me something besides his size to think about and his rhythm picks up.

I'm not sure how it's possible, but he does in fact, fit. I feel full and he was right, it's a tight fit, but when my hands take the time to explore his body allowing me to focus on all of him, my body follows suit and we relax into a steady cadence.

It's as though he already knows my body inside and out. He's not throwing me around like a rag doll and we don't change to any other positions. He kisses me throughout, only pulling back at the very end to hold my gaze as the corded muscles in his neck tense and his face grows a dark red when he finds his release, growling into the night air.

After catching his breath, he peppers feather-light kisses all over my face before he ever so slowly pulls out. He cleans the both of us up and then pulls me tightly to him. I feel an ache in my core that I'm sure will take a day or two to go away but more than anything I feel the loss of how it felt to feel so full. So close to him.

Pulling back, needing to see his handsome face to guage how he's feeling, the gold flecks in his eyes glisten in the soft light from the night sky. His chest and half his face are bathed in moonlight. A glow of contentment about him. The tidewaters splash on the shore and birds cry above. The tropical breeze floating in through the windows cools my body when it hits the dampness of my skin. It takes me a minute, but I connect the dots shooting straight up in the bed, pulling a sheet to my chest.

"Oh my God, Huck. There are no windows in your windows. They're just big open spaces."

"And?" He smiles knowingly.

Ugh! He's incorrigible!

"Every person in a five-mile radius probably just heard us!"

"So?" He has one hand behind his head and the other resting on his rock-hard stomach. He shrugs like he could care less if the entire island may have just heard us knocking boots. He tugs on my wrist forcing me to lay back down on his chest. "It's not my fault you're a screamer."

"I am not!" I huff, tapping his chest in a mock slap.

"Oh, but you are." He kisses the top of my head, trying to be sweet while lying about how loud I am. "I'd say that was pretty amazing. Even with the screaming."

He's so annoying. In the best possible way.

"Yes, it was," I agree. "I still can't believe it fit."

I feel the vibration of his chuckle in my chest. "Harper, it's not that big. You must have just been pretty unlucky in the past."

"Well, it's not like I have much to compare you to. I had the same boyfriend all four years of college but he…"

"Let me stop you there, Freckles. I love that you feel free enough to talk to me, but I do not want to compare penis sizes with your exes. I'd prefer to think tonight was your first time and nobody else has ever touched you, thank you very much."

"Aw, you're cute when you're jealous."

I squeal when he suddenly rolls us over so he's on top of me again. "I told you I'm all in, you get that, right?" The storm behind his hazel eyes searches my greens and I swear he's trying to look all the way into the deepest corners of my soul.

"I do," I manage to whisper.

"Good. Then you know it means no man will touch you again. You're mine, Harper Keaton."

"Is that so?"

"I think you know it is."

"Does this mean you'd do anything for me?"

"Name it."

I cover my face with my hands. "Why do I suddenly feel like I'm about to ask you to prom or something?"

He rolls off me to lay on his side, his head resting in the palm of his hand, an amused look on his face while his free hand traces figure eights over my belly.

"What is it, baby?"

God, I love it when he calls me that.

I pull the sheet up to my neck like it will shield me from my embarrassment. Why I'm making this such a big deal, I have no idea.

"Will you be my date to my dad's wedding this weekend? I totally understand if it's too fast or too serious or if you have other plans or—"

He covers my mouth with his hand, effectively putting a halt to my anxious ramblings. "Shh…"

"Sorry," I say in a muffled voice against his palm.

"Harper…"

"Yes," I reply into his hand still covering my mouth.

"I would love to be your date."

"You would?"

"I would."

He cautiously removes his hand. "Really? You get this is my dad's wedding, right? You'll have to meet my dad and my brother. My older brother."

"They make you who you are, Harper, and I can't wait to get a little glimpse into your life. Besides, I don't plan on missing a minute with you while we're here so you're kind of stuck with me."

"Every minute, huh?"

"Yup. Think of me like one of those little sucker fish that hangs on tight and doesn't let go."

"Hmmm…that sounds like a plan to me."

His hand slides up my neck and his fingers weave though my hair as his thumb traces my jawline. "Good," he says, leaning in for a sweet peck on the corner of my mouth.

8

Harper ~ Now

"Liza, I'm starting to worry. He's missed three appointments," I confide in my sister from another mister on the other end of the line. The one person who knows everything there is to know about me and me about her.

"I know sweetie. You've also been waiting two years to see him again but please don't do anything to risk your career for a guy who said he would call and never did."

"Liza, what exactly do you think I'm going to do to risk my career? All I said is that I'm starting to worry."

"Harp, I know you better than you know yourself."

Very true.

"Okay…what's your point?"

"I know you've gone through his file."

"Yes, but I was assigned to his case. It's not like I was breaking HIPPA law or invading his privacy or anything like that."

"Yet."

"If you're trying to say something just say it." I sigh into the phone.

I'm exhausted. I haven't slept in what feels like forever, even though it's only been since I opened the door to the waiting room a week and a half ago. I don't have the energy for anything right now and I think I might regret having called my best friend.

"His address is in that file."

I don't reply to her statement because she's got me.

"Sweetie, I know you want to see him. I know you want to help him. I know you want answers."

"You're right I do want all those things, but I also know the rules."

"I just don't want you to do something stupid."

"I'm not stupid, Liza. Besides, I've read his file. I know where he's been."

"Yes, you do, but it's bullshit he didn't reach out to you. He hurt you by not giving you the chance to be there for him. If he knows you at all, he knows you would have been by his side every step of the way."

I look at the compass tattooed on my left wrist and I know she's right. We said we would find our way back to each other no matter what. Our promise wasn't conditional. At least it wasn't to me.

My other line beeps and I take the opportunity to let Liza, and her common sense, go when I see Brian's name on my phone.

"Hey, I have to grab my other line. I'll call you later. Bye." I hang up before she can get another word in.

"Hey, beefcake, what can I do for ya?" I do my best to sound like my bubbly self even if it takes every last bit of energy I've got.

"What's up, Buttercup? When are you coming home? I feel like sushi."

"Well, my last appointment didn't show up so I'm actually free now." I try not to let my disappointment project in my voice.

"Best news I've had all day. Get that cute little butt of yours home and let's go. See you in thirty?"

"See you in thirty."

I gather my coat, throw my bag over my shoulder and pick up Huck's file. His file is burning a hole into my hand as I proceed down the hallway filled with patients who *did* show up and who *are* seeking the assistance they need. By the time I reach the happy color of Penny and the front desk, I know I'm about to risk my career and prove Liza right.

"Hey, Penny. Do I see an addition to your cast of characters here?"

She plucks up her latest crazy haired troll from the line-up on the credenza behind her and her round face lights up and the silver of her hair adds a little spark to those blue eyes of hers.

Penny's desk is an array of bright, neon colors courtesy of the up-combed hair of her mostly naked troll dolls. There are some in holiday or themed costumes, but for the most part, they're naked and quite frankly they freak me out. I think it's the big bugged out eyes. They're just so dang creepy.

"Oh, my goodness, Harper! Isn't it the cutest thing you've ever seen? Who knew they made unicorn trolls! I'm in Heaven!"

She hands the purple gem to me and I'm grateful it's a troll unicorn and not the usual naked little guy between my fingertips, if only I couldn't smell the synthetic plastic aroma wafting its way up to my nose.

"I had no idea they made unicorn trolls either. It's adorable, Penny," I say, holding it out in front of me for her to take, trying not to be rude.

She sets it back in its place next to a little blue-haired troll in a police officer's uniform.

"Looks like your three-thirty never showed? I called and sent him a text but no luck."

"Yep, he was a no show." I hand her his file. "So, I'm gonna call it a day and head out and get some sushi with Brian."

"Aw, tell that sweet boy I said not to be a stranger."

"I'll be sure to give him your message." I push through the door leading to the waiting room and wave over my shoulder knowing I've just lied to her. "Have a nice night, Penny. See you next week."

Who lies to Penny? She's the sweetest woman on the planet and a mother to all of us in the office. I am going straight to Hell.

I don't need the folder, now back in its place on Penny's desk, to know how to find him. I've had his address memorized since I read his file the day he ran out of the office.

My pulse pounds in my ears as I rush to the parking lot and to my car. The moment I turn on my car I'm programming my phone's navigation with his information. I'm sure to text Brian letting him know I'll be late for sushi. Once my Bluetooth connects with my navigation system it guides me out of the parking lot. It's a good thing too. I'm a nervous wreck and I couldn't find my way out of a paper bag at the moment.

As nervous as I am, I'm a woman on a mission and my sole focus is getting Huck to come in for his appointment. If there's any way I can help him, I have to try. I know I'm not only lying to Penny, but I'm lying to myself.

The other day when Tyler crashed into my legs hugging me like he does every week, my world stopped spinning. I thought my years of waiting had come to an end and my heart filled with hope underneath the initial wave of shock that blanketed my body. The moment I saw him sitting in our waiting room I swear the drab beige room full of uncomfortable chairs and people who wished they weren't there, lit up like Christmas had come early.

Seeing him overwhelmed me to the point of losing my ability

to speak. But it was clear my initial hope was ill-founded and Huck wasn't there for me after all.

He hadn't come looking for me like he promised he would.

Like I promised him I would.

That's the real reason I'm doing this.

We promised we would always find our way back to each other.

He may not have meant to find me, but he did, and now I'm holding up my end of the deal.

I should be angry, and I shouldn't care, but after reading his file and how his life had changed just seventy-two hours after he left me. I couldn't hold on to the bitterness any longer. He should have reached out and he should have trusted me enough to help him through everything, but I can't begin to imagine what he's been through.

Before I know it, I'm pulling up to a small house with beach-front access and a pretty scary looking motorcycle parked in the driveway. Turning my car off I stare at the simple home that doesn't look like all the pristine white multi-story homes in the area. It's older and the wood is greying from years of abuse from the wind and sea water, but it's perfect. This house, well, this house is all Huck. Rustic, manly and beautiful. Just like the man himself.

Not letting myself sit long enough to chicken out, I drag myself out of the car and tiptoe past his perfectly shorn grass like I'm about to break in and rob the place. I'm acting like a crazy person and starting to doubt myself. I'm thinking I should turn around to leave when my phone buzzes with a text from Brian saying he'll wait for me. Reading the text, my tattoo peeks out from under the sleeve of my sweater, reminding me why I'm here.

My feet stand on a welcome mat that says WIPE YOUR PAWS and I can't help but wonder if he does, in fact, have a dog?

I think it would make me feel better knowing he had a pet by his side.

My hand touches the old wooden door and I brace myself for what's to come. If his reaction to seeing me the other day is any indication he may not be too happy with my surprise visit.

I take in a deep breath and let it go along with my trepidation as I reach for the doorbell. My fingertip is a mere fraction of an inch from the bell when the door swings open and there he is.

Clearly on his way out, seeing me on his welcome mat was definitely the last thing he expected.

He stands motionless. Shocked.

His body bigger than I remember, completely filling the space of the door frame. He's still beautiful even with the addition of the scar that cuts through his eyebrow and down past the corner of his eye. His shaggy beach hair that had been lightened by the sun back in Bali is cut in a short regulation Army cut and a little bit of a darker blond than before.

It feels like we're in a stand-still and neither of us says a thing for what seems like forever. This wasn't the plan, so I start rambling, as I do.

"Hi, I know this is highly unprofessional, but I was worried I was the reason you weren't coming to your appointments. Dr. Cody is amazing and if anyone can help you, it's him. I'll remove myself from your case if you'll come back to see him."

My usual case of word vomit seems to have snapped him out of his state of shock, but it's clear he didn't hear a thing I said. And I've lost eye contact with him. His tan complexion is turning red. I couldn't say he was angry because there's no emotion of any kind on his stone face.

"Sorry, this isn't really something I want to talk about," he says, stepping out of the door forcing me to step off the welcome mat and to the side of the doorway. "Thanks for coming all the way here but I was just on my way out." He locks up behind him and doesn't give me another thought. He walks right off his porch leaving me standing there on my own.

The roar of his motorcycle rattles me to my bones and there's no stopping the cascade of tears streaming down my face.

Who was that?

He looks like the man I fell in love with two years ago, only the man I fell in love with was nowhere to be seen.

Huck, was emotional, sensitive, and funny. The man who just rode away on that bike was none of those things.

Where is the man who wore his heart on his sleeve in Bali?

I'm sobbing now because I know where that man went. I read his file. I know what he's been through.

What did I expect when he's lost so much? So many things that made him who he was? Does he not realize he's so much more than what he's lost? As much as his reaction or lack thereof hurts me, I know he's hurting so much more. I know now why he ended up in the clinic waiting room a week and a half ago.

We said we'd find our way back to each other and I can't help but feel fate has brought him back to me so I can help him find himself again. This thought steels my resolve.

Leaving his porch, I follow the sound of the waves around the side of the house and find a spot on the sand where I can think and try to figure out how I can help someone who not only doesn't want my help but doesn't seem to want to be in my presence.

9

Huck ~ Now

I've dreamed about this moment and here she is.

Standing on my front porch.

The amazing scent that is all Harper and mangos nearly knocks me over when the breeze picks up behind her. Instead of comforting me like it used to, all it does is cause the pain to well up from my stomach, lodging in my throat. I try my best to swallow it down, but I know my anger betrays me because I can feel the heat staining my face and tears beginning to well.

Fucking pussy.

I disgust myself.

I can't deal with this right now. Her pity is the last thing I need. All I want is for her to still love me for who I was. But how could she ever love me again?

Her lips are moving, but I'm too overwhelmed to comprehend what she's saying. I mutter something back to her not really sure what I'm saying just knowing I need to flee.

She has to step aside when I push past her, locking the house up to make my getaway. Simultaneously avoiding her and pushing her away.

Just like I do with everything else in my life. I rarely talk to my parents, avoid my friends and live like a shut-in when I'm not at work or the gym.

Seeing her is a reminder of everything I've lost.

Everything I loved.

When my weak ass makes it to my bike, I drop my damn keys at my feet when I pull them out of my pocket.

Fuck!

Way to look even more pathetic.

After I pick up the keys from the concrete driveway I take a deep breath and tell myself she isn't watching and to chill out. Wouldn't you know I take one step toward my bike and fuck me if I don't drop them again. This time I really step it up a notch when I accidentally kick them under my back tire with my boot.

I slow down and take another deep breath.

Don't look back, she might not have seen that.

Not wasting any more time, I forego my helmet quickly getting her started. She comes alive between my legs. I can't get out of there fast enough. In my haste, I don't even take the time to get the kickstand up before taking off.

Pulling out onto the street, I work the gears of the bike as fast as I can. Lusting for the speed and quite frankly the fear.

To feel that finite edge between control and oblivion.

To feel alive.

I gun the bike's throttle and pull out on to the highway. All the pain I was feeling at just the mere sight of her is only amplified as the bike picks up speed. Seventy, ninety, a hundred-ten miles per hour. The world around me a blur. The other cars and trucks on the road moving in slow motion. The cold wind against my face usually provides me with the rush I need. Not tonight.

Rolling the throttle all the way over, the bike lunges forward and there's no looking down to check the speed. I have no idea how fast I am going as I start to approach town.

The flashing red light hanging above the intersection ahead of me is about to bring me to a full stop and for a split second, I think, *fuck it, let's see what happens*, before coming to my senses. What the fuck am I doing? My actions are irresponsible.

I gear my bike down closing the distance on the intersection pulling up next to a Chevy pickup. Somehow, I manage to stop the bike before the white line.

A middle-aged woman with dark features and hair pulled up under a ball cap drives the truck next to me. When the young boy in the front passenger seat next to her points at me and starts to say something she reaches across her bench sheet to cover his eyes.

I'm staring at her, trying to figure out what the hell is so wrong with me she has to cover his eyes when I notice something strange in the glass windows of shops on the other side of the truck.

Flashing lights behind me.

Before I have time to react my left arm is grabbed and someone is trying to pull it behind my back. My training has me reacting on instinct, turning to strike the person in the head with my right fist. My bike rolls away from me as the person continues tugging on my arm. I pull my left arm free swinging, landing a punch and finally face to face with my attacker.

My attacker who stands a little over six feet, a stout two hundred and forty pounds, salt & pepper and oh yeah, he has a badge on his chest. He's bleeding from the small cut over his left eye and behind him is a patrol car with its overhead lights on.

I just hit a cop.

Holy fuck!

Raising my hands, I say, "I am so sorry."

But as soon as the words are out, my body locks up and

seizes. I swear, there's a goddamned strobe light going off in my brain. But instead of the light blinding me, it's like someone is slamming my body with a sledgehammer over and over again with each flash.

As if in slow motion, I feel myself falling forward and even though my mind is screaming at me to put my hands out to soften the fall, the message doesn't make it past my brain. In a matter of seconds, I'm flat on my stomach with a very angry cop on my back. The thin fibrous wires on the cement in front of me tie it all together.

He fucking tasered me.

Angry cop's been joined by another officer and they're pulling on my arms. With my body seizing uncontrollably from the electricity they're hitting me with it's impossible to cooperate with them. I'm not the guy who fights cops. I want to cooperate, but they won't let me.

The strobing finally stops just moments before my head's slammed against the asphalt. One of them has his knees on the back of my neck, while the other's knee is in the small of my back. Clearly, other officers have joined the fight because my thighs are pinned to the ground.

I can feel them trying to get my arms that are currently trapped beneath me, but with all of them on top of me, the situation seems impossible. I know they want to cuff me, and I want to help them. The thing is if they're trying to shout instructions at me, they aren't getting anywhere.

Things are getting fuzzy with the massive weight of all the cops on my back. I'm struggling to draw breath and if I were a betting man, I'd say I'm going to pass out soon. Closing my eyes, I take a deep breath in feeling the cold air fill my chest. The strikes against my legs and arms tell me they think I'm not cooperating, but I don't know what they want me to do.

Once my lungs are full to capacity I do my best to yell over the chaos. "I can't fucking hear you!" I feel a little pressure come off my lower back. "I can't fucking hear you. Goddamnit, I'm deaf!"

The nightsticks stop landing their blows, my legs are released and most of the weight is off my back. I pull my hands out from under my limp body giving them free access to cuff me. Escorted to a black and white police vehicle, they place me in the back seat leaving my hands secured behind me.

Through the window, I can see my precious Indian laying on her side. Officer Angry opens the driver's door and takes a seat then starts talking on his radio and typing on his computer.

"Sir. I am so sorry I hit you. I didn't know you were behind me and I just reacted."

He pauses looking at me through the rearview mirror. Noticing the cut above his eye he reaches into a bag on the passenger seat pulling out a handkerchief to wipe his brow.

I follow his hand when it drops back down to his bag and notice a Ranger tab across the side of the black bag. He catches me looking at it and we lock eyes in the mirror again.

"Hoora," I say in a low tone.

He gives me a nod.

"Officer, I know I don't deserve it, but I would really appreciate it if you take it easy on my bike." Officer Angry looks back at me giving me a thumbs up.

Before long, I've been transported to the local jail. Locked inside a small grey concrete cell. Sitting on a pale green paper-thin mattress atop a concrete slab on the back wall of the cell.

When they gave me my one phone call, I couldn't make it myself. They had to call Bradford for me. It's fitting I feel like a fucking teenager whose parents were just called because I was acting like one.

He lets me sit here an hour or so before he shows up and I'm on my feet coming to attention for my superior. Getting close enough to the cell bars to read his lips first things, first.

"Top. Man, I'm sorry. I really fucked up." I wonder if he can hear the shame in my voice?

Bradford takes a deep breath speaking slowly for me. "Fuck, buddy. You are damn lucky the cop you hit is a Ranger." The next part is hard to read, but I get the gist of it. He's willing not to press charges due to my issue. Bradford points to his ear when he mentions my *issue*, making it clear my pitiful state is the only reason I'm getting off so easy.

My body starts to relax anticipating the cell door opening when Bradford gets the attention of an officer, but he isn't asking for my release, he's getting a pen and paper from him. Quickly jotting something down on the pad and passing it to me through the cell bars.

I read his note back to him. "On one condition. You have to comply with the rest of your rehab."

"You're right. I know you're right. I need help," I say just to placate him. Even though deep down I know he's right.

Top reaches for the paper and I give it to him. He writes another note and hands it back through the bars.

"You have to cool your heels in here for the night. They need time to draw up the paperwork and have the judge sign it in the morning. I'll be back to pick you up." I read his note to him and his face says he feels shitty leaving me in here overnight.

"It's fine, man. I deserve a night in jail after my little stunt," I say, letting him know I get it. "I owe you one, brother."

Top moves in as close as he can and says slowly, "You don't owe *me*, shit." He points his index finger at me. "You owe it to yourself to start living again."

I nod my reply. What else can I say?

He slides me another piece of paper. "Look this over. I think you need to take a break from the bike and get this installed in your truck." When I begin to protest, he cuts me off real quick. "Don't fight me on this. Read it."

He walks away and leaves me with a brochure about systems I can install in my truck that will give me visual alerts to sirens, horns, and other noises I can't hear. I've heard about them but have purposely not looked into it. I'm sure it's safer to drive my truck and to install this device, but I'm just not ready to give up my bike yet.

The rest of the night I sit in the dark wondering what she was doing on my doorstep. So close I could smell her.

With the smell of Harper on my mind, I eventually close my eyes drifting off to a fitful sleep. Even thoughts of Harper aren't enough to keep the nightmares at bay tonight.

10

Huck ~ Then

"Blackbird to Delta 6."

"Go Blackbird." Dowd's voice fills my radio muffs.

He's posted up outside watching the van and will provide cover while we load the vehicle.

"Package is secure with three Tangos down. All Sierras accounted for. Ready for extraction."

"What condition is the package in?"

"Unconscious, but Doc says he's stable enough to be carried out. He'll need immediate medical treatment when we've arrived to the rally point."

"Roger that, load up, I got you guys covered."

"Copy. Delta 6. Oscar Mike."

Air support is en route to us, but still fifteen minutes out.

Taking pause, I have to admit this has gone much smoother than I would have expected.

We pulled right up to the front door of the target and found the door was open. Lucky for us, no one seemed to notice us entering the building. We contacted three armed men, and all were dealt with quietly with suppressed rifle fire. A single shot for each before any of them could get a shot off.

We located the doctor chained to a toilet upstairs. He was in bad shape, unconscious, beaten and maimed to an inch of his life but we got him out. Now, it's time to get him home.

"Load up, gents, exfil time," I say quietly into my mic.

Smurf leads the way to the front door. Snacks and Culp are carrying a backboard with Dr. Stafford strapped to it. Taking up the rear I make sure our six is covered as we load into the van. The Skipper can be seen from the shadows across the street. He casually walks to the van and takes his seat in front with Smurf.

Snacks says, "Last man, Jefe."

I moved to the back doors and the van already looks like a crammed can of sardines with all eight of them inside.

Doc is frantically working on Stafford already.

Doc is never frantic.

Something's wrong.

I feel it in my gut yet still step up into the van securing the two doors behind me hoping to get us out of here before the ominous feeling in the pit of my stomach is explained.

Smashed against the back doors I can barely move. Snack's massive back is pushed against my face making my helmet ride up, causing my earmuffs to scream feedback into my ears. I reach up and pull my helmet off to escape the noise.

Doc is manically yelling to Dowd in the front of the van and the ease of the mission seems to be taking a turn right before our eyes.

The roads here are rough. It feels like we're inside an old Maytag washer the way we're getting jostled around. Snacks' weight is the only thing keeping me in place. With the small view I have of the center of the van things with the doctor seem to have escalated. He's been freed from the straps of the backboard to give Doc more access.

"Doc, you good?" I yell.

"Man, he's in a bad way," he replies.

Pushing against Snacks I push myself up to get a better view when Doc cuts away the doctor's tattered clothing from his beaten body. When he rips his shirt open, the color leaves his face. Doc sits back on his heels taking a deep breath.

Not certain what I'm looking at but the hostage has a large incision in his stomach that's been recently stitched up. Poorly. The stitches look like a kid used football laces to fix an old stuffed toy or something.

I don't have a great view, but it's clear this is not a medical procedure we were looking at. His stomach is swollen, and Doc is pressing on the mass protruding from his midsection.

Doc jumps back against the side of the vehicle, hysterically trying to get as far away from the doctor as possible.

"MUDSLIDE!" Doc yells through the van.

Smurf slows the van down carefully. Rips his daughter's good luck charm off the dash of the vehicle and a heartbeat later jumps out of the driver's side door.

Mudslide.

A fucking bomb.

Dr. Stafford has an IED inside him.

I do my best to turn my body toward the door so I can access the handles I'm pressed against in the back of the van, but Snacks' body shifted as we went over one last bump in the road and he's got me pinned against the doors.

Suddenly, I'm blinded by a shock of bright light. Snacks' body slams against me pushing all the air from my lungs. Extreme heat smashes into me like a cinderblock wall. Smoke and dust everywhere.

Flat on my back, unable to breathe, I fight for air, finding it hard with the heavy weight compressing my chest. My eyes are filled with dirt and I can't see a damn thing. I manage to push the heavy object off my chest to take in large breaths of smoke burning my lungs.

My eyes are compacted with dirt, sand and a wet sticky substance.

My arms are burning and I'm desperate to see what's happening around me. Attempting to clear them all I do is make it worse when I rub my dirty glove into them. *Fuck!* My mouth is full of the same sand and dirt, along with blood… lots of blood.

Ripping off my gloves I wipe my eyes as best I can. My vision clears enough to see my rifle dangling to the ground in front of me as I crawl on my hands and knees. Looking to my right, I see Snacks. He was the heavy weight on top of me.

Only it wasn't all of him. Just his torso.

There's no stopping the vomit that comes up in a rush. But I push forward rising up on my knees looking at the metal frame that is all that's left of the van.

The walls of the shanties on both sides of the road are covered in scorched burn marks and coated in a reddish-brown mist, which I can only assume is blood. The blood of my men.

Get up, Huck. Get the fuck up.

I will myself to stand, moving toward the back of the van.

The ringing in my ears is unbearable. I've been in a lot of firefights and I've had the ringing before. It's nothing new.

Deal with it, motherfucker.

Blood continues to run into my eyes, but there's no escaping the scene in front of me. Surveying the carnage in front of me the reality that they're all gone shreds me. There are only burnt parts and pieces of my brothers left.

Somehow, I make my way to the front of the van to find Dowd's charred corpse in the passenger seat. But I don't see any sign of Dan and I know I saw him jump out of the van just before it blew.

Where is Dan?

"Smurf!" I scream out.

I see movement on the other side of the road, and I'm hit with a rush of hopeful adrenaline.

Dan's alive.

He's lying face down trying to push himself up. I move as fast as I'm able to close the distance between us. This is also when I start to notice that some of the locals have come out to investigate the blast. This is never a good scenario.

Move, Huck. I demand of myself.

Once I reach Dan, I waste no time bending down to roll him over to his back to assess his injuries. His face is burned. Barely recognizable. He's breathing, but the skin on his eyelids is so badly burned he can't open them.

"Dan, can you hear me?"

His mouth moves, but all I can hear is the damn ringing in my ears. When I look him over it only takes a moment to see his right leg is missing below the knee. Grabbing my tourniquet, I quickly go to work on his upper leg. Thank God, the blood flow slows.

Men with rifles are starting to move toward us from the south and they don't look friendly. I need to move before they see us.

"All right buddy, this is going to hurt," I say, grabbing Dan with everything I have in me. I lift his body over my shoulders placing him in a fireman's carry.

The rally point. I need to get to the rally point.

I start running, only to slow to wipe the blood from my eyes. I must have a pretty bad gash on my head.

Move Huck! Fucking run!

It feels like I'm sprinting, but the reality is I'm barely moving.

Falling several times, I pick us both up each time willing myself to keep going. I need to get Dan home to his family.

I need to get back to my home.

Harper.

I can smell her.

I can hear her calling my name.

Her voice fuels me, pushing me forward.

I have no idea where I am. I just started running in the direction the van had been aimed.

Panic has me spinning around checking in each direction with Dan still slung over my shoulders but when I finally still I feel a tug on my right hand that was grasping my rifle.

I look down and see the big chocolate eyes of a small boy gazing up at me. He's saying something, but all I can hear is the fucking ringing. Pointing to my ear I shake my head telling him I can't hear him.

The boy points down the street and tugs on my hand again as though he's trying to pull me forward.

He's wearing a dirty Denver Broncos t-shirt with a number eighteen on the front and he must be about eight years old. He looks malnourished and unkept but his smile warms me.

"We need to get to my friends, we need help."

The little man points to the Delta patch on my shoulder then points toward the street to the right of me.

"You know where they are, did you see them moving into position?"

I know you can't always trust the locals, even children, in these situations but when he takes my hand, I follow his lead.

We start to run, the boy looking nervously behind us and I know. We are not alone. Darting in and out of traffic and buildings I want nothing more than to stop. My legs don't want to continue.

Everything hurts.

I hear Harper's giggle in my head and it's the jolt of energy I need to keep going.

The little boy suddenly lets go of my hand and darts between two shanties. I don't hear them, but I see the bullet strikes in the dirt next to me. We're under attack.

Two men with rifles wearing paramilitary garb are shooting at me from a distance. Raising my rifle, I take the safety off with my free hand and start shooting in the direction of the men firing at me.

It works and the men turn away running in the other direction.

Run Huck, run.

I continue in the direction we had been running for what feels like miles. My body wracked with fatigue and pain. I trip. Falling to the ground, I feel Dan roll over my head as we hit the ground.

I pull myself over to him. "Sorry buddy, guess I need to work on my cardio." He's still and his chest no longer moves up and down. "Dan, you with me, brother?"

Fuck he's not breathing. Checking his pulse, I feel nothing.

Fuck!

I roll him over and start chest compressions, his ribs crunching under my hands but not from my attempts to save him. From the damage caused by the blast.

The skin on his chest was starting to cool. He's been gone for some time and I had no idea. Pulling him close to me I cry for my brother. For all of my brothers.

They're all gone.

There's a hand on my shoulder and I look over to see a team of US soldiers standing around me with rifles. I can see the sergeant's mouth moving, but I can't hear him.

The team of soldiers drag me to a tan armored vehicle, and they load Dan beside me. My gear is ripped off me as they search my body for injuries. My world starts to spin, and I feel like I might vomit again. Closing my eyes, I turn my head to still my stomach and don't attempt to open them again until they've finished wrapping my head wound with bandages.

They've finished treating me, so I chance a look.

They're all talking to me. No, they're yelling at me.

I can't hear anything.

11

Harper ~ Now

"Hey, Harper. What's up?"

"Liza, he showed up," I whisper from inside the office I use when I'm working in the Monterey County Audiology Center.

"Holy shit, Harp. You okay? Why are you whispering?"

"He's in with the boss right now. Couldn't tell you why I'm whispering. I'm kinda freaking out I guess."

"I thought this is what you wanted. Why are you freaking out?" she chirps on the other end of the line.

"What if he asks for a different speech pathologist?"

"Harper, you can't jump to the worst possible scenario, you don't know what's going to happen."

"Liza, you didn't see his face when he saw me at his place the other day. He was a total stranger and I was the last person he wanted to see."

"Sweetie, from everything you've told me he's lost a lot and probably not sure if he wants you to see this new version of him. Give him some time."

"He's had two years."

My best friend sighs on the other end of the phone. She's been with me every step of the way. Inseparable since high school, if it's happened to me she knows it and she knows how tortured I've been the last twenty-four months.

"I know he has, but he had a pretty good reason, wouldn't you say?"

"It depends on the hour of the day, I guess. Some days I get it and other days I think it would have been nice for him to have at least let me know he was alive. I mean he left me a note. That was it! For two years! I'm not sure he would have ever come looking for me if he hadn't ended up in the clinic, Liza. I may not have ever seen him again."

"Harper, just breathe. You've got this. Besides…"

There's a knock on the door and a handsome head pops inside the office.

"Hey, I have to go. Call you later."

Dr. Cody's giving me the look that asks if I'm ready for this and I'm not really sure I am. I wipe my sweaty palms on my pants and take a deep breath, just like Liza suggested and nod my head.

This is a good sign. He hasn't asked for a different pathologist.

The doctor opens the door wide and Huck looms large behind him. I remember him being tall and fit but he's much bigger than he was before. His arms are testing the strength of the cotton keeping his t-shirt together and his short hair does nothing to hide the size of his neck.

"Harper Keaton, please meet Ben Finnegan." He steps to the side to let him in the office and gives me a wink of support. Huck can't hear him and he's behind him so he can't read his lips. He's keeping it professional for me.

Reaching deep and finding every bit of boldness I have inside I step forward and offer my hand. "Hi."

"Hey, Harper. It's good to see you." He takes my hand and my eyes sting with tears that want desperately to fall with the simple touch of our hands.

I've thought he was gone forever or possibly dead for the last two years and here he is in the flesh. I'm actually touching him again and it's a handshake in a medical clinic. Not exactly how I've always imagined our first touch after all this time, but it's still overwhelming.

The click of the door signals the fact we've been shaking hands for some time now and Dr. Cody's left the room. As much as I hate to, I let go and motion for him to take a seat in one of the chairs in front of my desk. He looks shell-shocked. I know the feeling. The fact I'm actually functioning in any form at all is a miracle in itself.

He takes a seat overwhelming the chair as much as he does my emotions.

He's big, strong, devastatingly handsome yet, the cocky arrogance of his I loved so much is nowhere to be found. One glance at the bird on his arm and I can't help but think of the song that inspired it and how he sounded singing it. Music meant so much to him. I can't imagine how hard losing that has been for him.

The thought has my nose running and my eyes burning as I somehow keep the tears at bay.

Here's hoping I can make things a little easier for him.

As I do with all my clients, I'll speak and sign to him. This way he can learn to read lips and American Sign Language or ASL at the same time. Well, this is what I should be doing, but at the moment I'm sitting on the other side of my desk staring at him.

I've started this conversation a hundred times before, but I don't know where to start with Huck. I have so much I want to say to him but he's not here because we were once in love, he's here because he has to be. After getting pulled over the night I went to his place his boss has mandated his appointments. He's stuck with me unless he asks for someone else.

I nearly jump out of my seat when he starts speaking. "I know this is weird, Harper. And I'm sure I'm the last person you want as your patient, but here we are. I'm decent at reading lips but I don't sign at all. Dr. Cody gave me this." He holds up the tablet we use for our patients who don't know ASL yet. "So, if you want we can talk with these things."

"Right, yes. The tablets."

~

"What's up with you, girl?" Brian asks, sitting down on the couch in his usual spot. He takes the center cushion with me against the arm of the chair.

I snuggle against him resting my head on his shoulder. "Just a long day. Had a tough patient this afternoon."

"Want to talk about it?"

"Nope."

I'm not sure why I don't tell Brian about Huck. I didn't mention anything when I saw him in the office the first time or after I went to his place. My time with him today was a lot to take in and frankly left me exhausted. I trust Brian with my life, but for some reason, I'm not ready to tell him about Huck. I don't know what his reaction will be but I know I'm not ready for it. Rightly so, he has some very strong opinions about Benjamin Finnegan.

He interlaces our fingers together and we settle in for a night of TV and wine. He doesn't ask any more questions and I don't offer much in the way of conversation.

It's only nine-thirty when the facade that everything is okay becomes too much. "Hey, I'm gonna call it a night."

When I get up from the couch, he tugs on my hand. "You sure you're okay?"

Ugh, he knows me so well.

"I'm fine. Just tired."

"If you say so. You still up for breakfast with my parents in the morning?"

"Of course, I can't wait to see them. I just need some sleep and I'll be fine."

I leave him with a peck on the cheek and the full length of the couch to binge *Ozarks* without me.

Before I know it, I've gone through the steps of cleansing, toning and moisturizing my face, brushing my teeth and applying lotion to my hands and feet and don't remember doing any of it by the time I'm lying in the dark because my mind is still back in the office. Back to the thirty-minute consultation that was nothing but clinical. We discussed his injuries, surgeries and why he hadn't tried to learn sign language yet. Well, he didn't really have an answer to that question, but I have a sneaking suspicion his pride may have something to do with it. When I asked him why he hadn't tried to learn ASL or considered cochlear implants, he pretty much gave me non-answers and it was clear to me.

He sees his deafness as a weakness and Huck has never been weak a day in his life.

The only thing he did tell me was how he had figured out how to control his tone and volume since he can't hear how it sounds when he talks to people. Rehab helped, but reading the expressions on the faces of those he communicates with was the real solution. From what I can tell, he's done an excellent job at mastering this workaround, now if only he would give ASL a chance.

A few hours later lying in bed with no sleep in sight I hear the TV turn off and Brian going through his nightly steps to close the house up for the night. Rolling to my side, I try to count sheep, but it's useless.

Rubbing the compass on my wrist, thoughts of endless nights, his smooth voice and acoustic guitar serenading me, tattoo shops and bonfires, skinny dipping and the weight of his body on mine.

Is he thinking about our time together tonight?

Did seeing me today have the same impact on him?

If I don't get some sleep and clear my head, breakfast with Brian's parents could be a disaster.

I decide to go to my tried and true sleep remedy I came up with when Huck first left Bali, grabbing my earbuds and my phone from my bedside table. As always I select "Blackbird" by *The Beatles.* I make sure it's on repeat and push play. Paul McCartney and his haunting guitar sing me to sleep but not before I shed heartbroken tears knowing Huck may never hear this song again.

Silent tears soak my pillow as my mind drifts back to the first time he sang it for me. The passion and feeling that came through with every strum of the guitar and with every note he sang.

"Huck?"

"Harper?" he asks while continuing to drag his tongue in lazy circles around my nipple.

He asks like he doesn't know what I want. As though he has no idea what he's doing to me. We've spent the last few days in and out of his bed, and he's already found all the ways to wind me up. He knows my body inside and out and he's using his findings to his advantage.

I reach down trying to take what I'm in desperate need of, but he maneuvers his body so I can't claim my prize.

"Why are you doing this to me?"

He kisses my ribs as his hands glide down my sides and his body follows in the same direction. "What am I doing to you, baby?" He kisses me right above my aching core. "Does this not feel good?"

"You know it feels good. Too good." He kisses me applying pressure but not giving me more. "Huck, please. I need to feel you inside me."

"Oh, Freckles..." His tongue takes a leisurely lap between my folds and I lose my breath. "You know I love to hear you beg."

"Ugh! You are impossible!" I hate that he's getting what he wants, but I can't help but give it to him. I need more. "Huck, please I need you." I beg like the needy woman I am.

"What do you need. Talk to me, baby."

"I need you to do that with your tongue one more time, and then I need to feel you inside me. Please?"

"Is this what you mean?" he asks before doing that thing with his tongue yet again. That tongue of his, along with a certain part of his body that's brought me hours of pleasure should be insured for millions because if anything ever happened to either of them, it would be a travesty.

"Yes. Fuck yes."

He does that thing he does so well again only nice and slow and then without a hint of the urgency pouring out of me he makes his way up my body. Gently biting and then licking and kissing away the stings on my skin as he finds his way. "Such a dirty mouth. I like it."

The condom is already sitting on the bed at the ready when he positions himself between my thighs and talks to me while he covers his length.

"Is this what you want, Harper?"

He gently strokes himself once the protection is in place and I'm too mesmerized to respond.

"Use your words, Freckles. Tell me, is this what you want?"

"Fuck, yes."

"There it is. So, you want my cock, Harper?"

I do, I really do, but I want so much more. Making sure he sees the sincerity in my eyes, I answer honestly. "I just want you, Huck."

He doesn't reply. He doesn't need to. Our connection is enough. Our eyes are locked on each other and I swear we can read each other's souls. I know it's fast and I know the fact we're in paradise compounds things, but I have a feeling I don't stand a chance of not falling for this man.

He takes his time moving in and out of me while never breaking our connection. He's moving at his own pace and it's just fine with me. He's still up on his knees kneeling in front of me in all of his glory and glorious he most certainly is. With his hands on my hips, he guides our bodies together finding the most beautiful rhythm. I want him to take his time, to make this last forever. I never want our time together to end.

When he puts his thumb up to my lips, I know he's ready to take our leisurely tempo a little faster. I wet his thumb with my mouth and brace myself for what's coming. As soon as his thumb hits me in the place he knows will take me all the way there, he picks up his pace. The fullness of him hitting just the right spot as he moves in and out of me along with his thumb rubbing those perfect circles has me ready to combust.

"That's it, baby. I wanna feel you."

His words do nothing but fuel the inferno inside. My back arches and my hands reach for him. I need him closer. He brings his weight down on his forearms hovering above me without missing a beat. His thumb may no longer be working its magic, but there is still friction between us and the moment he crashes his lips to mine I'm there.

"Huck, I'm..." I pant against his lips unable to get a full sentence out.

"Come for me, Harper," he commands as his hips drive harder and harder thrusting deeper and deeper.

Just when he feels me start to fall over the edge, he arches his back and the view is one I could never tire of. His broad chest and his muscular traps tense, he clenches his jaw and rides my climax to his own and we come together.

"You really are amazing, you know that?" he says, following his statement with a kiss and pushing an errant hair off my face. "You know you don't have to beg though, right? I'd give you anything you asked for. No begging required."

He kisses me again and I slap him on the arm. "Liar. You were torturing me, and you know it! You are an evil man, Benjamin Finnegan!"

"Ah, Freckles, I don't think you really mean those hurtful words, now do you?"

He gets up to dispose of the condom, his fine ass a welcome sight. Not just welcome but perfect and he's right. I sigh, admitting my defeat. "I forgive you."

He looks over his shoulder catching me blatantly watching him. I don't bat an eye. I have no shame in my game and he just chuckles.

"Play me 'Blackbird.'"

"What?"

"You said you'd give me anything I asked for, no begging required. I want you to play me 'Blackbird.'"

"Right now, huh?"

"Yep, and just like that. Just you and your guitar."

He picks his beloved six-string up by the neck and the shit-eating grin on his face has me ready for round two in an instant. "Just me and Eleanor, huh?"

"You said you'd do anything I asked."

"I sure did." He winks at me. With not a hint of insecurity, he

brings his beloved Eleanor to the bed with him in nothing but his birthday suit.

His face is thoughtful as he situates himself against the headboard. His tan legs are out in front of him crossed at the ankles and his guitar is on his lap. His hair has that just got laid look going on and when I think of how the scruff adorning his chiseled jawline feels between my legs, I have to readjust myself to contain how ready he has me feeling again.

He strums his guitar and makes the needed adjustments to make sure everything is in tune. The moment he starts playing the haunting chords that mean so much to him, his eyes find mine and I feel the love we haven't yet confessed.

The moment he opens his mouth his soft, soulful voice fills the bungalow and my heart swells with the emotion of not just my feelings for the gorgeous man in front of me but because the song means so much to him. It represents the love he had for his grandmother and it's so much a part of him he had the imagery of the song tattooed on his arm.

When he gets to the chorus his eyes close. He sings from deep within his soul. Baring himself physically and emotionally. I am completely, utterly in love with every piece of him.

The song ends, his eyes open and his head tilts displaying a crooked smile as he strums the last notes of my new favorite song.

Claps and bravos can be heard from the surrounding bungalows and without missing a beat, he yells a thank you out the windowless window to his neighboring fans.

He reaches out and wipes a tear from my cheek. "Huck, that was absolutely beautiful. Thank you."

"Nowhere near as beautiful as you. Come here."

Eleanor set aside, I replace the instrument in his lap cuddling up as close as I can get to him. Skin to skin we hold each other and take in the beauty of the moment we're in.

Eventually, he kisses the top of my head and breaks the silence of the moment with his low husky voice. "I'm glad you liked it."

"I loved it, Huck."

I love you is what I want to say, but the words are stuck in my throat. It's only been a matter of days and it's way too soon.

But I do.

I love him.

12

Huck ~ Now

God, I hate a public gym.

Does anyone actually come here to work out? I'm on my twenty-eighth minute on this damn treadmill and I haven't seen anybody else really putting in any work. There are people talking, flirting, and staring at themselves in the mirrors. I mean the guys who work out on base are annoying, but at least they're productive.

Currently, my life consists of going to work and the gym and now weekly appointments with the girl I left behind two years ago. The rest of my time is riding aimlessly on my bike and sitting at home drowning myself in rum and Coke. Bradford and the guys are always inviting me to hang with them, but do I ever take them up on their offers? Of course not. In fact, the invites never stop no matter how many dinners, happy hours, poker nights, tee times or sporting events I turn down. Those fuckers just won't leave me alone.

All it took was one uncomfortable, yet fan-fucking-tastic appointment with Harper and I suddenly want to try.

Being in her presence was soothing yet scary as hell, hopeful and heartbreaking. I knew she was witty and smart but seeing her with her hair up wearing her white medical coat was very hot for teacher and more than worked for me. If she had thrown glasses into the mix, I may have had to get up and leave the room for fear I'd clear her damn desk of all of its belongings and take her right then and there.

Reconciling the bikini-clad woman from Bali with the professional woman she is today might take some getting used to but only makes me want her more.

That's why I'm at this goddamned meat market right now and why I said yes to drinks at the Old Cayucos tonight.

Sitting across a desk from her isn't enough. I need more.

The thing is…I'm nowhere near ready for her. I've hidden myself away for too long and I don't know what to do with myself anymore. What I do know is if there is even the smallest chance in hell our fateful situation could bring her back into my life, if there's a sliver of hope I might get to touch her again then I don't want it to be years from now.

After the first hour of our first date in Bali, I don't think we were ever not touching when we were near each other. I've dreamed of her every day and there we were face to face but in a medical office with a desk between us. A desk that felt more like an insurmountable wall keeping us apart. A wall I wanted to scale to get to her. To touch her. Hold her.

Somehow, make up for the last two years.

Instead, I was talking to her on a tablet.

The way she kept fidgeting with her necklace told me she was nervous, but the way she pulled her sleeve down to cover her tattoo was just plain awkward. Was she trying to keep it professional and not bring up the past? I noticed the compass peeking out from under her sleeve when I first sat down, and it was a punch to the gut.

Another reminder of the promise I didn't keep.

As we went over my file, my current health status and all the other basics she was required to ask about I was searching her face for something. I found another tell that said she wasn't just feeling awkward but that there was still something there, she was all business, but she still found a way to ramble. She likes to call it word vomit but I call it adorable.

When she asked why I hadn't wanted to use sign language yet I didn't have an answer for her. Well, I did but I wasn't quite ready to tell her what a pussy I was. That I was embarrassed. I would rather people think I was just a rude asshole who didn't answer when they spoke to me. Her brows creased at my answer because she knew I was spewing her bullshit. She didn't call me on it, this time, but with the list of homework she gave me, she is clearly quite the taskmaster and I'm not sure how long she'll let me get away with my half-ass answers.

She also mentioned that I might be a candidate for a cochlear implant, and I didn't have much to say about that either. I've read up on the implants and I don't know if it's worth it if I don't really hear sounds like her laughter again. An electronic signal that sends robotic sounds in place of the real sound of her voice or of the real sound of music seems almost worse than just not being able to hear at all.

Her eyes pleaded with me to talk to her. Confide in her. But I wasn't ready to climb over the wall still between us.

By the time I was letting go of her hand and saying goodbye, my feelings about getting my ass over that insurmountable space between us had changed.

Seeing her was the kick in the ass I needed, but it also left me feeling a little lost. She mentioned more than once that trying to get back to some sort of normal social life would be the best way to learn to master lip reading and to adapt to life without sound.

She said it could help with the depression that can also come along with such a big change.

I don't have to tell her she's right about the depression. She knows. It's in her eyes. She still knows me and because she does, she isn't pushing me to talk about it.

So, here I am. Getting out my aggressions at this piece of shit gym. Not because I'm depressed. Okay, maybe a little depressed, but Harper is a bit of hope in my somewhat dreary life. She also made me promise I would do my homework and that meant getting out into the real world. So, here I am following instructions and doing as I was told.

After forty minutes I slap the red stop button in front of me and as the machine slows down, I know the belt is making that whizzing sound it makes as it slows and the pounding of my feet is getting louder.

As the belt cools me down my eyes survey the gym and I see cast iron plates on the weight racks bang against one another and I know the entire gym can hear the clank of the weights as they touch. Just like I know there is music playing throughout the building and the dude lifting the two hundred fifty pounds over on the Smith machine is grunting like a son-of-a-bitch.

I know the sounds of a gym. I just can't hear them.

One step off the treadmill and my visual is full of breasts. Breasts struggling to stay put in a sports bra that is clearly a size or two too small for the twenty-something blonde who's bouncing on the balls of her feet just enough to threaten a nip slip.

She offers her hand and because I'm not a complete asshole I take it.

"Hi." This is all I offer, but she doesn't seem to notice because she's talking a mile a minute. All I hear is the voice in my head telling me to wear earbuds next time so I can ignore people without seeming rude.

Trying desperately to come up with a nice way to brush her

off I scan the gym for something. Anything I can use as an excuse to walk away. My wandering eyes stop their search when they land on Dr. Cody from Harper's office.

They don't just land on the good doctor but also the redhead he seems to be arguing with. Not sure if it's a lover's quarrel or what, but he has that same superior look on his face that he had whenever he wasn't playing the part of caring physician.

I watched him from the waiting room and noticed a smugness about the way he carried himself. In his mind, every woman wanted him, and every man wanted to be him. His demeanor during my appointment was completely different. He was kind to the assistant that typed notes into a laptop, and he was respectful and decent to me.

Like a modern-day Jekyll and Hyde.

The facade is gone today. At least for him.

Red is doing everything she can to make their conversation appear pleasant, but I can see the fear in her eyes. He pushes her thick red curls over her pale shoulder and leans forward to whisper something in her ear. She pulls back from him and although it's barely noticeable, I can see her trembling. He's pissed off and she's worried about the consequences.

She walks away while he puts the mat he was stretching on back on the stack where it goes. Of course, he doesn't wipe it down before putting it back, but he does, not so subtly, check himself out in the mirror one more time. Once he has his fill of himself, he follows behind her and without thinking so do I.

"Excuse me," I say, walking around the blonde still talking in front of me.

At first Dr. Cody's hand rests gently on the small of her back but as they approach a red BMW, he grabs her by the upper arm looking like a police officer helping his perp into the car. I've stayed inside watching through the window, but when he turns her and pushes her against the Beamer a little too roughly, I'm out the gym doors without a second thought.

Three hurried steps into the breezy afternoon air I stop in my tracks.

Red's free hand snakes up his chest and he releases her arm, grabbing her by the waist and pulling her to him. He kisses her roughly and she kisses him right back. Her hands are all over him and he pulls her by the hips only to push her back against the car again. A cat-like grin says she likes it a little rough and my first impression may have been off.

Instead of going back inside I decide to hop on my bike and call it a day. I feel better knowing she was in on the rough play, but I still have a bad feeling about the two of them. Something is rubbing me the wrong way just like it did watching him from the waiting room. I'm not comfortable treating a woman like that, even if she likes it.

Maybe I'm just old-fashioned. Maybe it's none of my business.

~

Huck: Dude, I'm gonna head out. Thanks for the invite.

I throw a twenty on the table to cover my untouched portion of the fried food frenzy I barely put a dent in, take the final swig of my beer and push back from the table ready to say goodnight, when my phone lights up.

Bradford: Sit your ass back down, asshole.

. . .

Huck: It's been a long week. I showed up. Give me credit for that.

Bradford: I know it sucks but stay a little longer. It might get easier.

How the fuck do you know if it will get easier? This is what I think in my head but don't say out loud. I keep a lot of things in these days. Before my appointment with Harper, I was on the edge of my breaking point and all the things I've been keeping in were about to bust loose. Since my appointment, I've stepped back from the edge and given myself some breathing room.

"Guys, I'm gonna head out. It's been fun," I announce to the table when I stop messing with Thomas' texts and lift my ass off the chair. "If any of you shit heads drink too much, text me and I'll come get you."

The guys protest, but luckily, I can't hear their bitching as I slap them all on the back when their handshakes pull me in for bro-hugs.

I can tell they're glad I came out and it really hasn't been too bad but if they all bang on the table in fits of laughter one more time and I'm not in on the joke, I may lose my fucking mind.

Isaac, Ford, and Shane are all single without a care in the world. Technically, I'm single too, but there hasn't been anyone since Harper.

Thomas is the old married guy of the group and I know he won't be here much longer. He hates being here as much as I do only for a much better reason. He can't stand to be away from Annabelle one second longer than he needs to be and damn it if I'm not a jealous bastard.

The other three don't even have to try to get women. They're all badasses and I guess rugged looking but there is something else about them that women love. I'm not sure if it's the fact they're always together and when the ladies see a pack of man muscle like that they all want a piece of it or what? Whatever it is, it means these three don't have to try in the least to get a date.

Isaac and Shane are the brawn of the group and Ford would be the beauty. He's just as big and scary as the other two but he's got that smoldering thing about him. I swear I've seen panties fall right off waitresses in the middle of the day with just the lift of his eyebrow. He's also the serious one. The other two never stop messing around and are always placing a bet on something.

I think I'll leave them to their own devices for the rest of the evening. They don't need their lame co-worker bringing down their cred with the ladies.

The night air fills my lungs replacing the staleness you get from an evening spent in a bar and cardroom like the Old Cayucos. One of the things I don't mind about Monterey County, you can actually see the stars on a night like tonight and I force myself to take them in. Clear my lungs and mind with the cool coastal air before shoving my head in my helmet.

It's a gorgeous night and I'll be spending it alone.

Until recently I had resigned myself to this life, but since those emerald eyes locked with mine, I've been wanting more.

The numbness has subsided and unfortunately, I'm starting to feel again. The problem with this is that I'm feeling fucking everything!

I worked pretty damn hard to block out the loneliness and convince myself I'm okay alone. Without music. Without the friends I've lost. Without Harper.

One look from her was a rude awakening, because it was proof I was far from okay.

When she showed up on my doorstep, her presence nearly brought me to my knees because it meant she still cared. And that hurt. It hurt bad. It meant that after everything I've done to her, after letting her down, she still cared. She still showed up. Even though I couldn't.

My appointment with her was the final straw that broke this idiot's back. She was so close but so far away. I remembered every facial expression and nervous habit. Her eyes spoke to me even with that poker face firmly in place. Being in her vicinity has me wanting more. Not just from her, but from life.

I only stayed out for an hour, but I did it. If I'm being honest with myself, it really didn't go that bad with the guys tonight. I got a lot of what was said but once the drinks arrived and their glasses were blocking their mouths things got harder. Most of the time they were talking so fast I could only get bits and pieces. It was frustrating to say the least.

Harper said this would happen. She warned me it would be frustrating but that if I let the people around me know to be sure I could see their faces and to let me ask questions to clarify, it would help. But this would be asking for help and not something I'm accustomed to. The guys don't give me shit and they would be more than cool if I asked them to accommodate me, but I don't have the balls to do it.

I could take on any enemy in the dead of night without a moment's hesitation, but my damn pride won't let me ask the guys to slow down. I know I'm being a pussy and I need to get over it, but for now, the fact that I went out at all is something.

In the past when things got shitty, I had my music to turn to. Without this outlet I'm lost, and I know what the rest of my night will consist of.

Rum.

13

Harper ~ Now

"And you guys, he is so great with the baby. Morgan just loves her daddy so much already."

"That's great, Liza. It's nice to hear parenthood is going well for you and Michael."

It's more than obvious Stephanie is simply placating Liza because her face and her tone is just as exasperated as I feel. We've been here for half an hour now and nobody has gotten to speak a word, except Liza. Liza, who won't stop gushing over Michael. I love seeing her happy and it's great they still feel like this after all these years together, but enough is enough already. If I didn't know better, I would think she was overcompensating for something. I can't help but wonder if maybe she has a case of the baby blues but doesn't want anyone to know so she's over the top about how happy she is?

"Ladies, please tell me we will never stop having our Monday lunches. As much as I love motherhood, I couldn't live without the three of you and I really need these lunches to stay sane. Now, fill me in on everything! Harper, you first! What's new with you? How's Brian?"

"Brian's good. He's training for his next Spartan race and busy with work, so he's gone a lot. Work is good and I'm just trying to get myself to the gym once a week let alone train for a Spartan, I'm not sure where he finds all that energy."

"Well, all that work certainly has paid off. I mean look at him!" Stephanie squeals.

"Behave yourself, Steph!" I throw a crouton at her but she ducks and it misses her.

"Harper, I may be married, but I'm not blind!"

"So, where are you ladies going on your travels next? Anything exotic coming up?" I ask, doing my best to get the topic off Brian's body.

Samantha, or Sam to her friends, and her cousin Stephanie are not only both from the same very wealthy family, but they also happen to be best friends and could pass as sisters, practically twins. Twins that would make Barbie feel insecure. Not only are they beautiful but they're sweet too. And smart. They own their own line of clothing boutiques in Los Angeles and San Diego but they pretty much run on their own so the girls have plenty of time to live the good life. And live the good life, they most certainly do.

They, along with Liza, have always been the epitome of the saying, blondes have more fun. This brunette has never had a hard time keeping up with their fun though. It's impossible not to have fun with these three in your life. Liza may not be herself right now, but once she adjusts to motherhood, I'm sure she'll be back and better than ever.

"Nothing too exotic in the near future," Sam replies.

"Unless you count Portland. We're going up next month to visit our friends Emily and Jonathan after their twins are born." Stephanie barely gets her sentence out before Liza takes over the conversation again. Just the mention of somebody else's babies, who aren't even born yet, sends her off on another tangent about motherhood.

When her phone vibrates, she checks her message and for a split-second stress washes over her face but not a moment later she's all smiles again.

"Sorry guys, it's Michael. He's so sweet, always checking on us and making sure we're okay. He really is so attentive and caring. I know you probably think I'm gushing a little too much, but he is just so…so…he's just so much more than I ever could have dreamed."

"Okay, you need to stop, or my soup may come back up and nobody wants that," Sam says only half joking.

It really is too much, and I am not quite sure what to make of it. I'll have to talk to her about it the next time it's just the two of us.

"Okay, okay, I'll stop. I have to go anyway." She tucks her phone into her purse and waves down our server.

"What do you mean, we've only been here thirty minutes?" I question her.

"I know, but Michael needs me at home, sorry Harp."

Stephanie chimes in under her breath. "If you can't go to lunch with friends for more than thirty minutes he can't be that great."

Liza pretends she doesn't hear her and pays her bill. She gives her goodbyes and hurries out of the restaurant like her hair is on fire.

"What in the world was that all about?" Steph asks once she's out of sight.

"I don't know, Steph, but she sure seems to be overcompensating for something. I mean, don't get me wrong, Michael's great but he's not perfect."

"Seems like it started after Morgan was born, maybe it's some sort of post-partum?" Stephanie says exactly what I was thinking.

"I was thinking the same thing. Maybe motherhood isn't treating her as well as we think and she's too embarrassed to tell us? I don't know since I've never been through it, but maybe it's something like that. I'll try to get some alone time with her and see what I can find out."

"Well, on a happier note…" Sam says with a little look to Stephanie as if I'm about to be hit with some epic news. "After Portland we're flying out to Amsterdam and then taking the train all over Europe for a month!"

"Oh, you guys, that sounds amazing! I want to be you two!" I say, not even trying to hide my jealousy.

"We were thinking you should come with us!"

"What? You guys are sweet, but there is no way I could take that much time off work. Besides, I would be a fifth wheel."

"You don't have to do the whole month. How about two weeks? You can meet us over there. Come on, you know you want to! And the guys will be golfing and fishing whenever they can, you won't even notice them." Sam winks.

Both of their blonde ponytails are bouncing with excitement at the prospect of me joining them in Europe and it does sound amazing, but now isn't the time. I know he's barely speaking to me but there is no way I would leave town as long as Huck is here. Of course, I don't tell them this, I haven't mentioned him to anyone but Liza.

"Guys, my caseload is packed, and I've got some clients who need me. It's not a good time but thanks so much for thinking of me."

"You sure?" Stephanie counters.

"Very. But I still want to hear all about it. Tell me everything you have planned!"

"Hey Harper, how goes it?"

I bump into Michael back in the break room and I can't help but think it's odd he's here at the office when Liza said he was waiting for her at home.

Interesting.

Not that working with your best friend's husband isn't already strange enough. I mean we don't work side by side, but we often share the same patients so there is cross over. At least we always have something to talk about if things get awkward at dinner parties.

What the heck is up with Liza? Why would she lie about leaving lunch? Now she's really got me worried.

"Things are good. How's your day? Getting enough sleep or is Morgan keeping you up?"

His face lights up at the mention of his baby girl.

"I have to tell you, Harper, that little girl already has me wrapped right around her little finger. Even if she does cry all night, she's still the sweetest thing I've ever seen. Besides, I have no doubt Liza will get her on a sleep schedule before we know it. She's really coming into her own as a mom."

"Ah, you guys are too cute. She was just gushing about you at lunch with the girls. I love seeing the two of you both still so in love after all these years especially now with parenthood in the mix."

"She was gushing, was she?" His smile says I've made his day.

"She was." I pat him on the shoulder as I pass him on my way out. "Thanks for making her so happy."

"The pleasure is all mine, Harper."

Leaving the blushing and in-love husband behind, I try to ignore the butterflies taking up residence in my stomach knowing my next appointment is Huck. Things felt really awkward during his last visit and I sure hope he's a bit more open to learning today. I also hope he's a bit more open to me in general.

"Hey, Little Miss Harper. Your three-thirty is here, and boy, is he handsome," Penny chirps as I pass by the front desk.

Shit! He's early.

"Penny, behave yourself." I giggle because I know she's referring to Huck and she's right, he is insanely handsome. Although, handsome doesn't seem like a strong enough word to express how truly breathtaking he really is.

I was hoping for another ten minutes to gather myself before facing him, but there's no time like the present, so I scoot around the front desk trying to ignore the light sheen of sweat I feel coating my body as I head down the hall.

"I may be a nana, but I've still got eyes, Harper!" Penny calls after me. I'm glad she's here for some levity because I have been worked up about this appointment for days.

When I get to the office door, I can't seem to turn the handle.

"Whatcha doin', Harper?" Michael asks with an amused smile on his face.

"He's in there," I say. No further explanation needed. He's married to my best friend, he knows who he is to me. Heck, after my tears the first day he was in the office, everyone knows there's something between the two of us. It's so embarrassing.

"Wow, this guy must be something else. I've never seen you like this," Michael says, reaching for the handle. "Shall I?"

"No!" I blurt out. "Hands off, mister."

"Okay, but you have to actually turn the handle to make the door open. You know that, right?"

"Be nice. You're supposed to be my friend," I say, wiping my clammy hands on the scrubs I purposely wore today. Hoping if I stay casual and don't act like I'm trying, he'll let his guard down a bit.

Michael steps behind me rubbing my shoulders like I'm about to enter a boxing ring and whispers, "Go get him, Tiger." He reaches around me and turns the handle and the door creeps open.

"Jerk."

I hear his laughter as he walks away and I'm forced to enter the office.

Expecting to see him sitting in one of the overstuffed office chairs in front of my desk, I'm surprised to find his large frame is actually standing right next to the door reading one of the posters on the wall.

"Hey, Harper," he says, taking a step back, giving me room to enter.

My heart stops for a beat.

Holy shit balls.

The sight of him in his uniform is a first and it's freaking hot. Undeniably. Hot! From his Delta t-shirt stretched tight across his chest, to the green belt cinched around his small waist, to the camo pants that fit just right tucked into his tan boots. He looks like he just stepped out of a calendar full of hot men in uniform.

"Hi. How are you?" I speak and sign so he'll get used to it.

"I think you just asked me how I'm doing and I'm good now. I'll admit, I was a nervous wreck sitting here waiting for you."

Oh God, his voice still sounds like melting chocolate. Smooth. Sexy. I could listen to him talk all day but hearing him say he was good now that I was here has the butterflies in my stomach worked up into a frenzy.

"Why are you nervous?" I ask before shutting the door and walking behind my desk where I take a seat, but he continues to stand with his hands in his pockets.

"Why am I nervous?"

He's pacing but he doesn't seem anxious, he almost has an energetic vibe going on, like he's on the edge of being excited about something.

"Huck," I say, trying to get his attention, but he's not looking at me.

"I'm nervous because well, you're you and I'm me. Last time things were a bit stuffy. Not like the you and me from before. We weren't the people I remembered."

You will not cry, Harper Keaton.

I attempt to reply, but he keeps pacing and talking to the ground. "I'm nervous because I have to tell you that you were right. I went out with the guys on Friday and it wasn't too bad. In fact, I'm glad I went. However, I didn't have the balls to tell them to slow down or not to cover their mouths with their hands or glasses. I'm not sure what my hang up is with that, but I'm working on it. In fact, I talked to my boss about it today and plan on talking to the guys too. So, there you have it. You told me it would be frustrating and what to do to make it better and I didn't listen, and it sucked. You were right. But I'm trying."

He finally stops moving and looks at me. I heard everything that came out of his mouth, but my heart keeps going back to the part about us no longer being the people he remembered. I know the other part is a bigger deal for him and I have to put my work hat on and focus on his feelings, not my own. But my heart sure wants to go back to the beginning of his rant.

"You being right and me asking the guys to make changes is a step forward. It's me trying. It's also me getting my hopes up. And that scares the shit out of me."

I slide a tablet in his direction so we can talk.

"Why do changes that will increase your quality of life make you nervous?" I ask via the tablet.

"I don't know. I guess the more I put myself out there, the more attention I draw to myself," he speaks, not needing the tablet to reply.

"You were never afraid of drawing a crowd before."

He reads my note and gifts me a small crooked smile while squeezing my heart in the process.

"What are you trying to say, Harper? You sayin' I was full of myself back then?" There's a smile in his voice, his demeanor beginning to relax.

"You were confident. The most confident man I've ever met."

His eyes meet mine and we hold each other with our stares and just when I think that confidence is shining through him again he pierces my heart. "Yeah, well, that was a lifetime ago and I was a different person then."

"Do you want to talk about it?"

"Not really."

"Okay," I say not sure where to go from here.

"Sorry, nothing personal."

"It's okay. I understand. But if you need me, I'm here."

He looks up from his tablet almost somber now. "Thanks."

Wanting the Huck with a smile in his voice back, I cross the line of professionalism. "You look good in your uniform. Like, really good. Just sayin." I know he's my patient but I'd give up my certification to make him happy in this moment and my compliment seems to work.

"Is that your professional opinion?"

"Yes, as a matter of fact, it is." I smile.

I'm on fire with embarrassment and I can only imagine the color of crimson covering my face. The humiliation is worth the sexy-as-sin smile hitting me from across the desk.

"Duly noted, Ms. Keaton."

His use of my last name gets me back on track even if reluctantly. If I'm right, he'll shut down the moment we push forward. But push forward we must, and I type my next question into my tablet.

"So, if I was right about what to expect when hanging with

the guys, does this mean you'll take me up on my offer to teach you ASL?"

And just as I had expected, his smile vanishes and his expression grows dark.

"Huck, why don't you want to learn?" I ask when he doesn't answer me.

"I don't know, Harper. I just don't, okay?" He's uncomfortable but still holds my stare.

"Are you afraid you'll stand out more? Do you feel like without the visual proof that you've lost your hearing the world will never know? Do you see your hearing loss as a disability? Because, I don't."

"I don't have a goddamned disability, Harper," he says in a low voice. I think he thinks he's whispering but his voice carries more than he knows.

When I place my hand over his that's white-knuckling his tablet he pulls away instantly.

"You know what, Harper? I don't need your pity and I don't need to learn fucking ASL." He isn't yelling and he doesn't get up and storm off. He's simply matter of fact about his feelings.

He just sits there without saying a word. His hazel eyes plead with me. But for what I'm not sure. To fix him? To leave him alone? To go back to the way things were?

Needing to break the connection of his stare I look down at my tablet and start to type a reply.

"Huck, I'm here to help you, not pity you."

"But I don't want your help, Harper. I know I'm required to get help after my little situation with the police, but I would really like it if that help didn't come from you."

His words burn a hole in my heart and tears sting the back of my eyes. I will myself to remember he's a patient and not to take anything he says personally, but it's impossible when it comes to him.

Everything about Huck is personal.

Maybe he's right. Maybe it's for the best.

"I can provide a list of other speech pathologists who you can work with if you don't think I'm a good fit. Here, let me print that out for you."

It hurts too much to look at him right now, so I direct my attention at my computer and pull up my list of recommended pathologists and hit Print.

The paper is warm to the touch when I pull it from the printer and the tear that finds its way loose brands my cheek with the sting of rejection. I slyly wipe it away before turning back to the silent man filling the seat five feet in front of me.

I slide the list in his direction. "Here you go. Any of the pathologists on this list are great. It was really good to see you and I hope that you find a good fit."

"Harper…" He starts to speak but when I round the desk and open the office door to imply it's time for him to go, he stops himself from saying anything more.

He walks past me and out the door. I watch his large frame eclipse everything in the office as his tan boots stomp down the hallway. When he reaches the door to the waiting room, he turns the handle, looking in my direction one last time with a sullen expression that says I've let him down.

Well, Huck. I let myself down too.

I know I gave up too quickly but after two years of thinking he bailed on me, and now after two weeks of hope I'm not sure how much more rejection I can take.

14

Huck ~ Now

Dude, what the hell is your deal? You don't want her help? Of course not, you tool, but at least if she's helping you it means she's a part of your life.

Storming out of the clinic it hits me that I've just pushed her away like I have everyone else in my life. I don't know who this man is. I know it's not me. I think of my friends and fellow soldiers as brothers. My parents were like my best friends. We were the three amigos and these days I rarely speak to them. And now, even though the forces of nature, karma, God or whatever you want to call it, have put Harper back in my life, I've pushed her away too.

There was no way she could hide the devastation in her eyes. Her always vibrant eyes dulled as if I had told her I didn't want her on a personal level. All I meant was it was too hard for me to feel weak around her. I wanted her to think of me as the man she knew before.

The man my family and friends knew before.

But I fucked up, as usual.

Before everything happened, I was the guy who could bring a smile to anyone's face. I worked hard and played hard and everyone in my life knew I cared about them. I didn't take friendships for granted and when I made a promise, I kept it. Now, I can't even keep a damn promise to myself, let alone another person.

Once out of the building and with enough distance between the two of us I can finally breathe again. The warm sun and the barely-there breeze feel good on my skin and knowing I'll feel the purr of my bike underneath me in the next minute calms me.

Lost in my own world, I almost walk right into the cute little kid I met the first time I was here. He's jumping up and down trying to get my attention. His pudgy cheeks are bright red and wet with tears and he's clearly panicking about something because he's signing furiously at me, but I don't understand a damn thing his chubby little fingers are trying to tell me.

"Hey, buddy, what is it? What's wrong?" I bend down to his level hoping to get a better feel for what's going on.

He signs again and still, I don't have a clue.

Where is his mom?

"Sorry, buddy. I don't understand. Are you hurt?"

Frustrated, he grabs me by the hand and pulls me toward a car and that's when it all clicks. The driver side door is open, and I can see his mom lying on the ground next to the car. Running around to the open door my heartbeat picks up and I start to panic right along with the poor little guy as I watch his mom seizing on the ground.

My years of field training kick into gear and I instinctually go into action. By the time I reach her, the seizure is over and she's non-responsive. I check her breathing. Nothing. My fingers find her pulse on her neck, but it's weakening. I wipe the foam from her mouth clearing her airway and start CPR.

Every time I catch a glance at her son, he's doused in fear and his tears haven't stopped. Once I can feel her pulse beating again and she takes a gulping breath on her own, I scoop her up in my arms.

"Come on buddy, let's get her inside where the doctors can help her."

I know he doesn't understand me, but he nods his head and grabs onto my camo pants pocket and runs along beside me.

Back in the building, I thank the man above when the elevator opens for us the moment he pushes the button.

When the doors open on the fourth floor, the receptionist sees us coming through the windows and opens the door for us while yelling through the office. Doctors and nurses come from everywhere and usher me back to a room where I lay her on a paper-covered table.

Not sure exactly who I'm speaking to but wanting to get the information out there to somebody, anybody, I start explaining the situation and while I speak I feel a tiny shaking hand grab onto mine as the medical staff crowd around his mother.

We're pushed to the corner of the room and I can feel the anxiety course through me as the little boy shakes beside me, so I pick him up and hold him tightly. I rub his back and tell him it's going to be okay while his tears and runny nose soak my shirt. He can't hear my assurances and I don't know how to sign it to him.

I don't know what to do.

I just want him to be okay. For his mom to be okay.

My body is swaying back and forth naturally trying to soothe him when I catch a glimpse of Harper across the room.

I don't have time for regret at the moment, but it's there. One look at her face and I hate myself for hurting her. It's been two years and she hasn't made me feel like shit once and yet I seem to hurt her over and over again.

"I'm sorry," I mouth to her and she gives me a nod and works her way through the white coats filling the room to join me.

The moment her hand touches the scared little boy's back, he lifts his head and I can feel his body relax at the sight of her. His arms reach out and she takes him from me. I'm surprised how much I wish I were still holding him. I think he was comforting me just as much as I was comforting him.

I get it, little dude. I get it.

When the paramedics arrive, the three of us move out to the hallway and she sets him down to sign to him what's happening. He asks questions back in the end, nodding his head and taking her hand.

While we wait, I can't help but notice how nurturing she is with him. I try not to remember how I thought of a future with her the day I left her in Bali. I could see the two of us becoming a family. I knew she was the one the day I met her. Hell, I knew I would marry her and she would have my children before that first night was over.

But somehow, we ended up here.

Lost in my own world, I feel a tap on my shoulder and Harper asks for my phone. I unlock it and hand it over. Her thumbs work fast and she hands it right back and pulls her phone out of her pocket. Her thumbs jump into action again and my phone vibrates.

Harper: I'm going to follow the ambulance with Tyler and wait for his aunt to get there. I'll keep you updated on Molly.

Harper: Oh, and I added my contact info into your phone so you can reach me too.

Huck: Okay, thanks. You want me to go with you?

. . .

Harper: Nah. We'll be okay. From the sound of it, she's going to be just fine. Thanks to you.

Not sure how to reply to her comment, I simply nod and put my phone back in my pocket. The paramedics wheel Molly out and thank God she's alert and reaches for Tyler as she goes by. Harper picks him up and walks alongside the gurney with him and his mom signs what I can only imagine are assurances but what he signs back I have no idea.

But I desperately want to know.

As the flurry of bodies storm through the door Harper looks over her shoulder and those greens hit me with a look that says what, I don't know, but the hurt from just a few short minutes ago seems to have subsided somewhat.

The crowd of doctors, aides, nurses, and Penny from the front desk start to float back to their patients and workspaces, they each stop and thank me. Some sign, some just speak to me but there are so many and they are all talking while moving and it's too much to understand much more than the occasional thank you.

The frustration I felt back in Harper's office begins to prickle its way up my spine and weakness and humiliation begin to infiltrate the momentary distraction the traumatic excitement of the last few minutes brought.

I leave them all behind and follow my previous path but this time I make it to my bike.

As I pull out of the clinic's parking lot, my bike wants to head in the direction of the hospital but I know I won't be any help. What will I do if that sweet little boy tries to talk to me again? My guess is he was born deaf because his mouth doesn't move along with his hands when he signs. I wouldn't even be able to read his lips.

Nope, heading home to wallow in my weakness, as per usual, it is.

My phone lights up on the table next to my laptop and I startle like I've just been caught surfing porn. Since the moment I got home I've been online trying to teach myself to sign.

The fact I couldn't understand what Tyler was trying to tell me today, the fact it took more time than it should have to get me to Molly and that this delay could have had detrimental repercussions, will haunt me forever.

I can't believe what an immature asshole I've been. Why should I be embarrassed to use sign language to communicate? To be able to talk to a kid like Tyler or to comfort him when he needed me, that right there is enough of a reason to get over myself and pull my head out of my ass.

Even though I've been consumed with teaching myself the basics online, my mind has been on Tyler, Molly, and of course, Harper. I've been waiting for her text for two hours now and when I see her name light up on my phone, my body starts to shake from the inside out.

Harper: Hi.

Why does her simple 'hi' scare the shit out of me? Her lack of details instantly has my mind whirling to the worst-case scenario and I hate myself already. Another person I wasn't able to protect, to help.

I am a piece of shit.

Huck: Hi.

Harper: I just wanted to let you know all is well. Molly is still awake and responding and they say you got to her just in time. Her family wanted me to thank you for them. So, thank you. From Molly's family, Tyler, me, and everyone else. Thank you, Huck.

Thank Christ! The cold sweat from the fear of what she might tell me turns into a hot embarrassed sweat. I'm relieved but her thank you was hard to take. I don't feel worthy. I exhale the breath I had been holding on to for dear life and look up above to whatever god may be out there and say thank you for not taking Molly away from Tyler. My belief in God was shattered two years ago and I swear today is the first proof I've had that God may in fact exist.

Huck: That's great news. How's Tyler?

Harper: He's good. A little scared but he's good. He thinks you're some kind of superhero though.

Huck: Nah, I just happened to be in the right place at the right time. No hero here.

. . .

Harper: It's a good thing you ended our session early. I guess, everything really does happen for a reason.

Huck: About that, I'm sorry I was such a dick.

And I really was a dick. I'm so embarrassed by my behavior. I swear Tyler is more mature than my dumb ass.

Harper: No worries. I get it. So, I'm gonna head home. Tyler's aunt is going to take him to her place and Molly will stay here for observation for a few days.

Huck: A few days? I thought you said she was fine?!

Harper: She is but it was a pretty serious incident and she was unconscious longer than the doctors would have liked. She's alert and seems okay, but they want to watch her and run some tests to make sure they haven't missed anything.

All because I didn't get to her fast enough. Because I was too bullheaded to learn sign language. I've had two years. Two fucking years! It's pretty sad it took something like this to see what a colossal dumb fuck I am. But I see it now and it's time for things to change. The list of shit I need to work on is gonna be long, but I'm putting Harper's name on the top of my new Get Your Shit Together list.

. . .

Huck: Please give her my best and let me know you've made it home safely.

Harper: Will do.

I swear it feels like hours go by instead of the twenty-three minutes that pass before I hear from Harper.

Harper: Home safe and sound.

Huck: Okay, thanks.

Lame. I am so fucking lame. That's all I say to the woman of my dreams. The one I let get away.

Harper: You okay, Huck? I know it was a stressful day for you too. I'm sure waiting to hear if she was okay was hard.

Huck: I'm good. Thanks for asking though. Just glad I could do something to help. It wasn't much but I'm glad I was there.

Harper: Huck, you saved her life. Tyler still has a mommy because of you.

. . .

My insides feel like headphone cords that have gotten all twisted and tangled. Even on my best days, I'm a tangled mess but when a person like Harper gives me a compliment I twist myself into a deeper spiral and I'm not sure I'll ever fully unravel. My ability to accept a compliment left me long ago. I'm not worthy of anyone's praise. Not after I've let so many people down. Not since the guilt took over and my friends never came home to their families.

Huck: Well, thanks for the update. Have a good night, Harper.

I put the phone down and without even thinking about it head to the kitchen, pick up a bottle of Captain and make myself a rum and Coke, guzzling it down as though I had just been without hydration for days. Then I pour another one and head back to the table but my want to learn ASL has fallen by the wayside.

I stare at the lifeless screen for several minutes when I catch the glow from my phone lighting up again.

Harper: Hey…

Huck: Hey.

Harper: It really is good to see you again. And I understand why you want to go to a different pathologist.

Huck: Listen. I'm really sorry about today.

. . .

Harper: It's okay, really it is. Besides, as much as I would like to work with you, I won't be begging you this time. That may have worked once, but I won't fall for it again.

Was that…did she just…is Harper flirting with me? Did she mean to sound as sexy as she did? Is she fucking with me right now? If she's not, do I play along?

I must take too long before replying because another text comes through and she's backtracking.

Harper: I am so sorry. That was highly inappropriate of me and I didn't mean to cross a line. Please pretend I didn't say that.

Huck: Please don't be sorry. It would be inappropriate if you were still assigned to my case but since I quit you today, I don't think you're breaking any rules. But, I'll pretend it never happened if you prefer it.

Harper: Thank you, I guess. I really do wish we were able to work together. It's been nice being around you again.

Huck: It has been nice.

Harper: Well, good luck with everything and hopefully, we bump into each other in the future.

. . .

Huck: Goodnight, Harper.

Goodnight, Harper! Fucking ‘goodnight, Harper’ is all I have to say? She flirted with me. She was downright naughty only to follow it by saying it was nice to be around me and I just let the conversation end.

What in the hell is wrong with me?

15

Harper ~ Then

"Wow, Freckles, you clean up nice." Huck winks at me as he crosses the room taking me by the hand spinning me around. It's hard not to get distracted by his beauty with the light breeze ever so noticeably blowing the white curtains framing the open French doors behind him, and the turquoise of the ocean the perfect backdrop. I could stay endlessly lost in him, but tonight we have to leave this room. My dad is getting married after all.

"Do you like it?" I ask as my long blue floral maxi dress pools at my high heeled feet.

"I love this color on you. A lot."

He leans in for a kiss but I only give him a tiny peck trying to step back, but his hands are on my waist holding me in place. Kisses always lead to more when it comes to the two of us and I don't have time for more, besides the fact I just spent an hour getting ready.

"Thank you. I'm glad you like my dress, but you need to keep these hands…" I say, peeling his grip from my body. "And these lips…" I sigh into the gentle peck I place on his lips. "To yourself. We can't be late and it took a lot of work to look like I haven't spent all day in bed with you. I don't want all that hard work to go to waste before we're even out the door."

It's true. We barely got out of bed long enough to eat lunch by the pool. Lunch only happened because we needed sustenance to keep going. Food was a must. So was our private outdoor shower sex we shared for dessert. My back pressed against the stone wall. The water cascading off his back and shoulders. The exhilaration of being outside, even if it was private. Just thinking about it now gets me all hot and bothered. But now is not the time.

"You don't mean it." I see the look in his eyes, and I know he's up to something.

"Do too." I grab my purse off the table while ever so slowly walking backward knowing he's about to attack.

"You love it when I touch you, Harper." His hands are in the pockets of his perfectly fitting linen pants while he casually stalks me like his prey.

"Never said I didn't, Huck. But right now, is not the time!" I squeal when he takes two giant steps and lunges for me before I can make my escape. My hand was almost on the doorknob, but I wasn't fast enough. I never am. His knees bend and he squats down. I know what's coming. He's about to throw me over his shoulder caveman style or at least I think he is. As I'm learning, this man is full of surprises.

Instead of hurling me over his shoulder he gathers my dress and lifts it off the floor high enough to leave an opening for him to slide his hand under. His hand gently caresses the inside of my foot exposed from my strappy three-inch heels and then makes his way up my calf. When his fingers tickle the back of my knee my legs nearly buckle.

"Huck, what are you doing?" I ask with bated breath bracing myself on his shoulder so I don't fall over.

"If I have to keep my hands to myself, then I want to be sure I give you something to think about for the rest of the evening."

His fingertips are steadily moving up my thigh and as he approaches the motherland, I open my legs farther for him, so he has room to get to where he's going. He smiles, standing up to his full height with the front of my dress gathered in his hand. "I love that we're always on the same page."

When he sneaks a finger into the side of my panties and finds me wet for him his lazy smile becomes a heated glare. The one he gets when he's really turned on. The one he gets when he wants me.

God, I love it.

His finger moves in and out of me just three times and I'm already a crumbling mess. When he finishes his teasing, he lazily removes his hand from under my dress and lets the material fall in a whoosh to the ground. He puts his finger in his mouth and sucks it clean and I'm so turned on, just the friction from my lace underwear is enough to leave me unwound.

He casually adjusts the collar on his white button up shirt and then the sleeves of his beige linen jacket. "Ready to go?"

"You are a horrible human, you know that?"

"Aw, you don't mean it. You love me and you know it."

My pulse quickens and I'm sure he can see my heart doing its best not to beat out of my chest. I want to yell at the top of my lungs, 'Yes! Yes, I love you! More than I ever thought it was possible to love someone!' But that would be ridiculous. I've known him five days and I have fallen so hard there's no turning back. But I can't say it. Not yet. That would be ludicrous. Instead, I recover and return to the humor he and I use so well as I duck under his arm holding the door open for me.

"You wish, mister."

"You got that right."

Forgetting what I said about my makeup and him keeping his

hands to himself I pause in the open doorway to kiss him long and hard. When I pull back, I use my thumb to wipe my lipstick from his face. "Ya gotta love being on the same page."

He knows exactly what I mean without elaboration and his hand lifts to my face and ever so softly traces over my bottom lip.

"I knew you were a game changer the moment I met you."

His hand, the one that was just bringing me to my knees, glides into mine perfectly and we walk through the villa hand in hand. The gardens of the resort are lush and full of fragrant flowers, the perfect setting for a wedding. But before we make it ten feet into the gardens, Huck's adoring fans bombard us with hellos and promises of the first round being on them, when in fact my dad is paying for everything.

Last night at the rehearsal dinner everyone in attendance fell in love with him. We're a small group of fourteen, well now we are, counting Huck, but man, did Huck help put on a party last night. He borrowed a guitar from the beach club where I first heard him sing, and he serenaded my dad and my new stepmom Sutton. Sutton, my sister-in-law, Tilly, Sutton's sister, Margo, and girlfriends all fell under his spell and I thought for sure I had lost him to his adoring crowd and song requests. He kept trying to bow out graciously, but they were relentless. After the fifth song, he finally cut them off.

Setting the guitar in its case and closing it he brought the attention to my father. "Mr. Keaton, this weekend is about you and your fiancée and I don't want to turn the focus on me in any way. I just wanted to sing you a little something as my gift to you during this special time." He shakes my dad's hand and then looks over our little group and says, "Now, I need to get back to my date. She's the prettiest woman here and I don't want anybody to steal her away, now do I?"

I could tell in that instant that my dad was on board. In fact, I'm pretty sure if I told my dad we wanted to make it a double wedding he would go for it. Everyone wanted Huck's attention, but for the most part, it was all mine. Even my brother Josh seemed totally smitten. I left the two of them alone for two minutes while I went to the bathroom and came back to the tail end of a conversation about baseball and the two of them going to spring training in Arizona together someday.

"Two minutes! I was gone for two minutes and the two of you are planning a trip together!"

"Listen, Harper, when you meet the one, you just know it. Josh and I both share a love of baseball, beer, and hot spring nights." Huck tries his best to explain the situation, but it's not enough.

"So, you're saying you both have the same online dating profile and you're a match?"

"Harp, don't be such a hater. I would think you'd want your big brother and your boyfriend to get along. You should be glad I don't want to kick his ass instead."

"Boyfriend, huh?" I chew on that label for a minute, pretending I'm not sure I like how it sounds, when in fact it makes me giddy inside.

"Damn straight," is Huck's reply. He swings his arm around my shoulder and that was that.

The rest of the night he was by my side laughing and listening to old family stories for hours on end and the entire time he was holding my hand, touching my shoulder, kissing the top of my head or simply pulling me into him and holding me close. He almost never lost contact yet there was no extreme PDA that would have been off-putting to those around us.

After the rehearsal dinner that turned into quite the party, we were the first to excuse ourselves. All of the touching had built up an anxious need in both of us and as much fun as we were having, we both knew the kind of fun we could be having back in my room. Last night was the first time he slept here at the villa with me and at first, the extravagance embarrassed me, but I quickly got over it. Even though there's actual glass in the windows here, he still made quiet, sweet love to me all night long. I know we haven't said the words, but that's what it was. Sweet, gentle, honest and all-consuming love-making.

The faint bubbling of the lily-pad covered reflecting pools we walk past as we follow the rose-petal covered path that will take us to our destination for the evening is quite serene. Luckily, it has a calming effect that takes me from wanting to stay in my room with Huck to do naughty things all night to wanting to be here with my dad and the rest of my small family to share in this special moment. Huck always seems serene, but even he seems to be taking in the moment and stays quiet as we make our way to the cliffside lawn where my father will marry the love of his life.

I couldn't be happier for my dad. He and my mom didn't work out and that's okay. There was no cheating scandal and no bitter war for custody. They split when I was eight but they remained friends and it made growing up with divorced parents pretty easy. I know divorce has affected a lot of my friends in the hardest way, but I was pretty lucky. In fact, it wouldn't have surprised me if my mom had been invited, although for Sutton's sake I think it's good she isn't here. Sutton is lovely and makes my dad happy and that's all that matters. She is also one of the most sought-after real estate agents in Monterey County and successful in her own right. They are a match made in heaven.

The cliffside is adorned with a simple wooden archway covered in hibiscus and sheer white fabric being kissed by the breeze. The simple setting is utterly romantic. Sutton's plan to keep things simple was the right choice. It's amazing how breathtaking a little archway with flowers and some rose petals on the ground can be when you pair it with our surroundings. With the ocean and its horizon stretched out before us, the view is awe-inspiring and the majestic waves colliding into the rocky shore below is the perfect soundtrack.

Just as the beautiful smudges of coral, lavender, and a fiery orange begin to blend together over the turquoise sea, my dad and Sutton walk down the aisle together for their sunset ceremony.

Simple.

Side by side every step of the way.

Beautiful perfection.

My brother became ordained online and is marrying them and I have to say it's pretty cool. It means a lot to my dad to have our support and I know my brother is proud as a peacock Dad asked him to have such a big part in his special day.

The wedding is short and sweet, and Huck holds one of my hands on his lap while I dab a tissue at my eyes with my other. Something about weddings always gets me misty but hearing my dad's poetic vows to Sutton and to see them both so happy really tugs at my frilly little heartstrings.

Huck brings our interlocked hands up to his lips and kisses the back of my hand bringing my attention to his face. The moment our eyes lock I feel like there's an elephant on my chest and it becomes hard to breathe and even harder to hold back my tears. It's not every day you realize you're sitting next to your very own beautiful perfection and possible future. I break our connection and turn back to my dad kissing his bride and my brother announcing them as husband and wife. The rest of us in attendance cheer, whistle, and cry as they walk past us on the rose petals strewn about the grassy aisleway.

Josh joins his very own blushing bride of just over a year, and the twelve of us follow the happy couple to the reception area where pictures are taken including one of me, Huck, and a sunset none of us are soon to forget.

"Milady," Huck says, pulling out one of the white chairs in the middle of the long matching table. The table is accented with rose-gold embellishments and there are several strings of white lights floating above us. Glasses of champagne are waiting at each place setting and Dad waits for us all to take our seats but remains standing.

Dad is pure class and so is his toast. He thanks each and every one of us individually, including my date.

"Huck, thank you so much for being here. Thank you for the fantastic music last night and for putting such a big smile on my little girl's face. Here's hoping we see much more of you in the future."

"Thank you, sir. I hope so too."

I'm turned in my seat looking at my dad and I thank the Lord above for that because I can feel myself turning beet red. Randall Keaton does not make statements like that nor does he like any male who has ever dated his daughter. I'm utterly shocked and I'm so glad the toast moves on to his new wife so I can cool down while my dad tells Sutton how much he loves her. By the time we all lift our glasses and say cheers I've calmed enough to turn and face my new 'boyfriend.'

"My dad really likes you," I whisper to Huck.

"The feeling's mutual."

"How do you do it?"

"Do what?"

"Make everyone you meet fall head over heels in love with you. Male…female…it doesn't seem to matter. They all love you."

I know what I've done before he says a thing. Verbal upchuck. It's a real thing.

"So, when you say *everyone* are you including yourself? Because if you are, then I think you just told me you've fallen head over heels in love with me."

"Huck, shut up."

He winks at me but not before Josh has to play the typical big brother.

"Hey, didn't Mom and Dad teach you anything. It's not nice to tell people to shut up, Harp."

"Shut up, Josh."

"Dad!" he whines jokingly to the man of the hour.

"You two behave and get along. I'm too old for this shit. Now let's eat!"

The four-course meal that follows is fit for a king. The cake is a small, simple three-tiered cake but there is sophistication and beauty in each tier. Frosting gives a marble effect and the top of each layer looks like an ocean wave. It's beautiful and delicious. More toasts are made, first dances are had and now we're all dancing to the old Motown hits my dad loves so much.

When the first notes of the classic "Ain't No Mountain High Enough" comes on, Huck lights up like a Christmas Tree. I think this may be his jam. Marvin Gaye and Tammi Terrell may start the song, but by the end, we're each singing their parts and pointing to each other making up our own choreography as we go. I know it's just a song, but the words remind me of what he said to me two days ago when I asked him what we were going to do after this vacation was over and he said he would always find me.

And just like that, I have a new favorite song.

When Sister Sledge starts singing "We Are Family" Josh cuts in dragging me away and we get down to the song my mom used to play for us and we bounce around just like we did when we were little kids. I'm glad my brother and I get along so well. Josh has always been my rock and the perfect big brother. Marrying Tilly has made him an even better man and I'd say on the whole I'm pretty fortunate in the family department.

While we dance, I catch Dad and Huck chatting over cigars at the same table where dinner was held. Not only are they talking but they both seem very serious and are giving each other their undivided attention. Two more songs play and they're still in deep conversation. When a slow song comes on, I slip my shoes off my aching feet and make my way to the table to join them. When they notice me, they both start to put their cigars out.

True gentlemen.

"Ah, there she is." I sit down on my dad's lap and he kisses my temple. "How's my princess?"

"I'm great, Dad, it's been a beautiful night. How are you doing and what kind of conversation are you two having over here that's so serious cigars had to be involved?"

"Oh, my sweet girl this has to be one of the best nights of my life." Sutton joins us and I switch to Huck's lap and Sutton sits on my dad's lap giving him a soft kiss on the cheek. "As for the cigar conversation…well, that my dear, is between myself and Mr. Finnegan." Huck pats my hip, but his lips stay sealed. "Now, if you don't mind, we're going to bid you all goodnight."

"Welcome to the family, Sutton," I say, giving her a big hug.

"Thanks for everything, Harper. I'm always here if you need me."

Moving on to my dad he pulls me in for one of his awesome hugs and whispers in my ear. "Sweetheart, I don't care if I see you the rest of this trip. Go enjoy your time and just check in and let me know you're alive once every day or so. I love you and I hope you have the time of your life."

"What was in those cigars?" I plant a kiss on his cheek. "Thanks, Dad. I love you and I'm so thankful I got to be here for your big day."

"Love you too, Princess. Now, go have fun and remember to check in from time to time."

The new Mr. And Mrs. Keaton bid us goodnight and leave us standing under the beautiful white decorative lights strung above where my dad and Huck were just deep in conversation. Smoking cigars. Huh?

"What in the world did you and my father just talk about?"

"That's between us, but I do have a proposition for you." He snakes an arm around my waist pulling me tight against his body while pushing my hair behind my ear.

"What kind of proposition?"

"You have one week left and your room here at the resort will be here for you, but pack your bags and come stay with me. Just you and me for the next seven days and nights. What do you say?"

"What are you doing standing there?" I yell over my shoulder, skipping through the grass that leads to the lily ponds leading to the villa where my things are waiting to be packed.

He chases after me and when he catches up, he sweeps me off my feet and carries me the rest of the way. His arms hold me with little effort and mine are around his neck.

This is all too good to be true.

The night sky is aglow with millions of twinkling lights putting on a show. They have to be sparkling just for us because I swear there is nobody else in the world but he and I.

16

Huck ~ Now

If I take any more deep breaths I'm going to fucking hyperventilate before she even walks out of the building. Then not only will I be a deaf asshole who never called but I'll be passed out on the ground looking like a bigger pussy than she probably already thinks I am.

It's 4:08.

In her text last night, she commented that her last appointment here at the clinic would be done by four and she couldn't wait to be free for the weekend.

So, here I am. Stalking her at her place of work. Still in my uniform with flowers in my hand. It's time to apologize and let her know I never stopped thinking about her and that I'm still madly in love with her.

I don't even have to look up to know she's just walked through the doors because I can feel it. I feel her whenever she's near. It's like some sort of static in the air that makes my heart beat a little faster than it was the moment before she's in my presence.

I stand up a little straighter when she cocks her head to the side looking confused but by the time she's standing in front of me she has a shy smile on her face. A twinge of hope squeezes my heart.

I can't read lips fluently, but I know the basics and I see her say, "Hi."

"Hi," I reply back, handing her the flowers and trying not to sweat through my uniform. After her flirtatious comments the other day you better believe I wore my uniform again.

I'm a nervous damn wreck.

I've practiced this over and over and it's really not that hard, so why am I just standing here?

I take one more deep breath and form an A with my fist and make a circle over my chest when I say, "I'm sorry I didn't call."

A tear falls down her cheek. She signs, "It's okay."

I'm not sure but I think her tear is a happy one or maybe relief, I really have no idea. She reaches around my neck with her free hand and hugs me. My arms slide around her body with ease just like they always did and the scent of mangos has me transported back to a time when things were simple. Easy. Perfect.

"Will you teach me?" I ask into her hair, not ready to let her go yet.

She steps back and starts to speak and sign at the same time, but I cut her off.

"I want to learn but not here. Can you teach me somewhere else? Not in this sterile office where everybody knows why I'm here."

Her face is beaming, and I think she likes the prospect of spending time together almost as much as I do.

"Of course!" I read on her smiling lips but her head swings over her shoulder and she lifts her hand up to someone.

A male someone.

An attractive male someone with a perfect tan, perfect hair and who looks like he could hold his own in a bar fight.

She reaches into her purse and wags her phone in front of me. I'm pretty sure she's telling me she'll text me.

She lifts up on her toes, gives me a swift kiss to the cheek and skips off. She's excited and two minutes ago I would have thought it was because of me but now I know it's the male model waiting for her in the red convertible.

They say hope springs eternal. Well, that shit is a lie.

I can still smell the mango of her shampoo and feel her body pressed against mine from mere moments ago, but it's clear the feelings we used to share are now one-sided.

Standing in front of the silver office building, like an idiot, I watch as she jumps into the car and gives him the same little kiss on the cheek. She lifts my flowers to her nose smelling them and smiles when she sees me watching. She waves and then he pulls away from the curb where he collected her, and she's gone.

The sudden desire to punch something overtakes me and I feel like Bruce Banner turning into the green hulking version of himself. The version of himself that destroys shit. That's what I want to do right now. I want to break something, but I'm in uniform and I don't want to cause a scene where she works. Besides, what am I going to do? Pick up a car and toss it across the parking structure? I don't think so, but I sure as hell want to.

I don't know why I'm surprised. It's been two years. I never called. Didn't text. Didn't think to email. Nowadays there are plenty of ways to get in touch with someone especially, someone you love, and I didn't.

The compass tattoo on my chest is burning a hole in my skin and reminding me I didn't hold up my end of the bargain.

We promised we'd always find our way back to each other.

But I didn't.

I may be here now, but she knows it was coincidental. There's no way she could take my pathetic fleeing from this very building any differently.

If I'm not going to hold up my end of the deal, I shouldn't expect her to. We knew each other a couple weeks, how long did I really expect her to wait?

We said we were forever but where was I? I'm sure she thinks I didn't have enough trust in what we had together to let her know I had been hurt but how do I tell her I survived when nobody else did? How do I expect her to want to be with a man who isn't the man she fell in love with?

No, her being with the male model in the convertible is all my doing. I'm to blame for her moving on, not her.

I'm just surprised she didn't tell me. When we've texted about Tyler and Molly the last week or so we've made small talk. Talked about what was going on in our lives but she didn't mention the boyfriend. It's clear she sees me as a friend and nothing more.

I finally make my way to my bike and climb on. The roar of the engine reverberating through my body is one of the closest things I have to hearing. I live for the sound of her engine purring beneath me. I know Top asked me to start driving my truck, and some days I do. But days like today, when I need to feel normal, it's the rumbling of my bike that gives me the confidence that's been slowly waning, Confidence. It used to ooze out of me. Confidence used to be my normal.

I take the long way home and let my mind wander to all the what-ifs filtering through my brain. The biggest is what if I had reached out to her? Even though I couldn't call her and talk on the phone, I could have done something. I could have figured it out.

In the end, all I want is for her to be happy and that is sure what she seemed to be. I guess that's really all that matters.

I'm thinking these positive thoughts as I pull up to the liquor store and replenish my supply of rum and Coke.

I may be glad she's happy, but it doesn't mean it doesn't still hurt like a son of a bitch.

I load up my ingredients for the pity party I plan on having tonight, into the saddlebags on my Indian when I feel my phone vibrate. Knowing it's probably the guys asking me to meet them out again, I don't know why I check it when my answer isn't going to change, but I do.

And thank God, I do.

Freckles: How does tomorrow sound?

After our first night of texting, I changed her name in my phone. Now, every time I get a text from her, it feels like old times. Not that we were ever apart long enough to need to text one another back in Bali.

Huck: Tomorrow is Saturday, Harper. I don't expect you to work on your weekend.

Freckles: Spending time with you is never work, Huck.

You know what I said about hope and that whole eternal thing? Yep, I get it now. I know I shouldn't read more into this, but I can't help it.

. . .

Huck: You sure?

Freckles: More than sure.

Is this really happening?

Huck: Where would you like to meet?

Freckles: Would you mind picking me up? My car is in the shop.

Huck: Not at all. How about 2pm?

Freckles: Perfect. I'll send you my address and see you at 2pm tomorrow.

Huck: See ya tomorrow.

Freckles: Can't wait.

I feel like I've been on a roller coaster ride since the moment I decided to show up at her office and apologize.

By the time I get home, I'm exhausted and end up just having a drink to settle my nerves but not to drink myself into oblivion. I need to be at my best tomorrow. No hangover and no excuses.

I also have to remind myself tomorrow is not a date, at least I don't think it is. She's going to help me learn to sign and I can't come off like a buffoon so it's one drink, albeit, a big one in a giant tumbler, and then off to bed at a decent hour.

17

Harper ~ Now

"I can't believe you didn't tell me he was back!"

Brian's pissed. I didn't tell him until about five minutes ago that Huck was coming to pick me up.

I don't know why I've kept it from him since he knows my history when it comes to Huck. I usually tell him everything.

"I'm sorry, it didn't come up."

Man, I am lame if that's the best I've got.

"That is some bullshit right there and you know it!" he bellows angrier than I've ever seen him.

He's right. If I'm honest with myself, I knew how he would react, and I didn't want to deal with it. So, I didn't tell him.

"Brian, I'm sorry. I really am. But he needs my help. It's for work."

I take another look at myself in the mirror and I can't deny he's right. When do I ever take this much time getting ready for work? Never.

"More bullshit! You don't wear tight ass skinny jeans, those booty things on your feet, and *that* sweater to work. I don't even think I've ever seen you take this long on your hair and makeup for fuck's sake!"

"Brian…"

"Harper, how can you keep shit like this from me?" He's exasperated and as he does when he gets worked up he's using his hands. "I mean, for fuck's sake we live together, and you keep something like this from me."

Before I can come up with a reply to his last heartbroken statement, there's a knock at the door. I only get two steps toward the door before Brian cuts me off nearly ripping it off its hinges.

Shit!

This is so not good!

"Brian! Please! Just be nice!"

He doesn't care what I have to say when he throws the door open red-faced and pissed beyond belief.

I'm waiting for Brian to say something. Anything. But neither he nor Huck flinch or speak. It's like they're having some sort of standoff or contest to see who can go the longest without blinking. Or maybe who can be the biggest, toughest idiot in Monterey County.

This is ridiculous.

I pop a kiss on Brian's cheek, hoping he'll be a bit calmer and more level-headed when I get home. I duck under his arm still on the door he threw opened but grabbed right before it hit the wall because there is no way he'd put a hole in the wall, no matter how pissed he was. He cares too much about the way things look to damage the plaster in this house in a fit of rage.

Huck didn't step back when I crossed the threshold and both men are still being idiots. Neither backing down.

I get why Brian is upset but what does Huck have to be worked up about? He's the one that never called. He doesn't get to act protective or even jealous.

All it takes to get his attention is my hand on his chest. Over his heart to be exact. The moment I come in contact with him his eyes find mine.

"Let's go," I say somewhat slowly so he can read my lips.

He nods and turns toward the street giving me the opportunity to swing around on Brian. "Mature. Really mature." I all but spit the words at him but start walking after Huck.

"Oh, there will be a conversation later. This is not over, Harper."

"You're not my dad, Brian. You don't get to tell me who I can and can't spend time with."

"I won't be home when you get back, I'm going out with the guys," he hisses, slamming the door.

I know his reaction to Huck's reappearance is only this strong because he loves me and I know I should have told him but I didn't and here we are.

When I finally look up, Huck is standing next to the motorcycle he took off on at his place. This isn't just any motorcycle, it's a big beautiful badass looking bike. Seeing him standing next to said badass bike in perfectly fitting jeans, worn and scuffed combat boots and a black leather jacket over a white V-neck t-shirt is probably the sexiest thing I've ever seen.

As beautiful as they both are my head starts shaking back and forth in protest as I stop walking halfway down the driveway.

"No way," I speak out loud along with signing.

He picks up the smaller of his two helmets and meets me in the middle of the drive.

"Come on. Where's the adventurous girl who went cliff-diving with me in Bali?"

I'm a mix of surprised and pissed. Surprised he brought up Bali and our time together and pissed that he wants to know where that girl is. *Where is that girl? Where is the confident man who knew without a doubt we were meant to be?*

"Huck, come on," I say, not addressing the feelings rolling

around inside of me.

He ignores me and pulls the helmet over my head. Over the hair I just spent an hour working on.

Gah!

Why are all the men in my life so exhausting today?

"Sorry, Freckles," he says, climbing onto the motorcycle that fits him like a glove. "I can't read your lips with the helmet in the way and I don't know sign language yet, so I guess you better get on the back of my bike and teach me so you can tell me what you really mean in the future."

He called me Freckles. I want to be mad but how can I be when his sass is back? Not only is it back, if even just a glimpse of it, but he referenced me telling him what I really feel in the future.

The future.

And just like before, all rational thinking is out the door and my leg is swinging over the bike. I don't know what to do with my hands once I'm sitting behind him. I know what I *want* to do with them, but I don't know what I *should* do with them.

The moment I feel the engine underneath us and my ears are ravaged by her growl I grab on to the sides of his coat. This is one powerful engine and I can't help but feel a little saddened that he can't hear it too. I know he feels it though, there's no way he couldn't and I wonder if the roar of the engine is the reason he rides.

Any question as to why he rides is answered as soon as we're on the open road. I was holding on to his jacket for dear life and honestly a little afraid when he tugged on one of my hands and brought it around his waist and I met it in the middle with my other arm. With my arms around him like this I had to lean against his back and in the end, I caved and pressed my cheek against his jacket and let his body and machine guide us.

Even though I wasn't skin to skin, it was enough. I had been dreaming about being this close to him for two years and it was finally happening. If only it wasn't under these circumstances.

When we finally reach our destination, one of my favorite trailheads, he helps me off the bike and then off with my helmet. I make a face because I know my hair is a big crazy mess now and he chuckles while he does his best to fix the rat's nest on top of my head. It's sweet and it means we're still in close proximity. I'll take it.

"Perfect."

I roll my eyes at him and lead the way down the trail grateful the picnic bench I envisioned us working at was free. It's right above the dunes and there's an ocean view. It's the perfect beach setting without being distracted by sand and sandy memories of the two of us together.

I pick up a couple of small rocks and pull some papers out of my bag using the rocks to secure the papers on top of the table.

"Let's get started," I say and sign. Trying to make this my norm when I'm with him. It will help him get better at reading lips and learning to sign. He has a lot to learn at once, but consistency is key.

We both take our seats at the picnic table sitting across from one another. As we tend to do, we look at each other for a beat longer than we should. I have no idea what he's thinking. This is all different for him. He's the one still healing from so much and I know this is hard.

For me, it all feels very surreal.

We're here. Together. In California. And I'm going to teach him to sign.

All of a sudden, I'm overwhelmed with emotion and my nose feels like it's about to run along with the tears puddling in my eyes. I sniffle and look up at the puffy clouds in the pale blue sky willing my tears not to fall. Now is not the time. He needs me to be strong.

With my eyes still on the sky above, I feel the warmth of his hand on mine, but I can't look at him. Not yet.

"Thank you, Harper."

Three little words. That's all it takes to remember why I'm here. I'm here to teach this phenomenal man how to find his voice again. The tears threatening to fall miraculously dissipate and I find him looking a little sad when I finally look at him.

"There is no place I would rather be."

He has no idea what I just said, but he smiles because I clearly showed the sincerity in which I meant the words.

I reach into my bag for a pen and hand it and a pre-test to him.

"A test? We haven't even started yet."

"I need to know what you know."

"Sure beans, Miss Keaton," he replies with a wink.

He can't hear my light chuckle when I think back to the night he coined this phrase but he can see the smile it brought to my face and I think it's enough for both of us right now.

Three hours later I'm standing next to his bike not wanting the day to end.

"Aren't you going to walk me to the door?" I sign, knowing he knows enough now to get what I mean.

"I don't want Brian to get the wrong idea," he says from his bike, holding his helmet in front of him not making any moves to stand.

"Brian? What do you mean?"

He can see the confusion on my face, and I can see his disappointment in me. What I've done to disappoint him, I couldn't tell you.

"Well, I don't know, Harper. I don't think I would want my live-in girlfriend being walked to the door by somebody she'd spent a pretty perfect two weeks with, even it had been two years."

I can't help the smile that spreads from ear to ear. I've been trying to suppress the butterflies that started floating around my stomach since the moment he said *sure beans.* The first sign he hadn't forgotten the fun we had together.

But now, hearing him say our time together was perfect, has those butterflies doing figure eights and partying like rock stars. He remembers our time together the same way I do, and I sure hope this is why he has been such a gentleman because I want nothing else, but for him to be so impolite with me I can barely stand it.

Taking my time to make sure he understands the situation I do my best to explain.

"First, it was only twelve days. But it *was* perfect."

He's focusing hard on what I'm trying to tell him, so I don't get much of a reaction.

"Second, Brian isn't my boyfriend."

This does the trick.

Confusion turns to relief but just as fast back to confusion.

"I don't understand?"

"Honey, he would rather sleep with you than with me."

"Slow down. I'm not sure I got that. Something about sleeping?"

I stop signing and speak slowly so he can read my lips.

"Brian. Is. Gay."

There's the smile I was waiting for. The lazy smile that draws you in and blinds you, knocking any sense of reason right out the door. Damn, his real, not smiling to make everyone else happy smile, is a beautiful sight to see. It's perfect, just like him.

He swings his leg off his bike resting his helmet on the seat. "So, are you saying you're single?" He's standing in front of me now and I can't help but feel as though I'm standing on the precipice of the rest of my life.

"Yes. You see, I never quite got over this guy I met on vacation a couple years ago."

I don't know if he got all that, but I had to hear myself say it out loud, because it's true. I haven't wanted to let myself believe it, but if I'm being honest, I've been waiting for him.

His knees bend slightly, and he looks up to the sky as if giving thanks or saying a prayer to a higher power. When his gaze finds mine the little flecks of gold in his hazel eyes captivate me just like they did two years ago when I spent twelve days getting lost in them on star-filled Bali nights.

The man I fell for is back.

He's back and there is a determination in his eyes. A determination that has him closing the steps of space separating us, taking my face in his big hands and crashing his lips against mine.

His kiss, although fierce and full of emotion, is tender and slow. He's not rushing a thing as he kisses me like only he can. All of the feelings I've held deep inside come rushing back and I know what we shared was real. What we had was just as special as I remember it being.

My hands are rubbing the back of his short hair and as good as he looks, I miss his longer beach waves and having something to grab on to. While my hands leisurely stroke the back of his head his hands leave my face and I feel the loss of their warmth instantly. But when he uses those hands to pull me closer to him, my body warms all over.

His tongue lightly traces my lips, asking for permission to enter and I don't waste a second granting him access. God, he tastes so good. Feels so good.

Much to my dismay, he pulls back, and his hands are back to my face. He pushes my hair behind my ear with shaking fingers and then his thumb slowly trails across my bottom lip.

He's just looking at me.

His eyes scanning every feature on my face as if he's trying to memorize them all.

"Freckles," he says with just the whisper of a breath but with so much emotion.

The breath I didn't even realize I was holding finds its escape and there is no stopping the tears welling up in my eyes and slowly falling down my face. Hearing him use his nickname for me the way he just did affects me more than I could have ever expected. I didn't know how much I needed to hear it.

And then it hits me.

I can't give him that.

He can't hear my words.

My heart breaks for him, but I am determined to make him *feel* what he can't hear.

I'll do whatever I can to make sure he feels it again.

"Baby, please don't cry." Hearing him call me baby feels good but I can feel some underlying anger building. It's been hovering just under the surface since he turned up at the clinic.

My tears turn into heaving sobs and I hide my face in my hands while my body shakes and I struggle for breath. All the pent-up emotion has taken over my body and it seems to be releasing all at once.

I can't talk. I can't sign. I can't function.

Just like he did so many times in Bali, he scoops me up and carries me. He sits us down on the bench on my patio and holds me as I sob into his chest. I can't see his face, but I can hear the pain in his words.

"This is the first time I've been glad I can't hear because I'm not sure I could handle hearing you cry like this. I'm not sure I'm strong enough to hear you say all the things you want to say to me. All the things I deserve."

I sit up using the sleeve of my sweater to try and dry my tears even though they continue to fall. I catch a glimpse of the agony on his face and the guilt in his eyes is enough to break me in two, but at the moment my anger wins.

Why didn't he call?

Why didn't he give me a chance to be there for him?

Did he really think my love was conditional?

I don't think he can take being eye to eye like we are because he gently pushes me back down so my head is resting in the crook of his neck before I can find a way to get all my pissed off questions out.

"Seeing you like this, because of me, hurts so much worse than I ever thought it would. I thought I was doing the right thing. I've been through so much, Harper. I've lost so much. I'm not sure I'll ever be the man you remember ever again."

I try to lift my head to reply, but he's not having it and gently holds me in place. "Let me get this out. Please?"

I nod and he feels my reply, taking another deep cleansing breath.

"Harper, there are so many things I regret. I regret not giving you a proper good bye. I regret not trying to sneak a phone call to you before we left on our mission. If I knew I was never going to hear your voice again I sure as hell would have found a way to call."

His leg starts to bounce up and down at a furious pace. He's anxious. This is hard for him.

"I regret not reaching out to you as soon as I was alert enough to do so, I truly am sorry about that. But Harper, what I regret even more is not being able to save my brothers. Eight of us left together and I'm the only one who came back. I regret everything I did or didn't do that day."

I had no idea he was the only survivor of that fateful day. He's lost so much more than I even imagined.

"Harper, those men were my family. They were a part of who

I am as a man. We took care of each other. We protected each other and I let them down."

My arms instinctually wrap around him and I feel a tear fall from his face onto mine as he tells his story.

"What I don't understand is why me? Why am I still here? Some of those men were fathers. There are five babies out there who will never know their daddies and there are wives and parents who will never see them again. How do I live with myself? How do I justify my place in the world when some of the best men I know are gone, but I survived? It's too much. It's just too much."

I turn so my legs are on either side of his and I hug him to me fiercely. He grips me so tightly it's almost painful and this time it's his turn. He sobs into my neck and I hold him with everything I have.

"I'm so sorry. I'm so sorry. I'm so sorry." He repeats these three words over and over and I am at a complete loss. I have no idea how to fix him. How to console him through something so painful and so tragic.

I hold his face in my hands and kiss him all over. "It's okay, baby." A kiss to the nose. "I'm here." A kiss to a tear-soaked cheek. "Let it all out, Huck. I got you." A kiss to the forehead.

He pulls back from me and uses his shirt to wipe his face. He's calmed, but the tears refuse to stop.

"Do you see why I couldn't call?" I nod. "It's not just that I was injured and needed several surgeries or that I couldn't hear you. I'd lost too much. I *have* lost too much. I'm a shell of who I used to be and honestly?"

"Always." He reads my lips and the faintest of smiles graces his lips at the throwback to what we would say to each other when the other says the word honestly.

"I haven't been strong enough. Worthy enough. I was afraid you would reject me and frankly I knew it would break me and there may be no coming back from losing you. I mean I know I lost you long ago by going MIA on you, but seeing you or reaching out to you only to have you turn me away would have been too much for me to take. I was a coward taking the easy way out."

His tired eyes are downcast, and I lift his chin to bring them to my line of sight. "Baby, you are more than worthy. You survived and I am so glad you did. I know I can't fix everything and make it all better but I'm here if you need me. For anything. I just wish you would have given me a chance to show you that from the start."

"Thank you. I know you've moved on with your life and I totally get it. But please know I really appreciate you helping me with everything."

"Moved on?"

He looks as confused as I feel.

"Huck, I'm not friend-zoning you."

His head tilt tells me he doesn't know what I'm saying so I use a language I'm pretty sure he'll understand.

Keeping eye contact, I slowly kiss his lips. One tender peck after another. Until we're both breathing hard, his hands are tangled in my hair and I'm moving on top of him causing friction that feels oh, so good to both of us.

I pull back out of breath. "I did not move on. I'm still yours." He's watching my lips but doesn't get it.

"One more time?"

Speaking slowing, I point to myself and then him. "I'm still yours."

His eyes light up fresh with new tears. He kisses me hard and the pieces of the puzzle of my life start to find where they fit.

"Fuck, Harper. I love you so much." I gasp from the surprise of his words. "I'm sorry if it's too soon and those words scare you, but we always said we'd be honest with each other." I nod with fresh tears of my own. "There hasn't been a day I haven't thought about you. About finding you." He pulls his t-shirt down so I can see the compass on his chest. "I'm sorry I didn't come find you."

"Shh…it's okay. I love you too." I lean down to kiss his tattoo and then kiss his lips.

After minutes, hours, I have no idea how long, we break away from the kiss that began when I reciprocated my love to him.

His eyes are closed and he presses his forehead to mine. "I'm so tired, Harper."

His confession breaks me into pieces, and I want nothing more than to fix him, but I know I can't. I can be there for him and I can help him any way he'll let me, but I can't fix what he's lost or the parts of him he feels are broken inside.

I stand up and offer him my hand. For a beat, he sits there looking lost. Exhausted. Eventually, he takes my hand and I lead him into the house. I'm grateful Brian isn't home, and the house is quiet and calm.

With his hand in mine, I don't take the time to show him around. Instead I take the stairs just to the right of the entryway and then take the hall to the left at the top of the stairs to my room.

Leaving the light off, I don't say or sign a word. I throw the clothes littering my bed to the floor not caring it's obvious I tried on hundreds of outfits before he picked me up today or caring they're all clean and now on the floor. I slide his jacket off his arms and add it to the collage of clothes and as curious as he is to know what I'm doing all I see is exhaustion. I take him by the arms and gently direct him to sit on the bed and when he does, I reach down and start to unlace his boots.

"Harper…"

"Shh…" I reply with my finger held to my lips.

I continue removing his boots and when they're off, I pull on his hands and stand him up. When I reach for the button on his jeans, he places his hand on mine.

"Harper, stop. I don't need sex, I just need you." He seems almost embarrassed.

"It's not what you think," I say, looking him in the eye. Trying my best to ease his discomfort.

Trusting me, he lifts his hand and lets me continue. Once I have his jeans off, I pull his t-shirt over his head leaving him in just his boxer briefs. His body was like art when I knew him before but now…now he is a Picasso. Even with the new scars adorning his body. He is a masterpiece.

I'm doing my best to stay focused and not to check him out but I'm only human and my eyes do take a tour of what's on display in front of me.

I place a kiss on the compass above his heart but keep my hands to myself. Stepping around him, I pull back the covers on my bed and motion for him to get in.

"Harper…what are you doing?"

"Just get in," I sign. I pull my boots off and then my clothes join his on the floor. It's clear he too likes what he sees only it's hard for him to hide his thoughts. I had remembered how big he was, I mean, how could I forget, but seeing him hard for me brings it all back to life and it takes everything I have to stay on course.

"Sorry," he says when he sees me notice.

"You're tired. Rest."

I climb into bed in just my bra and panties. Once I'm next to him I pull the covers over us, turn on my side and pull his arm around me. This is the way we fell asleep together in his bed in Bali. I have a feeling he hasn't had a good night's sleep since then and I'll do anything to give him at least one.

18

Harper ~ Then

I can't sleep.

I'm too happy.

His heavy arm is wrapped around me and he has me pulled in tight to his chest. So tight, I can feel his heart beat against my back. Like the ocean beneath our room breathes in and out from the shoreline the two of us breathe in time together. I've never felt so comfortable with or connected to another person in my life.

Gently touching the tattoo on my wrist, the events of the day replay over and over in my head. The words spoken. Promises made. There is no way I can sleep.

"I can't believe I have to leave in three days," I whimper into his neck. We've just made love and after we both climaxed, I collapsed on top of him and my head is resting on his pillow and my lips brush against his neck when I talk.

"I know baby, I know."

His fingers trail up and down my spine and he's quiet. Either he's deep in thought or recovering from his last orgasm. Maybe a little bit of both?

"I really have no idea how I'm going to say goodbye to you."

"Then let's not say goodbye."

Energized by the prospect of his last sentence I find the strength to pull myself off his body. I sit up pulling the sheet with me. He tugs it off, but I can't help but feel this conversation requires my body to be covered, so I take it back.

"Unless there is an emergency and I get called in, I still have a couple weeks left on my break."

"Huck, I have to go back. As much as I hate to leave you and this paradise we're living in, I have to get back to reality. Back to work."

"I know and I wasn't asking you to stay."

"Oh."

I hope I don't sound as dejected as I feel.

"What if I fly home and see my family for a couple days and then spend the last week or so in California with you. I'd love to see where you grew up."

Dejection quickly turns to elation and my mind is whirling with all the things I want to show him and places I want him to see.

"Really?"

"I mean, only if you wanted me to. I know you'll have to work at your mystery job. I still can't believe you haven't told me what you do, but I'd still like to come."

"If your job is a secret, so is mine but it would be really cool if you were to visit."

As soon as I say the word visit, *it hits me, that's all it will be. A visit and I miss him already.*

"Good, now ditch the sheet and get back over here." I do as instructed, finding my spot back in his arms.

I kiss his chest and then lay down with my ear over his heart. The beat of his heart is strong and steady. The thought of not being able to do this every day is well, depressing.

"Hello…" he sings as if he can't find me.

"Emm hmm…"

"Where'd you go? I thought me coming to visit was a good thing?"

Ugh. How do I explain this without him thinking I'm a whiny little baby?

"It is a good thing and I can't wait to show you my world, it's just that…"

"Honesty, remember?"

"It's still just a visit." I feel like a spoiled child, but it's how I feel. It's not enough.

He contemplates what I've said and rolls to his side resting a hand on my stomach. "Harper?"

"Huck?"

"You know this is real, right?"

"I do, but…"

"No buts. This is real. This is happening."

"How can you be so sure? With the distance and your mystery job, how do we make it work? It's all perfect here in paradise, but this isn't the real world, Huck."

His hand reaches up to my face and he brushes his thumb across my cheek. "Harper, I'm in love with you. Tell me you understand this."

I nod my reply.

"Good, so that means you know that this isn't a vacation fling. I know in my soul you're it for me. There is no distance too far or time apart so long that will ever change that for me. As for my job…well, it won't last forever. I can tell you this…I'm in the military and I'm part of a pretty exclusive team who goes on missions when we're needed. Because we can be embedded for

quite a long time, we tend to get extended breaks like the one I'm on now."

I ruffle his scruffy waves. "You don't look like you're in the military."

He flashes that lazy smile of his. The one that's been wooing me since the first moment he hit me with it. "Let's just say, with what I do, that's a good thing. The last thing I want is to look the part."

"Huck, I don't know how to tell you this, but you can't help but stand out. You're kinda special." I kiss the palm of his hand.

"Freckles, I'm trying to be serious here, stop making me hard."

All I can do is giggle.

"Fuck, I love that sound." He stares at me in bewilderment and gives me the softest of pecks on the mouth. "I'm telling you this about my job because you deserve to know everything. I may not be able to tell you what I'll be doing or where I'll be when I leave on a mission, but I can tell you this isn't a job I can do forever, my team is not for the faint of heart and it can take its toll. The military is my career and it's a part of who I am. A big part. Before I met you I never had a reason to want to be home and I've always traveled during my breaks, but who needs to travel the world when my entire world is waiting for me in California?"

Oh, be still my beating heart.

"I'm gone a lot, but it doesn't mean I can't relocate, so when I am home we're together. I can give you my heart, Harper, but when it comes to physically being together, this is my life for the foreseeable future."

"You would really make California your home base?"

He pushes an errant hair off my face. "Freckles, wherever you are is home." The sincerity in his words, the love in his eyes. I can barely find my voice.

"Okay."

"Listen, my life is a lot, I get that. Asking you to go from what we've had here to what it is to be with me away from all this is a lot to ask. But if you're willing, I promise I'll always find my way back to you, Harper."

"As long as I know in the end it will be you and me, I'm more than willing."

"My love for you will always lead me back to you. You're my True North, Harper."

Damn, he's romantic.

"Promise?"

"Promise, baby."

My stomach growls and I feel my eyes get big wondering if he heard it too.

"Nourishment," he says, jumping on top of me, confirming he heard the roar too. "I need to feed you..." He takes one of my nipples into his mouth and sucks hard enough to make a POP noise when he releases it. "...Hmmm...now that's one hell of an appetizer."

"Where's my appetizer?" I ask, trying to push him off and onto his back.

"Baby, don't distract me. I need to feed you, later you can have dessert. Deal?"

"Deal."

"Good. Now get dressed."

In no time I was dressed, and we were in the Jeep on our way to The Cashew Tree, the restaurant we can't get enough of. We gorge ourselves on frittatas, prawns, sweet potato and carrot soup, sushi bowls and our favorite homemade desserts.

Stuffed and barely able to form words he tells me he wants to go for a walk, so we stumble out of our favorite spot and head down the little village road. Oblivious to the fact that he clearly isn't just taking a leisurely stroll I'm surprised when he stops outside a tattoo shop and opens the door for me to enter.

"What? Why are we here, Huck?"

"Come on. I want to finish our talk from earlier."

"In here?"

I'm pretty sure he's lost his marbles but this man…this man is always a step ahead of me and always has a way with romance.

Thirty minutes after we crossed the threshold of the small shop, a design has been drawn up and a stencil of an ornately detailed compass is covering the spot on his chest over his heart.

We didn't talk about it and he didn't need to explain himself. I knew what this gesture meant.

It meant he loved me.

It meant he meant everything he said earlier.

It meant he would always find his way back to me.

It meant I was his True North.

My heart was full, and I wanted him to feel the same thing I was feeling in this moment. Loved. Secure. Sure, we could get through it all. So, when he stood up from the table I continued sitting in the chair I had been sitting on and without a second thought threw my arm up on the table and got the same tattoo. I may not have gotten it over my heart, but I did get it on the inside of my left wrist. The wrist connected to my left hand where the mythical vena amores or 'vein of love' is said to reside. I didn't explain my choice of location to Huck, because that part of getting the tattoo was personal. Only for me.

I could tell as he watched the needles dance across my skin we were in sync.

He knew I loved him.

He knew I heard everything he said earlier and I was on board.

He knew I would also always find my way back to him.

He knew he was also my True North.

And now here I lay.

In this perfect place.

With this perfect man.

Happy.

As much as I'm dreading the moment we have to say goodbye, I know it won't be the end. We'll get through whatever life throws at us and that's all that matters.

I'm not quite awake but not quite asleep as I take my time listening to the light lapping of the water below us.

Once I've resigned to waking for the day, I pull the sheet over my chest before rolling to my side to reach out for him.

My hand is met with a cold sheet. "Huck?"

Hmm…I wonder if he went to get breakfast?

Stretching myself awake my eyes finally open. I take my time rubbing the sleep from my face and sit up pulling my legs to my chest.

I've never been so happy. So content.

I know this isn't reality. But somehow, I feel like anytime with Huck, no matter where I am, would feel like paradise.

The thought of his rough hands roaming my body brings a smile to my face while thoughts of his love of throwing me over his shoulder dragging me around caveman style makes me giggle out loud. He's a big brut with the softest heart and the gentlest touch. Remembering all the times he's played and sang for me in this bed has me tightening my thighs together wishing he was here to serenade me right now.

In fact, where is he?

I get up to throw on the white tee he leaves for me every morning. It's become a thing. We putz around in the mornings with him in just a pair of shorts and me in his shirt. We already have a routine. And I love it.

My head pokes out of the V-neck and I pull my hair out and start to walk to the bathroom when my stomach tightens, and I'm gripped with fear when I notice his big sea bag is missing from the corner of the room. None of his things are scattered around the tiny space. The only things left of him is the shirt on my back and Eleanor on her usual perch in the corner.

Moving closer to the desk, I see a piece of paper with a pen laying next to it and I know what it says before I read a word.

He's gone.

19

Huck ~ Now

My eyes are still closed, but I swear the coffee floats through the air like a cartoon smell and hits my senses rushing straight to my brain. As my brain slowly comes alive, I find myself reaching across the bed looking for the delicate body I latched on to and didn't let go of all night long.

My anchor.

My True North.

My salvation.

She heard my story, watched me cry and gave me the only thing I needed. Her. She let me hold her all night and asked for nothing in return.

And I slept…really slept. No nightmares. No insomnia. All because of her.

My eyes flutter open and I see the indent from her head on her pillow and can't resist pulling it to me. Like a middle school boy in heat, I bury my face in it and take in the smell of her and of course, mangos.

Once my lungs are full of the smell that can only be Harper, I roll to my back and see that I've been busted by my green-eyed beauty. In only my shirt from yesterday, her shoulder leans against the door frame, her hip popped out, a coffee cup is in her hand and a shit-eating grin on her face.

She is music to my eyes, and I want to memorize every lyric.

"What?" I ask unabashedly.

Her eyebrows lift with a look that says, 'oh I think you know.'

Not missing a beat, I grab the pillow and smash it to my face. After my little display, I roll onto my side and watch her, watching me. Her smile lights her face and I know she's giggling. "Mangos and you. You weren't here next to me, so I had to go with the next best thing. Where you been?"

Watching her saunter across the room nice and slow like she is, is quite a way to wake up. She's putting on a show for me and I can't say I mind. Not at all.

With the coffee cup now on the bedside table, she joins me on the bed.

She's signing faster than I can keep up, but I'm getting enough to know she's referring to the night we met and our game of twenty questions and my love of coffee.

"You still mainlining Diet Coke these days?"

She looks off to the side and doesn't answer. Her playful mood diminishes just like that and I can't for the life of me figure out how a question about a caffeinated beverage could have this effect.

"Hey, Harp. What is it?"

"Honestly?"

"Always," I say, sitting up and resting against the headboard.

She blows out a breath. "When I came home from Bali I quit my…" She puts her finger up to the corner of her mouth and moves her head to the side like she's been fish hooked. Hooked…addicted!

"Oh, I get it!" Damn, I'm getting good at this shit. "So, you quit your addiction. That's great, but why do you look so sad?"

"Well, I quit because you were so hardcore about it. And then…"

"You quit for me and then I didn't come back, right?"

Her shoulders shrug up to her ears and her freckles do a little dance when she scrunches up her nose. She feels stupid. And that just won't do.

"I'm proud of you, Harp."

"Thanks."

I scoot closer pulling her to me. "I'm sorry I didn't come back sooner," I whisper into the top of her head. Her shoulders start to shake and the warmth of her tears falls down my neck.

I hold her.

I'll keep holding her as long as she needs me to.

If I have my way, it'll be forever.

My hand rubbing her back rises with her deep inhale and when she exhales her shaking has subsided and I feel her body calming.

Standing up, she says she has something for me.

"A present? For me?"

"Not really a present. More like a promise kept."

She's wringing her hands and has one of her feet turned in like she does when she gets shy about something. I can tell she's nervous, but her nerves in only my t-shirt are freaking adorable and sexy as hell.

She turns away from me and all it takes is a glance in the direction she's headed, and I swear there are two tons of bricks sitting on my chest making it hard to breathe. I move to the side of the bed and this simple movement has me feeling lightheaded with my old life flashing before my eyes.

Standing up in the corner of her room is Eleanor. In her case and on display like one of Harper's prized possessions.

My heart is pounding so hard I feel the beat through my entire body. I'm shocked by my reaction to seeing the instrument that went everywhere with me. At least she did until the urgent call I got to go on my final mission. I was told to report immediately and to pack light. Leaving Eleanor with Harper was another way for me to prove to her just how serious I was and how much I trusted her.

That I would always find my way back to her.

Harper picks up the guitar case with cautious hands and four steps later she's standing in front of me. The way she holds it out to me is reminiscent of a folded flag being presented to the family member of a lost soldier.

It's somewhat symbolic.

But I'm unsure if I want to take it. I stare at the case covered in years of wear and tear. Mementos from traveling the world, and taking her along for the ride.

My most prized possession.

With my continued lack of response, she starts to pull the case away and it's clear by the shine in her eyes she thinks she's made a mistake. I'm not sure if it's because all I want in this world is to make this woman smile but I take the case regardless.

The feel of the worn wood on my fingertips sends a wave of nostalgia through my veins. It's strange to think one item can hold so much history. Memories flash in front of me in a chaotic collage in my mind. All of it flashing through my brain at the speed of light.

Trying not to look in her sympathetic eyes I keep my attention on what's in front of me and can't help but explore the life lived on the wooden protection for what lies inside. As I drag my hands over the stickers that tell only part of my tale, I can feel the edges of some starting to lose their grip and I instinctually press on them to make them stay right where they are. Maybe if they keep their grip so will I.

When I finally brave a glance at Harper, she's stepping away. I can only assume to give me privacy, but I want to share this with her. I need to share this with her.

"You know, I got her for Christmas my junior year in high school," I finally say, unlocking the first latch on the case.

She stops, but I continue. "Best Christmas ever. It took me weeks to learn my first complete song. I taught myself how to play 'Three Little Birds.' I'm pretty sure I played it a thousand times in my bedroom that year. The first person I played in front of was my mom. I was so damn nervous, but she loved it. She and my grams were my biggest fans."

I flip open the second latch and open the case. A combination of feelings rips through me, tormenting me. Part of me wants to hold the wooden instrument to my chest and sob and another part of me wants to pick her up by the neck and slam her into the ground, breaking her into splintered pieces.

I feel the bed dip next to me and Harper's hand rubs warm circles on my bare back.

My callus-free thumb plucks at a string. I can't hear it but I feel the vibration and my emotions scatter even more.

"I wrote my own silly songs back in the day. My high school girlfriend loved when I would play for her around bonfires with all of our friends. She soon hated my playing because it earned me too much attention from other girls and she was jealous as hell. We eventually broke up and little Ellie here mended my broken heart."

I feel warm lips kiss my shoulder and the circles on my back continue.

Taking a deep breath, I lift her out of the case and hold her as though I was going to play her causing Harper to scoot behind me so she isn't impaled. It feels good to hold her, but I don't strum her strings yet. I'm not sure I'm ready for that.

"You know, when I first started playing for people I was

always afraid I was going to forget the lyrics and I would tape the words to certain sections of songs to the top right here," I say, dragging my finger along the shape of her. "God, I would get nervous to play. Even if I was just sitting in the corner of a coffee house and nobody was paying attention, I would be scared shitless. I was fine with impromptu playing, but planned gigs had me scared out of my mind."

Harper is up against the headboard holding a pillow in her lap. She's letting me talk my way through this and isn't trying to interject or distract. It's just like yesterday on the porch. She's just letting me get it all out.

"I always took Ellie with me everywhere I went. I couldn't have her in boot camp but my mom brought her to my graduation and she was forever by my side after that. Me and the boys would make up stupid, immature songs in the barracks and I would torture them every time I taught myself a new song. 'Blackbird' really did them in. It seems like a pretty simple song but until you've got the tempo down, it's pretty painful to listen to. Especially since it's not in my range and I couldn't sing it for shit. But, it got me this." I lift my arm to look at the tattoo that also represents who I used to be.

She scoots closer and her soft skin caresses my arm and calms me. "She's a part of our story too, Harper," I say, referring to the instrument.

Her lips kiss my shoulder in reply.

"She was there that first night and helped me woo you." I feel the lips pressed against me spread into a smile. "I left her with you so you would know how much I trusted you. That I loved you."

Her tears burn a trail down the back of my arm, and I can't have it. No tears. I set Eleanor back in her case on the ground.

I face Harper and she looks shy and embarrassed. "Please

don't cry. I know I hurt you and I am sorrier than you will ever know but…" She places her finger against my lips.

"I'm not crying because I'm sad. I'm crying because it feels so good to hear you say you loved me." With her confession, she starts crying hard and I have no idea how I got so lucky when she could be holding the last two years against me.

Pulling her into my lap, she wraps her legs around me and we hold each other so tightly it feels like we may meld into one.

As much as I would love to put this bed to use and bury myself inside her, I'm not ready. It's been two years not only that we've been apart but since I've been with anyone and I'm just not sure I'm there yet. Besides, I know she says she's mine and she hasn't moved on, but I need her to be certain. Because one thing that hasn't changed is the fact that once I have her there is no going back and I want her to be crystal clear on exactly what she's getting into.

"Wanna go for a ride?"

She pulls back in a rush, a smile on her face and her eyes big and it's clear the fact that she's straddling me and can feel my growing erection gave my question an entirely different meaning than I intended.

"Get your mind out of the gutter, Freckles. I meant on my bike."

She pouts for a second but then the thought of going for a ride on my bike lights her up and the glimmering emerald in her eyes sparkle with the light of morning and the hope of the new spring leaves.

Harper. My light. My hope.

20

Huck ~ Now

The firelight cast a golden hue on her skin, and I swear it's as though the stars from the night sky are dancing in her eyes.

She's happy.

Her feet are in the sand in the backyard of my place and she's happy.

The usual glee and mischief in her eyes are enough to make any man stand at attention and take notice, but tonight there's a fire burning inside her. Knowing all of her attention is on me and the resulting fire is because she wants me has my chest puffed up with pride, yet full of air I'm fucking terrified to release.

The fact that she's here, sitting on my lap and a part of my life seems too good to be true. Life had felt so dark and desolate for so long. We've had a great night. In fact, we've had a great night every night for the last several weeks, but I've been putting off something that's been bothering me, and I need to rip the band-aid off.

"Penny for your thoughts," she says, always signing along

with saying her words out loud. Because of her consistency, I'm actually progressing much faster than expected. Not only is reading lips, especially hers, getting easier but I've been spending all my free time studying my ASL and I'm surprised how quickly I'm picking it up.

I'm still uncomfortable communicating in public with my hands, but if it means I don't miss another conversation with Harper, I can get over it. Also, not being able to help Tyler was a real wake-up call and my pride can suck it up if it means I can help a kid like him when he needs it most.

"Babe, at dinner did you notice…"

Her phone lights up and she holds up a finger letting me know she needs to get it. I saw Liza's face pop up on her phone and I can't help but wonder why she's calling. Of course, I think the worst after what I saw at dinner but the smile on Harper's face says it's not a call for help.

When we walked into the Cody's home and Michael was standing in the living room swaying back and forth with the baby in his arms, I momentarily stopped in my tracks. At first, I couldn't reconcile what he was doing there. Harper introduced me to Liza and as we shook hands, the good doctor kissed her on the temple and handed the baby to her so he could shake my hand.

In my head, I was doing the math. He's my doctor, but he's also married to Harper's best friend. Her best friend who I happen to know he's cheating on. Well, ain't this a bitch? I have to tell Harper what I saw all those weeks back, but when? How?

Not only do I know he's cheating, but I'm pretty sure he's abusing her as well. I saw bruises on her biceps when she lifted the sleeve of her dress to scratch a spot on her shoulder. I also saw her realize her mistake and pull it back down as quickly as she could.

They always say that when you lose one of your senses the ones that remain become heightened. This has to be why nobody else at the table seemed to notice how shaky Liza was. Or how subtly subservient she was to her husband. Her entire evening was spent trying to be perfect. The perfect wife and mother. For him. Harper, Stephanie, Samantha, and their husbands seemed oblivious to the entire situation.

His demeanor at home is much different than the white coat version of him at work. I didn't particularly like him when I met him on my first visit, but I thought it was just because I didn't want to be there. I thought it was me. But the button-down shirt and pressed jeans version of him seems almost arrogant.

During dinner there was a smugness about him that said he knew he was better than the rest of us. He was nice to everyone, but I could see it laying just beneath the surface. Not to mention his wandering eyes. Am I really the only person in the room tonight who saw the way he looked Samantha and Stephanie up and down every chance he got?

I made sure I was glued to Harper. If he thought he was going to eye fuck her in my presence, he needed to think again. I think Harper thought I was uncomfortable and kept my hands on her to settle myself. There was something to that premise, but there was also a possessive need to protect her from the dirtbag hosting our meal.

"Sorry, it was Liza," Harper says when she hangs up. "Now what were you going to say?"

"Everything okay?"

"Yep." She smiles shyly and seems embarrassed. "She called to tell me how glad she was to meet you and how much she likes you." Holding up the index finger on her left hand and pressing her right fist against it she signs, "You were a hit! Now you were asking me something about dinner."

Shit! I do not want to do this. Her face is lit up. Hearing her friend liked me, liked us together. That same friend who I'm about to suggest is being abused.

"Shit, Harper. I don't really know how to say this."

She goes from the top of the world to scared and wondering if what I have to say is about us. I didn't mean to scare her like that, but I'm not sure I'm going to be able to get anything about this conversation right.

"What is it, Huck? I thought the night went well. Did I miss something?"

"Baby, I'm fine. We're fine." Her entire body relaxes, and I feel like an asshole.

"Okay, so what is it?"

She slides off my lap and sits next to me on the outdoor couch, pulling her big oversized sweater closed. She stays close but turns so she can see me and I turn facing her too.

"Harper, has Liza said anything about any problems between her and Dr. Cody?"

"Michael and Liza? Problems? No, they're great, why?" Her hand hangs motionless with her thumb and pinky finger leaving the word *why* hanging in the air.

Her smile still graces her face. I hate this conversation already.

"Do you like Michael?"

She looks confused. "Michael's great. A little serious but Liza loves him, so I love him."

"You didn't see how shaky she was tonight?"

"What are you talking about?"

"She just seemed a little off and I noticed some bruises on her arm, I don't know, something just didn't feel right."

Her face falls. I've blindsided her.

"What do you mean bruises?" Worry and concern paint her features. Nope, she didn't see what I saw.

"Listen, I'm sure I'm wrong, but the bruises on her arm looked like they were from someone grabbing her and she seemed a little anxious is all."

What I don't say is they look like the same marks he probably left on the woman from the gym.

"No way." She shakes her head defiantly. "Michael would never hurt Liza. I'm sure it's a coincidence, but if it will make you feel better, I'll talk to her. But, I think you're worrying about nothing."

"Okay."

Okay? Come on, Finnegan, you're just gonna leave it at that? What about him kissing the woman at the gym? That you know for sure.

She tells me how sweet I am for worrying about her friend, thanking me with a kiss. At first, I feel like a dick for not telling her about what I saw the other day, but she quickly distracts me.

Crawling on my lap, she stares at me with a look that says she wants to show me just how thankful she is. When she bites her bottom lip while her fingers undo a button on my shirt her face says she's feeling frisky.

"Whatcha up to, Freckles?"

Her answer is to undo one more button so she can lean forward and kiss the tattoo over my heart. Her lips blaze a red-hot trail up my chest to my collarbone. By the time she reaches my neck she's scooted tighter to my body so she's centered right on top of my hardening erection. When her tongue flicks my earlobe and I feel her breath on my ear, I wish I could hear the moan I know went along with it but feeling her body on mine, as she ever so subtly moves just right on my lap deters me from pouting.

Her tongue outlines my ear and then when she presses her lips against me I feel the vibration of her moan on my skin and it breaks me and puts me back together at the same time. I hate that I can't hear her but feeling the vibration and remembering what she sounded like moaning in my ear has me losing my mind.

"Fuck, Harper. What are you doing to me?"

She pulls away from my neck so I can see her lips tell me she misses me.

"I've missed you too, baby."

"We can fix that, you know?"

She lifts up on to her knees and slyly sneaks her hand down my stomach and over my straining jeans. The moment her hand starts to stroke me you could see her playfulness become serious.

"And how exactly do we do that?" I ask her while my hands cup her ass and my head falls back to my shoulders. It's been awhile and I'm not sure how much of this I can take before the evening comes to a disappointing end for both of us.

"I think you know how," she says with her hand still gently stroking me. I bring one of my hands up to cup her breast and then flatten it on her chest so I can feel her heartbeat. Her lips gracefully kiss mine and are followed by her tongue outlining my lips and the rhythm of her heart picks up.

I know what she wants and fuck if I don't want it too, but it's been so long, and I hurt her so badly. Just like before, once I have her again, she's mine. Only I'm not quite the package I used to be.

When she starts to lift her dress, I know a conversation is in order before we go any further.

"Harper, wait," I say, taking her hand in mine and stopping her. "Do you remember what I told you before our first time in Bali?"

Her smile is coy.

She remembers.

"What did I say?"

"You said that I would be yours."

She kisses the corner of my mouth softly.

"Harper, that hasn't changed, but I have. If we do this, I'm all in. Not that I was ever out, but I won't be able to let you go ever again."

She tries to reply, but I stop her hands and cover her mouth.

"Harper, I have scars. Not just physically, but emotionally."

I release her hands and mouth and rest my hands on the top of her legs under her dress. Her skin still as soft as silk.

"I have wounds that may never heal. When I tell you I love you, and you say it back, I can't hear you. If you scream for help, I won't know you need me to rescue you. I may need therapy for the rest of my life. Which reminds me, I should probably start going." This earns me a small smile. "What I'm saying is, if you don't want a lifetime of *this* version of me, I get it. No hard feelings."

My hands nervously rub up and down her thighs as she stares at me without saying a word. I'm not sure if this is a good or bad thing but when she leans forward and kisses my tattoo again things look up. But I also need to know she gets how serious this is.

"Baby, when I say I'm all in, I mean it. Since the day I met you, it's only been you, Harper. If we're gonna do this, you need to think about what you're getting yourself into. Really think about it. I don't think I can take losing you again. And yes, I know the first time was my own fault. We don't have to do this tonight. Take all the time you need, Harper, but please be all in if we do this. Not horny. Or reminiscent. But all in because you love me as deeply as I love you. As deeply as it would take to live a life with a man like me."

A tear falls down her cheek and how I've kept my emotions as in check as I have is a miracle. I'm giving her the chance to walk away and I'm scared shitless. I'll never be the man she deserves me to be and to say I'm feeling insecure would be an understatement.

She starts to lift off my lap, my heart dropping to my stomach and I swear I might vomit if she walks away. Even though it's probably the right choice for her.

She finds her footing, but her hand stays on my shoulder to balance her while she slips off her heels.

When she lifts her dress over her head and drops it in the sand, my heart rights itself as she gives me her answer. Standing in front of me, in only her pink lace bra and panties. Exposed. She's giving herself to me.

I can't help my own lone tear that falls because she's just said she's all in.

She's mine.

She loves me enough.

She crawls back onto my lap and a cascade of tears stream from her eyes and I'm pretty sure she's yelling at me through her tears when she says, "You are not hard to love! You are not a sacrifice! You loving me is all I've ever wanted. After living without you, having your love again has rescued me from living half a life." She wipes her face to rid the tears, but they just keep falling. "I love you. I need you. I'm all in."

We're both sobbing into each other's mouths as we devour one another. The salt of our tears mixing together and burning our lips. Her arms and legs are wrapping around me frantically as if she can't get close enough to me and it feels like she's trying to crawl inside my soul.

Out of the corner of my eye I see a dog running down the beach, the reality of where we are hits me and the thought of someone seeing her vulnerable like this has me taking action.

She clings to me and I have a hold of her ass again, so I stand and kick sand over the fire, effectively putting it out.

"I need to get you inside. Hold on tight."

I can feel her speak something into my neck, but I'll never know what she said. And in this moment, I'm okay with that.

Because she's mine.

She peppers kisses all over my neck as I make our way inside the house. They feel good, but her kisses are torturing me at the same time. I need more.

So much more.

Barely inside the dark house, I can't go another step without tasting her again. Pressing her back against the wall, I crash into her kissing her fast and rough. There isn't anything gentle between either of us. She rips my shirt open and I'm sure buttons now litter my floor. She's trying desperately to get my shirt off me, but the arms are too tight.

The wall isn't going to work.

I walk us to the bedroom and toss her onto the bed. The moment she bounces onto the mattress, she is on her hands and knees scrambling to get to me. Just as my shirt is finally off, her fingers have found my belt and her body is practically shaking as she fumbles to pull the belt not just open but right out of the loops so she can toss it across the room.

It's hot and adorable and mesmerizing. I'm so awestruck I let her take the lead. She's on her knees in front of me with her butt on her heels unbuttoning my pants one button at a time with her lower lip between her teeth and when she gets to the last one she lifts her sparkling eyes to mine and she lights up the darkened room. Her skin is bathed in streaks of moonlight as the night sky peeks through the open blinds. Love, passion, and excitement shine back at me and I can feel my life changing in this instant.

She pulls my pants down and her eyes are instantly drawn to what my straining briefs are no longer keeping contained. Her lips form the word *fuck* and I have to grab myself and squeeze tightly so I don't come on the spot.

Seeing her reaction makes me feel more like a man than I have in years. Feeling her delicate fingers pry my hand off my dick sends me into overdrive, and I swear I feel my heartbeat all the way down to my balls. But when she takes the waistband of my briefs and pulls them over my ass and down my thighs, the sight of me escaping brings a hungry smile to her sweet little face and it's impossible for her to hide her eagerness. Watching it all play out in front of me is nearly enough to kill me.

She stops pulling my Calvins down and leaves them above my knees. She's feeling needy. Needs to touch me. With awe in her eyes, she slowly caresses me. Her hands are steady and soft, not applying any real pressure. She's exploring. Teasing. When I see her tongue dart out to wet her lips, I know what's coming and if I don't stop her, it will be my undoing.

But I can't stop her.

With one hand around my shaft, she brings the other around my hip and latches on to my ass. She leans forward and presses her lips against my head and chances a look at me. Her smoldering eyes dancing with lust.

God help me.

Her tongue now circles my head and I watch in rapt fascination as she opens her mouth and takes me in. She may not be able to take but half of me but the sight alone has my balls tightening and me gently pushing her back by the shoulders.

"Harper, baby. I need you to stop."

She pulls her perfect pink lips off and I swear the way my dick bounces if I *could* hear I would have heard a popping noise when she released me. God, I would kill to hear that. Quickly after this fleeting thought, I see the look of concern on her face.

"What's wrong?" she asks.

I mount the bed, forcing her to lay back for me so I can place myself on top of her. Knowing if she touches me anymore the night will be over before it's started, I situate her on the pillows and lift her hands above her head holding them still.

"What's wrong, is me coming before I'm inside you. It's been a long time, Harper. I want to take my time giving you what you need before I get mine."

Her hands are trapped but when she asks me *how long* I can read her lips clear as day here in the moonlight room.

"Two years."

Her mouth falls open and her eyes fill with tears once again. I'm not sure what I expected her response to be, but I'll take this. I'm not going to ask her the same question because I'm sure the answer won't be the same but I'm glad she knows there hasn't been anyone but her since the day I met her. There's no shame on my side of things. I told her there was no going back once I had her. I meant it.

She tugs on the hand holding hers above her head asking me to free it. Of course, I do. She tells me she loves me and then takes my face in her hands and kisses me with pure abandon.

After our lips are swollen and sore, her bra and panties come off. I explore every inch of her and bring her to climax twice before I finally ease into her with nothing between us, finding my release as she finds hers yet again.

The fact that we didn't use a condom isn't some mistake that either of us will feel guilty about in the morning. Neither of us may say it, but it was a conscious decision on both our parts. We needed the closeness. We needed each other in the most intimate of ways. As a symbol of giving ourselves to each other completely.

21

Huck ~ Then

I wake up to an all too familiar sound of the "bat phone" vibrating on the table in the opposing corner of the bungalow. The face of the device lighting up the room. Cautiously rolling away from her, careful not to wake her. Her breathing is heavy. She's out cold.

My gut is twisted in knots because I know what I'm going to find when I pick up the phone. In the past, a call like this would send a jolt of adrenaline through me. I lived for the sound. But not now. Not while I'm here with her. I grab it to silence the vibrating but when I look over to make sure she's still asleep my insides twist even tighter. She looks like a dream. Half her body is out of the sheets bathed in waves, moonlight glistening off the ocean below.

Why now? I ask myself before reading the encrypted message. *Why fucking now?*

Attn: 1st Special Forces Operational Delta (Section 2)

Report to Camp Lemonnier Djibouti Africa within 48 hours for mission
Brief.

Fuck!

Did I know this was a probability? Of course I did. It's always a probability. The thing is I've never cared if my plans were interrupted for work in the past. The beauty in my bed has quickly become my home and I don't want to leave her. I can't help but wonder what this is going to do to us.

With trepidation, I send my confirmation text back to my command staff with a feeling of dread. How can I say goodbye to her? She looks like an angel with her long waves of chestnut hair against the white sheets. The golden glow of her sun-kissed skin outshining the moon outside.

She is perfection, and I have to leave her.

Quietly, I collect my things, putting them in my Army-issued duffle and finally sit back down at the table and write Harper a note.

Harper,
Baby, I got that call you were afraid I might get and duty calls. Please forgive me for not waking you. What we have is too perfect to have tears so early on. I can't tell you where I am going, but as soon as I can, I'll call to let you know I'm safe. I hope you know I meant every word of what I said. I'll always find my way back to you, Harper. You are my True North. Please don't forget that because it means I'll always find my way back to you. I'm leaving Eleanor in your hands for safe keeping. You know what she means to me, please take good care of her.
I love you,
Huck "Your guy."

Keeping my distance, I must stand next to the bungalow door for five minutes just watching her sleep. I know if I get too close I'll have to touch her. If I touch her, I'll wake her, and if I wake her, I'll have to see the hurt in her eyes when I tell her I'm leaving.

I'm not brave enough for that.

Two long flights and forty-eight hours later I find myself in the ready room in Camp Lemonnier getting briefed by a joint CIA and Military Intel group about a hostage situation in Mogadishu. A United States citizen working as an emergency medical aid doctor here in the city had been kidnapped and is being held for ransom by a local warlord. Intel believes Dr. Mike Stafford was targeted due to his affiliation with the UN.

The CIA had multiple informants in the local criminal organizations stating that Dr. Stafford was being held in a small two-story building near the Bondhere District. The area was surrounded by densely urban populated shanties and large open-air markets. The target building was surrounded by "unfriendlies," which meant there was no safe approach and an air insertion would compromise the Dr's. safety.

Far from the paradise I left just hours ago, the windowless government grey room with only a table to hold a large projector, a large projection screen on the wall and three rows of tan plastic tables and black chairs facing the screen is a sharp contrast to my bungalow in Bali.

Our team commander, Major Pete Dowd, walks up to the front of the room bringing our attention to the power point on the wall.

"Gents, we've been tasked with a hostage recovery. Dr. Stafford's condition is believed to be dire. His captors have posted videos showing the brutal removal of the good doctor's ears and three of his fingers. Due to the location of the target building, and the fact it's surrounded for miles in each direction with unfriendlies who sympathize with the warlord, we only have one option for insertion and exfil.

"Blackbird, you and your team will convoy to the target in a cargo van that has been mocked up with some local business facades in hopes that it will blend in and not draw attention to your team before you arrive. Intel has provided a diagram of the building, looks like a two-story commercial building with several small rooms and very tight hallways. So, light loads gentlemen, you need to be able to move quickly and quietly.

"CIA informants put Dr. Stafford in the second story in a large great room with access to the entire second floor. We can expect six armed guards with rifles and small arms. We have no information on booby traps or countermeasures. We have confirmation that they are running counter-surveillance in the blocks that surround the building."

I raise my hand, and the Major looks my way permitting me to speak. "Skipper, do we have any support at all? Helos or any reaction teams in the blocks?"

Dowd shakes his head. "I wish we could, Huck, you'll be on your own during your transit to the location, once you radio that you've secured the building and Dr. Stafford is in hand, two Blackhawks will head your way and act as air support, but it will take about fifteen miles until they're on target. Your closest rally point will be four blocks away to the south of the target location."

He points to the map on the screen, and I can see the building that will have a reaction team and medical staff to assist with Dr. Stafford's care. "It's approximately half a mile away from the target." The look on the Major's face says he knows this has the potential for lots of problems.

Four hours later we're in rehearsals in a sizeable empty aircraft hangar. The Intel teams have placed bright yellow duct tape on the concrete floors representing the walls and doors of our target building. These are never perfect, but it's always good to practice our movements and go through contingencies.

"Snacks" is working on some breaching charges on a large table in the corner of the hangar. A giant bear of a man. He stands at six foot six, and his hands are the size of catcher's mitts. You would never imagine with his Paul Bunyan stature he would be the mad scientist of the group, but when it comes to explosives, there is nobody better. He knows just the right amount needed to safely breach a door and keep people safe on both sides.

"Are you fucking kidding me?" I hear Dan Berry's voice yelling at someone. The Staff Sergeant is looking at the panel van that we'll be traveling in.

"What's the problem Smurf?"

"They couldn't even put fucking plywood up to slow down the bullets. There's no ballistic protection here, Jefe. Just fucking fiberglass. Fiberglass is all that will be between us and all those heavily armed fuckers out there." Smurf's reactive personality is a stark contrast to Snacks and his easy-going demeanor.

You'd never know the five-foot-five dad of two small girls would be a member of any tactical team, let alone a team as elite as our Delta team. He proudly sports the "Dad Bod," but do not let his soft exterior fool you, the man is as hard as stone with no quit in him. He always carries a small Papa Smurf figure with some stickum on the bottom. It goes everywhere we go and is stuck to the dash of any vehicle he drives. His oldest daughter gave it to him for luck years ago. He doesn't leave home without it. To say Smurf is superstitious would be a gross understatement.

Dan, the redhead in the van, is our transportation expert. The man can drive anything with wheels, tracks, skies, skates; they say that he once stole a hovercraft on a drunken dare and parked it on the beach in San Diego.

He looks at me and I know without a word he doesn't feel good about this.

"Do your best, buddy. Just make it as safe as you can." I try to reassure him. I mean it's not his fault this is all we have to work with.

"Huck, I can't. If I add any weight to this heap, it'll tip over if we have to take a turn over fifteen MPH."

"Shit."

I have an awful fucking feeling about this fucking mission.

"This op sucks, Huck. You know that, right?" Dan says matter of factly.

"I know, brother, but they all suck. That's why we get paid the big bucks."

We both start laughing, knowing that most of the guys on the team with families can barely pay the bills with what a soldier makes these days.

"You okay with rehearsals, you ready for any contingencies that might come up?"

Dan rolls his eyes, and with a huff, he half-heartedly says, "Good to go, boss."

Over at the tape-out the rest of the team huddle up talking amongst themselves. The three amigos stand shoulder to shoulder looking at me with grins that can only mean they're up to no good. Jason Culp, Blake Wilson, and John Riggins can always be found together. Delta teammates for six years and best friends for years before that. How they got assigned together, I'll never know. Having these three yahoos on the same team is a blessing and an annoying curse at the same time.

When we're not deployed they spend time together traveling

the world climbing, diving, and exploring the deepest caves on the planet. Total adrenaline junkies.

"What are you three smiling at," I ask?

"We're placing our bets," Riggins responds with a toothy grin.

"On what? How may hostiles we will come in contact with?"

"Nope. Whether or not she's blonde, raven-haired, or a redhead?"

"What the hell are you idiots talking about?"

"Come on man; you've been distracted since you got here. We have a bet going, and the pool is up to three hundred bucks," Culp quips.

"Jesus. Are you guys ready for the mission? Any questions?"

"Yes, Romeo, we're good to go. All the gear is ready, and our contingency plans are in place," Culp responds with a Cheshire Cat look on his face.

"Good. You all owe me three hundred bucks, she's a brunette."

"Shit!" Riggins complains, dropping his hands to his waist.

He looks like a G.I. Joe action figure in all his gear. Massive shoulders, tiny waist, the poster boy for the US Army.

Doc, Hicks, and Butler are working on one of the small point man robots when I join them. They're down on their knees huddled around the tiny wheeled machine. "Is this thing gonna work, fellas?"

Butler is our squad's tech lead and responsible for keeping all the gear up and running. He's living proof playing video games for hours on end might just lead to something one day.

"I know this little fella has had its issues, in the past, but it is running great right now," he responds.

"Last time it made it into the doorway and got taken down by a pair of dirty panties," I poke at him.

Doc interrupts, "Uh, pretty sure that was user error."

"Fuck you, Doc," Butler snaps.

"You guys have everything you need for this?" I ask, getting us back on track.

"Of course, Huck, we were born ready," Doc replies with just a slight sign of sarcasm in his voice.

"Boys, this one could get nasty. Keep your heads on a swivel and be ready for anything."

I turn around in time to see Major Dowd walk in.

"Bring it in, men." He's in his full tactical kit, indicating he'll be joining us on the Op. "Take a knee, fellas." Dowd drops to a knee and takes off his helmet.

We gather in a small circle, joining our hands and dropping our heads.

Dowd calmly speaks with a low voice. "Then I heard the voice of the Lord saying, whom shall I send? And who will go for us? And I said, here am I. Send me!"

"Hooah," we all chant.

"Gear up and let's squeeze into our new whip." I give them a confident smile grabbing my rifle and helmet.

Her smile flashes in my mind.

I can smell her hair.

Hear her giggle.

Get your ass back to her in one piece, Huck, I tell myself.

My helmet secured, I'm the last to load in the van.

"Let's roll."

22

Harper ~ Now

"Hey, Penny. I've got a couple of hours before my next appointment so I'm going to head out for a bit. Text me if anything comes up."

"Will do, sweetheart. Enjoy your break and we'll see you later this afternoon."

Waving over my shoulder my head buzzing with Liza on my mind. I haven't been able to stop thinking about her since Huck brought up his concerns.

I can't imagine not knowing if there were problems with Michael. Liza and I tell each other everything. Don't we?

Since my brief conversation with Huck, I've thought back to the last few lunches we've had and how she's been going what seemed to be overboard to me and the girls. I can't help but wonder if I missed a sign.

I'm sure she's fine, but I won't be able to shake this nagging feeling in the back of my mind until I talk to her. So, with the next couple hours of my schedule free I'm gonna go check in just to keep my sanity.

Pulling into the expensive neighborhood Liza and Michael live in, all I see is perfection projected from all of the perfectly manicured lawns and beautiful homes. In a neighborhood like this, image is everything.

Liza and Michael and now baby Morgan are the picture-perfect family, but no family is perfect. I'm sure most of the neighborhood doesn't know about the two miscarriages they've been through or the year and a half of IVF they endured to finally be rewarded with my beautiful goddaughter.

Parking my Mini in the driveway, I look up at the palatial home that is more than Liza ever envisioned or wanted in her life. All she ever craved was a family. Michael and Morgan are really all she ever needed and this lifestyle and all that comes with it is simply a bonus.

There's no answer when I knock on the front door, but I still have my key from when I took care of their cat, Aristotle, the last time they went to Europe.

I know Michael was with a patient when I left the office so she should be alone.

When I yell for her in the entry, there's no reply. The cat rubs against my legs, his purrs vibrating against them, but otherwise the house is silent.

I don't find her in the kitchen, so I take the stairs to the second floor to look for her in her bedroom. I pass Morgan's room and can't help but pop my head in since her door is open. All buttoned up in the pink footy pajamas I got her last week, I smile as she sleeps soundly like the perfect little angel she is.

Leaving the door cracked behind me I continue down the hall to Michael and Liza's room. I don't see her, and I don't hear her, but I feel her. I poke my head in her massive walk-in closet and my heart drops.

Sitting on the floor under a rack of clothes clutching the baby monitor in her hand Liza is sobbing and so distraught she doesn't even seem to notice I'm in her space.

In this moment I know he was right. My best friend's husband is hurting her.

Dropping to my knees, I grab her free hand. "Liza, sweetie, what happened? What's wrong?"

Her reply is to shake her head violently not wanting to tell me what's happened.

"Liza, it's me. You can tell me anything."

"Harper, I just can't."

"Liza, is it Michael? Did he hurt you?"

Her eyes grow big and the fear in them is undeniable, but she still hasn't confirmed whether or not he's hurt her or not. I pull her into my arms so she can break apart in my arms.

After some time, I pull back wiping the tears and pushing her hair off her face. "Did Michael do this to you, sweetie?"

"Harper, I really can't talk about it."

"Yes, you can. It's me. You can tell me anything, you know that."

She takes a couple deep breaths and I think she's about to talk, but instead of confiding in me she picks invisible lint from her pants and stays quiet. It's okay, I'll wait as long as she needs me to.

Morgan adjusts in her crib and adorable sleeping baby noises from the monitor seem to shake her from her desolation.

"Harper, I'm just so tired."

I take her hand in mine. "I know sweetheart, I know."

"I know everybody thinks Michael and I are this perfect couple, but, Harp, things aren't always what they seem."

Man, Huck was really on to something.

"Liza, nobody expects you two to be perfect. But I would say sobbing on the floor of your closet is a bit more than not being the perfect couple. Are you gonna tell me why we're sitting down here? I mean I love all your beautiful shoes even if I'll always be bitter my best friend doesn't have the same size shoe as me so I can never borrow any of these beauties, but I'm still not sure why we're down here."

"I'm just so tired."

"You already said that, honey. What are you tired of?"

"He's been cheating on me since before we got married."

What the hell?

"Before you got married? Liza, why didn't you ever tell me? More importantly, why are you with him? Why did you marry him?"

"Harper, you don't understand."

"No, as a matter of fact, I don't. Why don't you try to make me understand?"

"I tried to leave in the beginning, but he has a way about him."

"Liza, I don't care how charming he is, you deserve better than a cheating husband."

"It's not that he's so charming, he can be…he can be a little harsh. I guess *cold* would be the word. And sometimes he can intimidate me a little."

My mind instantly goes to the marks Huck saw on her arm.

"Honey, does he…has he hit you?"

"What? No! Harper, I wasn't saying that. He can just be a bit cold sometimes." She bolts up from the floor and starts pacing the large closet space in a panic. Her closet is bigger than my bedroom with a luxurious marble topped island smack dab in the middle of it. The island has tons of small drawers filled with jewelry, scarfs and other expensive items that don't mean a thing if your husband is abusing you. "I shouldn't have said anything. It's hard to explain but…"

She trails off. I can tell there's more. Something she's not telling me.

"But what?"

"Listen, I know he's cheating, he has been for years, but he takes good care of me. I mean look at this. All of this. He provides a great life for me and Morgan. My little girl will never want for anything. And, Harper, he's a great daddy. He really is."

I can't wrap my brain around what she's telling me. My strong, independent best friend, or so I thought. Is she really saying she puts up with all of his cheating and what I'm pretty sure is abuse because of money?

"Liza, you don't have to live like this. You and Morgan can come with me right now. Brian and I would be more than happy to have you. It will be just like the old days. Let's pack a bag. What do you say?"

"Harper, we don't want to leave. He's a great father, and I don't want to take him away from her. She deserves to have both parents in her life."

"Liza?"

What does she mean she doesn't want to leave?

"Listen, it's my life! I love him! I'm not going anywhere!"

"And what would happen if you were the one cheating? Would Michael accept it and stay with you?" I ask, rounding the marble-topped island, closing the distance between us.

"Harper, it's none of your business!"

"What's none of Harper's business?"

A chill spills up my spine and we both hold our breath when we realize Michael is leaning against the closet door.

I can feel her stiffen next to me and there's no way he doesn't know that I've clearly discovered something. I've known this man for years but now, knowing what a piece of shit he is, he looks completely different to me.

No longer the handsome, charming doctor in my eyes, all I see is douchebag and the sight of him sends me into an internal rage but I know a freak out from me won't help Liza.

Thinking fast on my feet I wipe at my face and lie through my teeth. "You know us girls. What better place is there to talk about our sex lives than here surrounded by beautiful things."

He doesn't buy it, but he plays along. "Aw, thanks for keeping our private life private, darling. I appreciate that."

We all know what he really means and the cocky sneer on his face says everything. And since when does he call her *darling?* Ugh, it sounded so creepy coming out of his mouth.

Morgan chooses this moment to wake up and her whimpers come through the monitor quickly turning to cries. Liza starts to move toward the door, but Michael says he'll get the baby and leaves us on our own.

"Harper, you need to leave."

"No way!" I shout in a whisper. "There is no way I can leave you alone with him. He knows what we were talking about and he looks pissed. I won't feel right leaving you right now."

"Liza, if you don't leave, you'll only make it worse. Besides, I don't like what you're implying. Just because he sleeps with anything that moves doesn't mean he would hurt me. Please just go," she begs, pulling her hair back and herself together before he returns.

"Are you sure?"

The sounds of Morgan's whimpers are fading in the monitor meaning Michael is likely on his way back. I can see the fear in her eyes, and I don't know what to do, but when she takes me by the arm and walks me out of the closet and through her bedroom where we're met by Michael and Morgan, it's clear she's not giving me a choice.

"There's Mommy," Michael says, handing Morgan to Liza. The baby snuggles up to her mama and Michael kisses Liza on the temple. "Looks like you're headed out too, Harper. I'll walk with you."

His arm is around my shoulders and he's guiding me down the

hall and away from Liza. I look over my shoulder and she mouths a thank you to me and holds her little girl tight to her chest.

"What were you doing here in the middle of the day, Harper?" He asks in a voice I've never heard before. There's something sinister about it and now I'm fearing for my own safety. He knows his secret is out and he's not happy about it. On the big staircase, I step out from under his arm and step closer to the banister to help my shaky footing.

"I had a break in my schedule, and I stopped by to see my goddaughter. I've been so stressed about things between me and Huck and she's the only one that can ever talk any sense into me."

"I'm not sure what you're worried about. He should be lucky you're still willing to give him a second chance. I don't think you need to stress about him bailing again. He'd be a fool to let you go again."

"I'm sure you're right," I play along.

"Oh, and Harper?" He holds the door open for me motioning for me to pass.

He walks next to me though all the way to my car, but he doesn't speak until I'm inside with him holding the door open, hovering over me. "Liza's right. Our personal life is none of your business."

He slams the door with a sweet smile and a wave. Keeping up the facade, I wave back. Anybody driving by would see two friends saying goodbye and would be none the wiser. If they only knew their charming neighbor is a disgusting, arrogant, cheating pile of shit.

Smiling as I back out of the neighborhood, I wait until I'm at least a mile away before pulling over to the side of the road to text Huck.

23

Huck ~ Now

"Dude, I can't wait to spend some time with you and the infamous Harper this weekend. It's nice to have you back," Bradford says through the last mouthful of his double bacon burger. But it doesn't matter because the fucker is signing everything he says.

Yep, turns out shortly after he found out about my diagnosis the asshole started learning sign language even when I didn't. He knew I was a stubborn fool but he also knew I'd get there eventually and he wanted to be there for me. So, after I told him I had finally started learning ASL, he shared his little secret with me.

The first time he signed a simple *How was your weekend?* on a Monday morning, I stood stunned and completely unsure how to reply. My first emotion was blind rage, even though I knew it was irrational, it's how I felt. In the end, I buried the immature temper tantrum I wanted to throw deciding to go the mature route and ignored him for the rest of the day.

But, being the fucker he is, he didn't quit and kept using ASL every time he talked to me. Now here we are, just like the old days stuffing our faces with burgers and fries over our lunch break. I'm one lucky bastard to call this man not just my boss but my best friend and brother.

"Bradford, you're gonna love her, it's impossible not to. I'm telling you right now though, I don't want to hear 'I told you so.'"

"And what makes you think I would say that?" He dips his fries in the ketchup that is unlike any other ketchup. Not sure what it is about it but *The Cork & Plough* ketchup doesn't taste like ketchup, yet it's the best you've ever had.

"Because, when you meet her it'll confirm that I should have reached out to her. I should have given her more credit than I did. I wasted a lot of time we could have been together. Most of all you're gonna be pissed I hurt someone like her."

"Huck, I already know all that. You were a fucking mess until she came back into your life. My friend is back. I know a lot of that is because you finally pulled your head out of your ass, but it's all because the love of your life finally found you when you wouldn't find her. Always the stubborn asshole."

Yep, he knows me better than I know myself.

"Well, now that we have that out of the way you won't have to say it after you meet her."

"No promises," he says, shoving a fist full of fries down his throat. "So, what do you want Annabelle and I to bring?"

"Let me check with the hostess and I'll let you know."

My phone lights up and I feel the vibration on the table. "Speak of the devil." I wipe the pub sauce from my fingers unable to help the excitement I get knowing there's a message from my sweet Freckles waiting for me.

But that excitement turns to panic the moment I read her text.

Freckles: You were right. Michael isn't who I thought he was.

He's a cheating bastard and he pretty much warned me to keep my mouth shut.

Huck: What do you mean he warned you?

Freckles: He told me it was none of my business but in this creepy evil way. I've never seen this side of him.

What the fuck?

Huck: Where are you right now?

Freckles: I just left their place but I pulled over to text you. Can I see you tonight?

Huck: Harper, if you haven't already figured it out you'll be seeing me every night unless you say otherwise.

Huck: He threatened you, Harp?

Freckles: Not like that. Calm that overactive imagination of yours. He's creepy and an asshole but he's not going to hurt me, Huck.

Huck: You know I want to go find him and rip his damn throat out right now, right?

. . .

Freckles: But you won't, right?

Huck: Right.

But I fucking want to!

Freckles: Thank you. Can't wait to see you. My last appointment will be over at 3:30.

Huck: I'll see if Bradford will let me leave early for the weekend. My place or yours?

Freckles: Your place, please. I don't want to share you with Brian.

Huck: I fucking love you, Harper.

Freckles: Love you.

Even though the end of our conversation left me with a smile, I want nothing more than to haul ass out of this place and hunt down Michael Cody and beat him bloody for even thinking about threatening Harper, but I don't.

She's okay.

He didn't hurt her.

He did creep her out and basically told her to keep her mouth shut, but he didn't actually threaten her. The fact he creeped her out means she better be prepared to be stuck to my ass like glue. I'm not taking any chances when it comes to Harper.

Harper stuck to me isn't such a bad predicament to be in. I'd say it's a more than decent silver lining.

When I look back at Thomas, his arms are crossed, and he looks beyond confused.

"What?"

"What? What the hell was that? You went from looking like you were going to rip somebody's head off to looking as though somebody gave you your very own puppy. Talk about a case of whiplash."

I explain the text conversation with Harper and his only response is to be the prick that only he can be. "Damn, you're whipped already, my friend. She really must be something."

Because I know him and I know this is his way of saying he's happy I ignore his comment. "Thomas, she's fucking everything."

"I know she is, man. I'm happy for you."

"Thanks."

This is about as emotional as we get when it comes to the female species so it's not surprising when he changes the tone.

"If that doctor she works with becomes a problem and you need me to go with you to pay him a visit, I got your back. You know that, right?"

"I do. Hopefully, for everyone's sake, it doesn't come to that. I have a feeling Liza didn't tell Harper the whole story today though. I know he's abusing her and that's what worries me. I'm not saying he would be stupid enough to touch Harper, but I saw him with the chick at the gym and I'm pretty damn sure he hits his wife. You just never know, man."

"No, you never really do." He slams what's left of his ice tea and throws his napkin on his plate. "Got to get back. We've got training in an hour. Don't want to keep your adoring fans waiting."

We each throw cash down on the table and more than cover our meals and tip. I pick up my phone and her last message, her '*Love you'* message is still on the screen when I push the button to check the time.

This is all it takes and I'm walking out of here high as a fucking kite.

~

Her blue Mini Clubman is parked in my driveway when I pull up in my truck. Yes, my truck, not my bike.

Last week after dinner Harper gave me a little present. I could tell she was scared shitless and I couldn't figure out why until my phone lit up with a playlist link in a text message.

At first, I was pissed. I was embarrassed. It didn't make sense. Before I could say anything or find a way to dismiss the playlist she got in my face and got my attention. Signing and speaking like she and now my best friend always do when talking to me.

She told me to trust her. That she had an idea. A way for me to possibly enjoy music again. She drug me to the garage and opened the driver's side door of my truck. I couldn't figure out what she was doing until she got in the passenger seat and plugged my phone into the adapter. Next, she pushed the button to turn on the truck's power and her lips said *trust me*.

The playlist was full of songs she knew I would know. She nearly broke me when I saw the first song come on and I saw it was *The Beatles* on the display. She pushed my leg against the speaker in the door and told me to put my hands on the dashboard near those speakers as well.

She messed with the treble and base on the stereo settings and pushed play. A few seconds later I felt the song. I felt it down to my bones. The base reverberating in my chest and a sense of relief because I found the song deep inside after about ten seconds. It was a song I knew by heart and when the chorus kicked in, I swear I could have sung along word for word.

The magical woman who was making my life better every single day was bouncing in the seat next to me singing along. Singing the words, I knew she was singing because I could feel it.

When I sang the words "get back" along with the song she stopped bouncing and her hand covered her mouth and her eyes, those glimmering green eyes that brought me back to life after the darkest of days grew large. Her eyes that showed me the light and my way back home.

She was my hope.

My home.

We sat in the cab of my truck listening to her playlist for a good hour and I felt more alive and more like myself than I had in two-plus years. We sang along to old school rock, rap, hip-hop, country, pop and everything in between. I could feel the beats, the rhythms. They hit me deep in the chest and resuscitated the piece of my heart Harper hadn't gotten to yet.

Yet, she had. It was because of the giggling woman who opened a water bottle with her thighs on a beach chair in Bali that I had the other love of my life back. Maybe not the way it used to be in my life but still, it's there.

Wallowing in my self-induced misery for the last two years I've kept myself from so much of the good stuff. I could have turned up my stereo and figured this out on my own, but I've been in such a deep well of self-pity I hadn't even tried. I didn't want to learn ASL. I didn't even attempt to feel music. I didn't want to be happy again.

Not without her.

But now…now I'm happy and I'm pulling myself out of that damn well. In fact, I'm all the way to the top. My eyes burn from the daylight and I've thrown my leg over the edge of the well's ledge, but my foot hasn't quite found solid ground yet. All because of her I'm almost there.

The freedom I feel being able to communicate with Thomas and Harper is stronger than I could have imagined. Then there's driving my truck again. You'd think I was a sixteen-year-old who just got his license the way I'm riding around with my music cranked to eleven.

Oh yes, this one most definitely goes to eleven.

My neighbors must hate me. I've no doubt they assume I've gone mental.

And now here she is waiting for me. My petite, freckle-faced beauty is leaning against her adorable little car waiting for me. I have to say life is pretty damn good. Her light brown locks fall over her shoulders and even in a plain white t-shirt, jeans, and flip-flops she is stunning. If only my girl didn't look like she had had a such a shit day.

"Hey baby," I say, kissing her on the forehead after she patiently waits for me to take my helmet off. "How long you been waiting?"

"Not too long. Glad you're home though. I missed you."

"Missed you too." I don't even need to think about what I'm about to do when I reach into my pocket and pull out my keys searching for the one to the front door. "Here."

There's nothing to think about when it comes to the two of us.

We just are.

Her eyes bulge and I wish I could have heard the gasp of air she just took in.

"Huck…"

"No more waiting in the driveway. You said you were glad I

was home but Harper, it's only home if you're here waiting for me."

Her nerves are getting the best of her and I can see in her eyes she's warring with excitement and fear.

"Are you sure?"

"What did we say that night by the fire? Before I took you to my bed?"

She doesn't say anything.

"Harper, what did we say."

"All in. We said we were all in."

"We did."

Standing in the middle of my driveway I'm having one of the most important discussions of my life.

Her hands cover her heart, one on top of the other and she looks at me just like she did in Bali. Like I've hung the damn moon.

"Babe, you're my home. I don't want you to ever have to ask me if you can see me after work. I want to see you. Every. Night. I want to know I'm going to fall asleep with you in my arms. Every night. Well, I'll sleep with you until you get too hot and throw your leg out of the covers and eventually roll over and smack me in the face when you throw your hand out next to you. Then I'll have to move to my side of the bed, but until then, you're in my arms."

I can see she's giggling and I would give anything to hear that sound again. "I do not smack you in your face when I sleep."

"You do, and I love it every time you do."

She lifts up to her toes, takes my scruffy end-of-day face in her hands and kisses my lips. The smile on her lips evident when she presses them against mine.

"I know it's quick, Harp. But I'm so fucking in love with you and…" Her lips cover mine again, effectively silencing me. I taste the salt on my lips and I know she's crying but I also know from the giggle reverberating through my soul, I'm tasting tears of joy.

Stepping back, she presents her hand palm up bopping up and down with anticipation. When I place the eagerly awaited key in her hand, she closes her fingers around it quickly as if it might vanish into thin air.

She puts the key in her pocket and although the smile on her face isn't going anywhere, she dons a sheepish demeanor when she rounds the front of the car and opens the passenger door and signs, "Your little gift sure does make this a lot less embarrassing."

She hurls the biggest duffle bag I have ever seen—outside of a military issued sea bag—over her delicate shoulder and unlike the Grinch's heart that only grew three times its size, mine grows as big as it possibly can without bursting out of my chest.

"Glad to see we're on the same page," I say, meeting her next to her car and taking the gargantuan duffle from her.

"Honestly?" she asks with one eyebrow raised as she signs the word by sliding two of her fingers over her open palm and over her fingers to sign the word.

Moving my index finger in a circle in the air next to my head, I sign and say, "Always."

"I've had that in my car the last two times I've stayed over." She scrunches her nose and those freckles I love so much do that thing they do.

"Like I said…same page." I chuckle and motion to her to use her key to open the front door.

She puts her key in the lock making a cute little show of the act. After I drop her bag in my room, I find her in the living room. She's standing in the middle of the room, her hands in her back pockets and biting her bottom lip. In the seconds I was gone, her entire demeanor changed.

"What happened? I was gone for like two seconds."

"Huck…" She pulls her hair up off her neck clearly worked up about something, but what, I have no idea.

"Harper, what in the world is going on?"

"I feel so stupid." She's signing at lightning speed, but these days I can read those lips of hers like the back of my hand. "You gave me a key, Huck."

"Right. I was there."

She looks at me like she wants to smack the smirk off my face. "You didn't ask me to move in. You gave me a key. But I brought a closet full of my stuff. I think I may have gotten a little too excited. I'm so sorry."

The flush on her chest and neck shows just how embarrassed she is. I wish she knew how ill-founded that embarrassment was.

"Baby, I'm the one who's sorry for not making myself clear."

"Do you think I'm a stage-five clinger now?"

She still isn't getting it.

"Freckles…just so we're crystal clear…I a*m* asking you to move in with me. I'll let you decide how much notice you want to give Brian, but you're in my bed every night from here on out. My truck will be parked in the driveway and your car will go in the garage with my bike. I'll grab the garage door opener for you later. Got it?"

"Got it." She's beaming, though still embarrassed and it's damn cute.

"We can pack you up and move you in this weekend or if you need more time that's cool. Just let me know and these"—I flex my arms for her—"are at your disposal."

"I don't need more time."

"Good, so it's done. How about you give Brian, as many months' notice as you want but we move all your things Sunday after the BBQ. No need to drag it out but I know you won't want to leave Brian in a lurch or have boxes all over this place when we host our first get-together here. Work for you?"

"Works for me."

"I couldn't be any happier, you know that?"

It's true. This right here is what dreams are made of.

"So, we're moving in together?" she asks, still shy and I'm pretty sure a bit in shock.

"Get over here."

I pull her into my arms and as much as I want to take her to bed and celebrate, I know she has things to talk about. Scooping her up in my arms I move us to the couch and settle her on my lap.

"You're moving in. Now, tell me about Liza."

24

Harper ~ Now

Uneasiness and dread have been needling me for close to a week now. This past Saturday Huck and I had everyone over for a BBQ and it was awesome. The day was full of love and laughter from all of our favorite people. Great food and drinks, a roaring fire on the beach, and all hosted at my new home. The home Huck didn't waste any time filling with my belongings. If only the images of Michael and Liza would stop flashing through my head.

Having our family and friends over to *our* place for dinner was great. I had imagined a day just like it for years while I waited for him to come find me. To say the day was surreal would be an understatement.

I finally got to meet all the guys Huck works with, including Thomas and his wife Annabelle, who I know Huck holds as close to his heart as his own family. Every time I would see them signing and laughing it took every ounce of strength to hold my tears back. Annabelle caught me watching them out the kitchen window and made sure I knew that she and Thomas would do anything for Huck, even if it meant they all learned to sign.

Apparently, Thomas and Annabelle took online classes together and even taught their toddlers along with them and it's so sweet to watch them use it without Huck being around. It's true, kids really do pick up on things quickly and these two sign almost as well as their daddy.

Thomas and Annabelle have two boys so close in age you would have sworn they were twins. They're almost five and the most adorable little guys I had ever seen. Following in their daddy's footsteps, they were big for their age, probably the biggest in their classes. Short brown hair cut to match their dad's, and olive skin gifted to them from their beautiful mother. They're sweet and energetic yet well-behaved little men.

It would be impossible not to like this little foursome and I'm glad to know my future holidays and family vacations for years to come will include them. Dad, Sutton, Josh, and Tilly were there as were my girls Sam, Steph, and their husbands. Then there was Liza and Michael.

I'm not sure if it's because I now know the truth about their relationship, if I had not experienced the cold side of Michael first-hand or if Liza had lied to me and there were more than indiscretions happening in their fictional fairy tale world, but something felt off with them all day.

Liza looked exhausted. To anyone else, they probably thought this was due to just having a baby, but it was more than that. Every unexpected loud noise had her jumping out of her skin. She laughed too loud and doted on Michael like he was the light of her life and not the man who drove her to a puddle of despair at the bottom of her closet.

Michael, on the other hand, looked like he hadn't missed a minute of sleep. He was attentive and sweet to her. And if you didn't know what I knew, you would think they were the perfect couple from the outside looking in.

Our day in the closet wasn't discussed and Michael acted like nothing had ever happened. But something wasn't right. The light behind Liza's eyes had burnt out and no matter how loud she laughed her eyes were still filled with storm clouds. The problem is I couldn't tell if the storm had already made landfall or if it was still making its way to shore. Either way, I didn't like what I saw.

I've tried to call, but she doesn't answer. Her texts are brief and the selfie of her and Morgan at the park this morning I'm sure was sent to ease my mind, but all it did was worry me even more. I'm worried about my friend and this is why I'm taking my lunch break to go to her and make sure she isn't at the bottom of her closet again. At least this time Michael is out of town for a conference. Here's hoping this means I can get her to hear me and maybe consider leaving her disgusting cheat of a husband.

As I pull into the Cody's driveway my phone pings.

Huck: Hey Freckles. Hope you're having a good day. How does tri-tip on the grill sound for dinner tonight?

I love these everyday, mundane questions from him. After our time apart, I never take for granted just how lucky I am to make a simple decision about what to have for dinner with him.

Harper: Sounds perfect. You know how I love your meat.

Huck: Someone's feeling frisky.

. . .

Harper: Not really. I just got to Liza's. I've had a bad feeling all week and wanted to check on her. Just gonna pop in real quick and make sure she's doing okay. I can only stay for 15 mins and then I have to leave for a client appointment so I should probably get going.

Huck: Okay, give her my best and text me after and let me know how she is.

Harper: Promise. Love you.

Huck: Love you, baby.

Smiling from the inside is what I'm doing when I end our texting. I don't even mind the awful drizzle in the air from the fog that never quite burned off today. Never in a million years did I think I could be this happy, but I am. I really am. Once I ease my worried mind about Liza, I'll be content.

The last time I showed up unannounced, I found my best friend in a heap. I'm pretty sure I'm about to find her in the same condition but knowing I have Huck to go home to sure does help me actually get out of my car and walk myself up the drive.

Most of my appointments were with kids today so I wore scrubs, knowing I'd spend a lot of time on the floor. When I don't get a reply from my knock on the door or ringing the doorbell, I use my key letting myself in. I'm glad I'm dressed as I am because I break out in a sheen of sweat the instant I enter the house.

Chills race up and down my spine when Morgan's screams echo down the staircase from the second floor. I rush the stairs not wasting a second getting to my goddaughter. These aren't regular cries, they're screams.

Something is wrong.

I feel it in my bones.

I know before I get to her room she isn't in there but I glance through her open bedroom anyway. Just like I thought, she's not there, but things are in disarray with piles of clothes all over her floor.

The adrenaline coursing through me spikes as I run in the direction of the master bedroom. Light pours from the grand bedroom into the large hall and the moment I cross the threshold, I see Morgan bouncing in her little pink bouncy Jeep. When she sees me, her footy covered feet go crazy in a fit to get out of her bouncing contraption, her arms are outstretched reaching for me and her chubby candy apple red cheeks are soaked with tears.

"Hey pretty girl, what is it?" I brush her hair off her sweaty forehead and wonder where her mom is. "Your mommy told me you were finally big enough for your Jeep. I can't believe it." I try to make small talk with the six-month-old as I pick her up and bounce her on my hip but the hair on the back of my neck is standing on end.

"Liza, it's Harper. Where are you?" I shout over Morgan's cries.

I'm only a couple of steps into the closet when I see Liza's signature red toenails peeking out from the other side of the island. I squeeze my goddaughter tight to my chest and make sure her little face is tucked into my neck as I round the island.

The room is large, and the carpet is plush but the moment I finally catch sight of my best friend's blue face and bulging eyes, I feel like I'm in some kind of horror film and the vastness is closing in on me.

She's dead.

I'm in a room that is basically soundproof and I have a feeling Michael didn't go to his conference after all. I need to get the hell out of here.

My mind is reeling and I know I need to get help, but I can't stop staring at my best friend.

She's gone.

Liza is gone.

But the beautiful baby girl squirming in my arms is still here and as much as I want to fall apart and spill the acid burning in my throat, I know there isn't time for that.

I may not have been able to save her mama, but I can try to save her.

Still bouncing Morgan in my arms, I back away from Liza, not wanting to turn toward the closet door until I'm out of view. I know she's only a baby, but she doesn't need to see what I just saw.

When I do finally turn around, Michael is leaning against the door frame, just like the last time I was here, dripping in nonchalance. Arms I once found attractive and muscular crossed, as are his ankles.

"You really do have to stop coming by unannounced like this, Harper."

I'm choking on the breaths I can barely catch and the fear I'm trying to keep at bay. "What did you do?" My question comes out in a barely audible whisper.

"What needed to be done."

"Why?"

"Like my late wife once told you, it's none of your business." There is no remorse in his tone and the sneer on his face says he won't feel any remorse when I find the same fate as my sweet friend.

Trapped.

I am completely trapped in this windowless room.

The air grows thick and cold sweat coats my body and soaks through my scrubs. He has the advantage. There is only one exit and he's standing in it. He's bigger and stronger than me, not to mention the gun in his waistband he's *not* trying to hide one little bit. And then there's Morgan in my arms.

Fuck!

It's clear he has no intention of moving and he looks very pleased with himself. I've caught him and he could care less.

Huck knows where I am, but he also has no reason to come looking for me.

Fuck! Fuck! Fuck!

"Michael, whatever happened with you and Liza…whatever it was…I'm sure it was an accident. I know you didn't mean to hurt her." He knows I heard him say he did what he had to do, but I'm just pretending he didn't admit to murdering Liza. That would make him a sociopath and I can't be trapped in a closet with my dead friend and her baby in my arms.

I can't be.

Won't be.

Think, Harper! Think!

"Harper, can I have my daughter please?"

If you think I am just handing this little girl over to you, you are sorely mistaken.

"It's okay, Michael, I can hold her while you tend to Liza. I'm sure 911 is on the way, right?"

Pushing off the doorframe and removing the gun from his pants he enters the interior of the closet heading straight for us. I back up and try to get to the other side of the closet so I can put the island between us.

My ankle twists when I step on what I am pretty sure is my best friend's arm. I gasp and tighten my grip on Morgan, but don't let the heartbreaking feeling resonate long enough to stop me from getting the hell out of here.

"A for effort, Harper but I'm pretty sure you've figure out 911 isn't coming. In fact, you've just added a whole new twist to things. I always knew you two liked to do everything together, it's only fitting you'll both die on the same day. It really is romantic."

"Michael, you don't want to do this. I promise I won't say a word. Besides, what about Morgan? You don't want her to witness something like this."

He's the hungry lion and I'm the timid antelope.

We're walking in a circle around the closet acting like I don't notice the game of chase we're playing so when the time comes I can try to run for my life.

For Morgan's life.

"Oh, she won't see a thing, Harper. If you'll just hand her over to her daddy, I can make sure of it. Now give me my fucking daughter."

He's reached the end of the island where his deceased wife lays and the metallic clank of the gun on the granite countertop sounds when he puts his hand down to brace himself as he looks down to step over her. I take the moment to bolt for the door. Morgan starts screaming again as I jostle her around and run out of the bedroom and down the hall toward the staircase. The plush carpet under my feet doesn't make a sound and gives me no clue just how close behind me he is.

About to take my first step down the stairs, I swear I'm being scalped when he grabs me by my hair jerking me to the ground.

"I said to give me my goddamned daughter."

I hold on for dear life but he pries a screaming Morgan out of my arms and I see him set her on the floor. Scrambling to my hands and knees, I try to get to her, but everything goes dark when I feel cold metal slam against my temple with the force of a freight train.

. . .

I'm so sorry, Liza.

25

Huck ~ Now

"Dude, relax. You're gonna wear a goddamned trench into the floor if you don't stop with the pacing," Thomas signs, stepping in front of me as I pace the training room.

It's been an hour since Harper said she was checking on Liza. She said she was staying for fifteen minutes and heading back to the office.

"I know you think I'm being overprotective, but something just doesn't sit right, man. Something's wrong."

When I start my anxious pacing again, he grabs me by the shoulders. It pisses me off but it also gets my attention. "Do you have her office number? Why don't I call and see if she turned up? Maybe she's in with a client?"

I pull up the number on my cell and tell him to explain who he is to Penny. Penny loves me, and she'll tell him where she is if she knows he's calling for me.

I hate that I can't make a regular phone call in situations like this. I feel helpless watching him make the phone call in the same uniform I'm wearing. The uniform that feels stiff and stifling. I don't deserve to wear it and I would rip it from my body if I could. Why am I trying to pretend I can still protect my country if I can't even make a simple phone call to try and find my girlfriend?

I'm a goddamned waste of space.

Disconnecting the call, his forehead creases in concern and I know he has bad news. "They've been texting and calling and can't get ahold of her. She didn't show up for her last appointment, man. What do you need from me? Tell me and it's done."

"Fuck!"

Yelling profanities at the top of my lungs doesn't solve anything and I don't feel any better, but I don't know what else to do with myself.

I need to get a hold of myself.

"Listen, I'm sure she's still with Liza. Something bad must have happened and she didn't want to leave her. It's still not like her not to text. Will you take the two p.m. briefing? I'm gonna head over there and make sure everything's okay."

The second I see his head begin to nod confirmation I'm out the door and on my way to my bike taking off the moment she springs to life.

A mind is a terrible thing sometimes because mine is too preoccupied with all the things that could be wrong to pay attention to the lanes of traffic I'm weaving in and out of and I nearly get sideswiped.

Do I reduce my speed? Of course not.

Am I going to look like an overprotective ass when I get there and everything is fine? I sure as fuck hope so.

Pulling into the Cody's neighborhood my loud Indian Chief stands out in this stuffed shirt, white-collar neighborhood and I could give a fuck.

I nearly go ass over tits when I screech to a stop on their

street. There are people everywhere. And smoke. Lots of smoke. One of the houses is on fire and there is no getting through the commotion.

No fucking way.

It has to be a coincidence.

Leaving my bike next to the curb, I push my way through the neighbors littering the street. About five houses down, I lose the ability to breathe when it finally hits me.

The inferno garnering all the attention is the same home Harper called me from a little over an hour ago.

My world crumbles in an instant and without thinking I run straight for the house looking for a way in. The flames dance from the roof licking the sky while they reach out at all of the onlookers from the windows on every floor. The entire house is engulfed, and I have no idea if Harper or Liza and the baby are inside.

Fucking assess the situation and act accordingly. This is the shit you are trained for. Clear your head and take care of shit.

Swinging around to the crowd of mostly stay-at-home moms, the soldier in me takes over and I start barking questions.

"Has 911 been called?"

Heads nod and lips say yes.

"Did you see anybody come out of the house or has anyone gone in?"

Heads shake back and forth and they all start to speak at once but it's too much to focus on and none of it's making sense. They're panicking. I'm panicking. We're getting nowhere.

A silver-haired woman in a cream cardigan approaches me. She's assessed my situation and tries to communicate with me when she points to my feet.

"I'm sorry ma'am? I don't understand."

Her hands form a small box and then she pretends to drive a

car. She points to the driveway again and makes the same motion only this time it hits me!

“There was a Mini in the driveway that drove away! Was it blue with white stripes?”

She shakes her head and points to the garage.

“The Mini was in the garage and then left?”

She nods her confirmation.

“And was it blue?”

Her yes is easy to read, and hope engulfs my heart. Even though it doesn’t make much sense that her car would have been in the garage.

“Was she alone?”

She shrugs her shoulders and says she didn’t see who was in the car.

My hope is short lived. Harper may have driven away but what about Liza and Morgan? Are they inside? I still need to find a way in.

Flames have broken through the windows on either side of the front door as though a fire-breathing dragon was screaming at us issuing its warning.

Do. Not. Enter.

I’m just daring to get closer when I see the flashing lights out of my peripheral. The sea of neighbors part and the two trucks pull up. I join the crowd across the street and let them do their job.

As I wait, I text Thomas and fill him in. The house was on fire, but a witness had seen Harper’s Mini leave the driveway before it started. I asked him to go to my place in case she had gone there and as soon as I had confirmation Liza and Morgan weren’t inside, I was going to try her office.

About thirty minutes later the firefighters come out to update the woman who I had learned ran the homeowner’s association.

The kind woman who had talked to me before approached me with a piece of paper.

One body inside.

An adult female.

Liza.

It had to be Liza because Harper drove away.

Please, God, tell me Harper drove away.

My heart hurts for the loss of Liza, but my worry and concern for Harper is still ever present.

Liza is dead.

Harper's friend is gone.

Where was the baby?

How long after Harper left did the fire start?

How do I tell Harper?

Where the fuck *is* Harper?

Head as thick as the damn smoke now billowing out of the partially extinguished house. Body numb from emotion yet nauseous knowing in my gut I hadn't discovered everything that had happened today. Radio silence from Harper wasn't like her. Not at all.

Time to figure this out. I had been texting Bradford while I waited so he was up to speed and headed to our place in case Harper showed up at home. I'm going to drive her route back to the office and look for her car on the side of the road. Better yet, she will have made it to the office safe and sound and tell me she lost her phone.

With the weight of the world on my shoulders, I screech out of the neighborhood and surely leave my mark on the asphalt now behind me. I follow the path I'm sure Harper would have driven.

I ride slower this time. My head is on a swivel trying not to miss a thing, but to no avail, I arrive at the office damp from the relentless mist in the air. My fear and anxiousness have me twisted up inside and I'm as edgy as fuck as the elevator moves at a glacial pace up to the fourth floor.

When the elevator doors open, I frantically burst into the lobby area of her suite but I know I'm not going to find what I'm looking for when I see Penny's face. Her grimace and sad eyes tell me everything I need to know.

I've reached the front desk and I'm about to find a way to tell Penny about the Cody's house and more importantly Liza when I feel a chubby little hand tug on mine.

Tyler.

This time when he brings the hang loose sign up to his chain and subtly shakes his head, I know he's asking me *what's wrong*. The thing is…this time I can communicate with him but what do I say? How do I explain without scaring him?

"Hey buddy, nothing's wrong. How are you?"

He shakes his head and asks me again.

"Well, little man. I'm trying to find Harper, but I'm not sure where she's hiding. Don't you worry, I'll find her."

"Like hide and seek?" he signs.

"Sure, buddy."

A spark lights his eyes and he brings his hand to his face like he's trying not to give away the ending to Harry Potter or something. Not the reaction I expected.

When he asks me if I want a hint, I'm not sure I understand.

"A hint? What do you mean, Tyler? You know where Harper is?"

He nods and smiles like he has the best-kept secret ever and the floor drops out from under me, the room spins and I grab the edge of the front desk in search of stability before I squat down to his level.

"Where is she, buddy?"

He looks up at his mom to make sure it's okay and she assures him it is and his little hands get to work.

"I saw her car by the big bridge."

Turning my attention to Molly. "Big bridge?"

She's stunned but clarifies. "Bixby Creek Bridge. We take the Bixby to get here and there was a lone car on the bridge. I thought it was strange because with the fog and mist there isn't any visibility, so why would somebody pull over today. But I didn't put together it was Harper's car. I believe him though. He's been obsessed with Mini Coopers since he rode in Harper's."

That's right. When Molly went to the hospital he rode with Harper and her car is one that would be hard for a little kid to forget.

"You sure, Tyler?"

He nods furiously signing again. "Blue. Two white stripes. I love Harper's car."

"You did good, buddy!" We high five and he's proud and amused with himself for spoiling what he thinks is Harper's hiding place. "Thank you!"

I tell the crowd of staff who've gathered around Penny's desk what happened at the Cody's, bringing most to tears. Penny is beside herself but still manages to promise she'll reach out to Michael at his conference and she'll also call Brian to see if he's heard from Harper.

Racing back to my bike my mind feels like a Tilt-A-Whirl thinking of all the reasons she might be on the side of the road in such a dangerous area. All of the tragic accidents that have taken place on the bridge are flashing through my brain amid all the possible scenarios of just what exactly is going on.

I'm sure it's not safe for me to drive at the moment but I've got a one-track mind and that's getting to her.

My Freckles.

The love of my life.

Reason for breathing.

The air that I breathe.

26

Harper ~ Now

Slowly and reluctantly, I pry my eyes open, only to be met with darkness and blinding pain. I blink them closed and squeeze tightly before opening them again. Still, I'm met with darkness only now I realize it's not completely dark. There are flashes of daylight as well as cold air blanketing me. My body begins to shake from the cold but even more so from the intense pounding in my head. I instinctually try to wrap my arms around myself to warm up, but I can't move my arms.

The ground under me sinks and I swear I hear a car engine zoom past and then the surface I was just laying on lifts again and my entire being is bounced back onto carpeted metal underneath me. My head is aching already but when it comes in contact with whatever the plastic above me is and then hits the hard surface below me on the way down, lightning bolts of pain shoot through my vision. When I try to rub my aching head, I once again realize I can't move my hands. It takes me longer than it should, but it all comes together.

I'm tied up.

Pulling at my restraints only makes things worse because they're attached to my ankles. Stretching my neck to see through the cracks of daylight on the sides of the space, my head hits something hard and the smallness of the space I'm trapped in becomes clear. The fog over my brain starts to lift and flashes of Liza remind me where it is I'm coming from.

"Michael?" I ask from the trunk of my car.

"There you are. How was your nap, Harp?"

Holy shit! Your friend's husband has kidnapped you, Harper. He's already killed Liza. You're next if you don't find a way out of this.

Stay calm.

Think.

Keep him talking but don't piss him off.

"Michael? Where's Morgan?"

"Aw, always thinking of others, aren't you? That's what got you into this mess, Harper. But don't you worry, Morgan is just fine, aren't you baby girl."

When the baby coos from the back seat my held breath whooshes out of me.

"Michael, what are you doing?"

He's clearly pulled off the main road if the rocking and rolling I'm doing back here is any indication. Seconds later the car comes to a stop and the engine dies.

"What am I doing, Harper? I'm changing my plans, that's what I'm doing." The voice coming from the front seat is sinister and calm. Not a good combination.

The driver's side door opens and then closes, and I start kicking and pulling, trying to undo the ties binding me before he opens the doors to the back of the Clubman. He doesn't come to the back of the car though. I can hear his feet walking in what sounds like gravel and then it gets quiet. Could there be other people here? Is he checking the area for people?

Shit! People! What if there are people outside?

"Help! Hello! Is there anybody out there?" I'm frantically trying to get loose from the ropes around my wrists and ankles. "Help! Please help! I'm inside the blue Mini-Cooper. Please! Help!"

Before I'm anywhere remotely close to getting loose, light floods the small space I'm trapped in when the doors swing open and the security screen that's been hiding me rolls back into its case.

Pure evil stands over me and my brain is trying its damnedest to reconcile how he is the same man who has been a part of my family for years now. Then a picture of Liza's toes peeking around the island in her closet flashes before me and common sense finds me and the need to survive the situation is at the forefront of my mind.

Because I will survive.

I have a little girl to protect and a man to love for many years to come.

"You weren't a part of the plan, Harper. You've fucked it all up. Looks like I'll just have to make up the rest as I go." He looks around him, surely looking for witnesses and when none appear, he proceeds. "Get out."

I wiggle in my restraints, but with my wrists tied to my ankles, I'm not going anywhere.

"Michael, the way you've got me tied up makes it a little hard to move. If you want to untie me, I'll do whatever you ask."

Inside, I'm a freaking mess, but I'm doing my very best to keep my tone soft and sweet. I don't know the version of the man I'm speaking to and I can only hope if I stay calm, he'll follow suit.

"Fuck." He rolls me off my side and onto my front smashing my face into the hard rubber cargo cover.

The moment he releases my restraints and my legs and arms

are free the tension in my body eases allowing hope to sink in and my mind starts racing with ideas on how to plan an escape for myself and Morgan.

Any kind of hope vanishes when searing pain shoots through the back of my head as Michael drags me out of the back of the car. The thin material of my scrubs tears open and I can feel the gravel embedding deep under the skin of my hands and knees. Fighting to get away or at the very least right myself to gain some footing. The damp mist from the fog that never quite cleared today is an eerie backdrop to the situation I find myself in.

"Stop being such a cunt and fucking cooperate, Harper! You're just going to make all of this a lot harder than it needs to be."

The stinging pain in my head becomes a dull throb when he lets go and tosses me up against the car. I scramble off my hands and knees pressing my back against the passenger side rear door. Michael stands to the side of the car with his back to the road and a gun in his hand. Pointed at me.

"Get up."

I do as I'm told, never turning my back to him but also catching a glimpse of a nearly asleep Morgan in the backseat.

"Open the door and take the car seat out." I do as I'm told, releasing the baby carrier from the base he must have installed in my car before leaving his house. "The whole fucking thing. I don't need any trace the two of us were here."

Gently, I place the baby carrier on the ground next to my feet keeping her as close to me as possible while I unhook the seatbelt from the base of the car seat. Michael motions with the gun to toss the base of the seat off to the side and I do as instructed.

"Good. Now, why don't the three of us go for a little walk."

Picking up the baby carrier I ask, "Where are we going?"

"Wherever the hell I tell you to go." He reaches into the car pulling out a duffle bag. "We have some work to do before our little field trip is over." He throws the bag over his shoulder with his fingers tightly guiding me by my neck. I do my best to search my surroundings, but when I catch a glimpse of the giant of a bridge behind me, I know exactly where we are and it isn't too hard to figure out how he plans to get rid of me.

We've gone down the dirt path just enough to not be seen from the road when he tells me to sit on a large rock. The freezing cold wakes my fuzzy brain when I take my seat on the damp stone covered in the day's cool mist. I keep my hand on Morgan in her seat, never letting go. This place is usually crawling with people stopping for pictures with the usually stunning view as the focal point for their next social media posts. The weather causing a lack of visibility must be keeping people away.

Michael sits on the rock next to us unzipping his bag. The first thing he pulls out is a bottle of tequila followed by more rope and duct tape which he throws at me.

"Here, put that over your mouth."

I try desperately to rip a piece of tape off but I'm too shaken to do it with one hand and I don't want to let go of the car seat.

"Jesus, you really are helpless, aren't you? Give me that." He pulls the roll of tape out of my hand and uses his teeth to tear the piece of silver adhesive and slaps it over my mouth. He pushes on my face so hard my feet leave the earth below my feet but I right myself before slipping off the rock and losing hold of the baby.

As though the knowledge that I can't speak back frees his vocal cords he starts talking and doesn't hold back.

"You know. You and Liza both ruined my plan. Neither one of you can just let shit go, can you?" He slams a gulp of tequila, replaces the lid and sets the bottle aside next to the gun he set down to rummage through his duffle. "I needed one more day. That's all, but neither of you could leave well enough alone."

The baby fusses and I rock the carrier back and forth settling her with ease.

"I still have paperwork to do. Arrangements to make. Morgan and I don't have tickets to fly out until tomorrow and with our house currently in flames we'll have to rough it for a night." He sees the confused look on my face. "Oh, you missed that while you were taking your little siesta. I packed us up and then set my house and Liza on fucking fire. Sorry you had to miss it. He smiles, proud as a peacock.

Tears burn my eyes and fall with no regard for their audience. I told myself not to give him any more advantage than he already has. So much for that effort. He pulls my hand off Morgan's baby seat and ties my hands together in front of me this time.

"For fuck's sake, she was already dead. You saw her. Stepped on her your own self. Why are you crying? A little late don't ya think?"

I fight him as he continues to tie up my hands but a slap to the face slows me down and when I see big blue eyes looking up at me from her car seat, I know that struggling isn't the best option if I'm going to save us both.

"I needed the house and everything in it to go so I could have the insurance money so I just left her in the closet when we left. It was kind of the perfect storm, wouldn't you say?"

The furrow in my brow must show my confusion because he feels the desire to elaborate as he checks over the passports and paperwork he pulls out of his bag.

"I'm sure you're wondering why I would burn my house down with my wife inside, yes?" he says, keeping his eyes cast on the paperwork in front of him. "Things aren't always what they seem, Harper. Your dear friend liked nice things and I gave them to her. The problem is I gave her too much, not that the bitch appreciated how hard I worked to provide for her. I'd say it's fitting she met her end in that monstrosity of a fucking closet. I couldn't give her enough so you'd think she could give me a fucking child without all the drama. Two miscarriages after two years of costly IVF is fucking expensive, Harper. The bitch couldn't even bother to lose the baby weight, after all I did for her, she thinks I want to be seen with a heifer on my arm? Anyway, throw in some bad investments and we're about to go bankrupt."

Michael and Liza bankrupt? How is that possible. The clinic is successful and he's a renowned doctor in his field. None of this makes any sense whatsoever.

"That's right, Harper, the Codys are bankrupt. Well, except for the account in Caymans that will take care of myself and my daughter for years to come. I always liked the name Sarah for a girl. Sarah Williams has a nice ring, don't ya think? Morgan and I will be living a carefree world as the Williams."

He holds up two passports. One for him and one for his daughter. He really does have this all planned out and his solution was to kill his wife. Doesn't he know he won't get any insurance until after they do a thorough investigation about the fire? How does he plan on leaving town tomorrow with a new identity yet still collect the insurance money? None of this makes any sense.

Watching him manically shuffle through the stacks of documents he brought with him not only confuses me but makes it clear as day that something is wrong with Michael and it isn't just his finances. He doesn't seem to notice the thick mist from the low-lying fog slowly but surely turning the papers into mush. They're limp in his hands, but he continues to flip through all the pages not actually reading a word. He is a man unhinged and seems to be having some sort of mental break.

With him frantically rambling on and on nonsensically I slowly, one centimeter at a time slide my foot in the direction of the gun still sitting on the ground between my rock and his. I stop breathing when he starts laying his papers on the ground. The brown dirt soaks through the pages essentially ruining them and yet he smooths them out and meticulously lines them up just inches away from my sneaking foot.

"Shit!" Rummaging through his things I take this as my chance and stretch my leg out trying to get my foot on the gun.

Morgan chooses this moment to start crying causing me to freeze and Michael to look up. He smiles a sinister sneer before backhanding me. Rolling off my rock with my hands bound I slide farther down the path, the juniper bushes tearing at my skin when they rip through my scrubs. I don't feel a thing though. The view of the steep canyon hundreds of feet below makes the cuts on my skin irrelevant. We have to be two to three hundred feet up with nothing but a rocky terrain and the crashing waves below.

I stop myself on one of the vicious junipers and scramble backward as far from the edge as I can. With my hands bound it's a struggle to get to my feet at this angle and stay upright but determined it's exactly what I do. Not only do I not have any intentions of going off the side of this cliff but I need to get back up to the baby.

Before I get too far, Michael helps me along when he meets me on the path and drags me back up to our spot and back to my rock.

"Enough of the bullshit. Let's get this over and done with, Harper."

The foul-tasting adhesive takes a layer of skin off my lips when he tears it from my mouth. There's no time to enjoy the momentary relief. Michael has my hair around his hand—I have no idea how there is any hair left the way he's been dragging me around by it—and tilts my head back.

"Open up," he sings and roughly pushes the tequila bottle against my lips. When I don't open up, he starts shoving the liter of booze against my lips until the glass is clanking on my front teeth. "Open the fuck up, Harper. You really have to stop making everything so hard."

He finally pushes the glass bottle past my teeth and it feels like a tooth chips, but there's no time to think about a chipped tooth as my throat fills with the putrid liquid I threw up too many times before I was twenty-one.

I shake my head trying to fight him off, but he tightens his grip until I can't move my head at all. I'm writhing, trying to kick him, anything to get the tequila water torture to stop.

"Damn it, woman! Do you do anything you're asked to do? I need them to find this shit in your system when your body is recovered on a river bank somewhere." He tosses me to the ground like a piece of trash. "If you aren't going to drink it, fine, let's just get this over with."

You'd think he was creating his very own Jackson Pollock the way he shakes the Jose Cuervo all over me. My eyes burn when the alcohol splashes across my face so my sight is blurred, but I can still see the frantic pathological look on his face and the gun back in his hand.

He's feeling desperate.

My gut tells me I'm about to run out of time.

27

Huck ~ Now

Sure enough, Tyler was right. I spot Harper's car at the north end of the bridge near the turnout. If only it took away the anxiety buried deep in my chest.

My heart is racing as I park my bike next to the car that is just so *her*. Peeking inside the driver's side window, I slowly make my way around the car looking for what, I have no idea. When I come across a set of footprints next to what looks to be a body or something large being drug around the back of the car to the passenger side of the vehicle only the worst thoughts of what could be happening cross my mind. When I see two sets of footprints in the wet dirt heading away from the car, I waste no time rushing to follow where they lead.

I don't have to follow them far before an all-consuming rage seizes control of my body.

Just off the dirt pathway, the rage boils in my gut while the horrific scene plays out in front of me. Harper lies on the ground bloodied and dirty while Michael pours what looks to be a bottle of tequila all over her while his left hand holds a gun at his side.

Her hands are bound in front of her and she's helpless. I see the baby seat off to the right wedged between some large rocks breathing a sigh of relief when it starts rocking back and forth.

Morgan is still alive.

In my haste to get to Harper, my foot slides in the loose gravel blowing my cover. Michael spins around and the sick bastard gets a grin on his face that says he couldn't be happier to see me. He's not upset or worried I've arrived, he's happy as a clam about the addition to his little party.

Unfortunately, my presence has him pulling Harper to her feet and pressing the gun to her already crimson coated temple. She has a piece of tape hanging from the corner of her mouth, but I can still read the words she speaks to me. If only it didn't feel like she was saying goodbye.

"I love you so much. Thank you."

"I love you too, Freckles."

Michael takes the gun away from Harper's head and uses it to motion me to step back.

"Dr. Cody, what do you need? Name it. What can I do to help? You're one of the smartest, most accomplished men I know and I'm sure this is all just a big misunderstanding."

Yes, I'm stroking his maniacal ego while trying to make him think I give a rat's ass about him when the only thing I know for certain is that Harper will be walking away from here today with that baby in her arms and he won't be going anywhere.

He laughs at my attempt to reason and communicate with him. I know we won't be talking our way out of this but whatever I can do to draw him away from Harper is my primary focus at the moment.

The gun is back at her temple and he's ranting and raving so fast I'm only getting bits and pieces of what he's saying. I did catch the words *soldier boy* and I think there was even a *tough guy* thrown in.

Slowing down to make sure I don't miss a word he says, "Don't try to be a hero, Huck. Trust me when I say today is not your lucky day."

"Michael, there's no hero here. Just want to help make whatever's bothering you better." My hands are in the air next to my head making it clear I don't have any weapons.

Within fifteen feet to them, I chance a step forward not taking my eyes off him and he instantly does exactly what I had hoped he would when he removes the gun from her temple and aims it directly at me.

Keeping my hands up, I take another step toward them. "Come on, man, you don't want to do this. You've worked too hard to become a successful doctor. The best in your field. You don't want to throw it all away like this."

"Would you just shut the fuck up?" he says, punctuating each word with a thrust of the gun in the air. I'm riling him up and even though he still has a firm hold on her, he's stepping farther away from her and toward me with each annoying word I speak.

I take my next step and as soon as I see the gun jolt, I feel the burning sensation in my shoulder. Dropping to the ground, my head hits one of the big rocks next to me and the world goes a little fuzzy before it comes back in focus again.

The bastard fucking shot me. The front of my shoulder is on fire, but it's just my shoulder. The fucker doesn't know what he's doing and clearly hasn't heard the term shoot to kill.

He's going to wish he was a better shot.

I'm in pain, but I'm not going to die. Laying on my side with a face full of dirt, things aren't crystal clear, but I can see he's heading my way and Harper is behind him, a pleading and sobbing mess. I'm not certain but if I am seeing things correctly, she's trying to pick up a piece of the broken bottle.

She's a fighter. Never gives up.

God, I love that about her.

I decide to stay where I am and let him come to me because a man with an ego that big will be sure to finish the job up close and personal. Making sure I'm dead.

His boot comes in contact with my ribs not just kicking me but using it to roll me to my back. I don't move and I try to keep my breathing as calm as possible. He let Harper go and that was the main objective.

Now, to end this motherfucker.

My eyes are closed, and I may not be able to hear what's happening, but I feel the dirt kicked into my face and then another swift kick hits my ribs. Not wasting another second, I open my eyes to see his satisfied grin fall from his smug face when I grab his ankle and pull him off his feet and on to his ass.

The gun falls out of his hand and skids down the trail landing under a juniper.

I leap to my feet and can't help but laugh at the sudden change of events. He's scrambling on the ground trying to get back to Harper. Harper who has armed herself with the broken neck of the tequila bottle. With trembling hands, she holds the sharp ends of the broken glass pointed at him ready to defend herself and Morgan. She's placed herself between him and the baby. Her legs are bent, and her perfect face has a fierce snarl on it that says 'stay the fuck away, asshole.'

Yep, that's my little fighter.

I grab him by the legs flipping him over and kicking him in the ribs just like he did to me.

"Harper, I've got this. Take Morgan and get to the car. Call 911, baby. It's gonna be okay now."

Knowing I can't take my eyes off the piece of shit on the ground in front of me but also sensing Harper isn't following my instructions, I bark a little louder this time.

"Harper! Now! Get the fuck out of here!"

You don't need to see what I'm about to do.

He's smart enough not to try to get away again but when I see Harper pass by in my peripheral, I break my own rule taking a glance in her direction and this was all he needed to pull the same move I did by catching me off guard and pulling me to the ground. We wrestle around for a moment and at first, he's on top of me and he gets in one good punch before I alpha roll him to his back and beat the shit out of his face with one punch after another. My shoulder be damned.

I feel his nose break and his cheek shatter from the force of my fists, and it feels damn good. My hand is gonna hurt like a son-of-a-bitch later and I will relish the pain. But when I take a break from swinging my fists at his face, the sadistic fucker smiles through a mouth full of bright red blood and broken teeth.

"You fucked with the wrong soldier, Michael. Harper will not find the same fate as Liza. Not on my watch." His eyes also full of blood widen at the mention of his wife's fate.

"I fucking knew it. You killed your wife and burnt your own damn house down. You really are one sick piece of shit, aren't you?"

He's a puddle of broken bones beneath me and I'm not worried about what little fight he may have left in him. This is why I don't notice him reach for his knife with his right hand while giving me his middle finger with his left. When I feel the cold metal pierce my thigh, I realize my mistake. And to think I had considered not ending his life.

Without a second thought, my hands are wrapped around his throat and it only takes a moment before I feel his windpipe crush underneath my fingers. I didn't think I would ever feel the life of another man slip away at my hand again, but here I am.

There isn't anything I wouldn't do for Harper.

She's my life.

I'm nothing without her.

If I have my way, she will never go through anything even

close to this again. It's clear now that there was a reason I made it out that day when my brothers didn't.

It was because of Harper.

I survived for her.

For this day right here.

I don't need to check his pulse. I felt his soul get sucked to the depths of Hell the moment his throat filled with blood and the death gurgle vibrated through my hands and up my arms. Still, I'm not walking away from his body unless I'm sure. My fingers at his neck are met with nothing beating below them. I swing my leg off him and check for a beat on his wrists and again, nothing.

Leaving him behind like the trash he is, I make my way up to the turnout to find her waiting for me.

Shaken.

Dirty.

But in one piece.

She's bouncing Morgan on her hip and it's the most beautiful sight I've ever seen. I know she's scared to death, clearly in pain but damn it if seeing her alive with that baby in her arms isn't all I need in this moment.

"Freckles, you okay?" I bend my knees to look her in the eyes checking for a concussion. Sure enough, her pupils are larger than they should be. I'm no doctor, but I know a concussion when I see one.

She simply nods.

"Harper, baby. I think you have a concussion and I need to know if you're hurt anywhere else that I can't see." I move the hair stuck to her temple and she winces, so I let it go.

"It's mostly just my head and some scratches. I'm fine." Her eyes dart to my shoulder. "What about you? Huck, you were shot." Her hand cups my face and I place mine on top of hers to keep it there.

"I'm fine, baby. It's just a scratch."

She strips her hand away so she can sign as best she can with Morgan in her arms. "It's not a scratch! You were shot!" I try to catch the hot tears before they make it down her face but they're falling so fast I can't keep up. "You were shot because of me! You killed a man, because of me!"

Her reaction isn't just because of my injury, it's because I killed her friend's husband. With my bare hands.

"Harper…"

Harper looks over her shoulder, and I see the blue and red lights of the emergency vehicles on the bridge.

Our conversation may be interrupted, but it's certainly not over.

When the officer steps out of his squad car and the ambulance pulls up behind him, I brace myself. I just killed a man and now I have to explain myself, and Harper is going to have to translate.

This should be fun.

28

Harper ~ Now

"Harper."

Somewhere in the background, I hear a familiar voice saying my name, but my brain can't register any more information. My heart simply cannot endure any more pain. My entire life has flipped inside out in one day and it's too much to take. I'm afraid one more piece of news is all it will take for me to break.

Truth be told…I'm already broken, but I have to hold it together. Not for me, but for Huck and Morgan.

"Harper. Hey, you okay?"

The hand gently resting on my shoulder now adorning fresh scrubs finally pulls me out of my hazy reality. I know the voice, but until I turn to the left and actually see Molly's face, I'm still not sure who's trying to get my attention.

"Oh, hey Molly. What are you doing here?"

"I'm here to check on you."

"Oh, I'm fine, thank you."

"Sweetie, where are you headed?"

"Um, I have to find Morgan. I'm supposed to meet with the social worker."

"How about I walk with you. I think you may be a little lost. You left your room and the nurses have been looking all over for you."

Checking my surroundings, the look of concern on her face makes perfect sense. I have no idea how I got here, but the double doors in front of me tell me I've reached RADIOLOGY and I know this is not where I need to be.

"Uh, yeah. Thanks, Molly."

Walking along the corridor, I hear an annoying dragging sound following us. Matching us step for step. I stop walking and the sound stops. As soon as our feet start moving, I hear it again and realize it's me. My feet are dragging. My body unable to lift them off the ground only able to push them along.

"Let's sit down for a minute," Molly offers, guiding me to some overstuffed leather seating.

I fall into a chair while Molly drags hers in front of me taking a seat and my hands in hers.

"If you want to talk, I'm here."

Staring off into the distance I make a point of not looking at her. I'm not ready to face it all. Everything I had in me went into the letter I left for Huck. All my heart and all my strength went into those words and left me empty.

"Sweetie, I know I've never been through anything close to what you're going through, but as a single mom I know what it feels like to be scared and sad and most of all wondering how you're going to make it through the day. So, if you need someone to talk to who will just listen, I'm your girl. You've been there for Tyler and we're here for you too."

"Tyler!" Those two syllables are the fuel I need to function again. "Oh, my God, Molly! He saved my life! Your little boy saved my life and Morgan's! I owe him everything!"

"Sounds like you two are even then. Huck saved my life and Tyler saved his." She smiles at my confusion. "Harper, if you had seen him when you were missing, it was heartbreaking. The prospect of losing you was killing him right before our eyes. He could barely breathe or think a coherent thought, but when Tyler said he had seen your car you could see the life slam back into him. He had hope and a mission. A mission to find the love of his life."

Drowning in tears, I allow myself to feel again.

If only for a moment.

"I love him so much, Molly."

"I know you do."

"But…"

"Harper?"

"Everything changed today. Nothing will ever be the same. *I* will never be the same. It may be too much."

"Too much what?"

Resigned, I cry the words. "Just too much."

Squeezing herself into my overstuffed chair, she wraps her arms around me and pulls me close.

"It's gonna be okay, Harper. I know it doesn't seem possible at the moment but you're strong and you will get through this. So will he. As long as you two have each other, you can make it through anything."

I want to believe she's right, I really do, but after everything that's happened, I simply can't muster up her optimism. The thought is sobering and following in Huck's footsteps from years back, avoidance is how I'm going to choose to deal with the situation, at least for now. Huck will find my letter when he wakes up and whatever happens from there is what is meant to be. Right now, I have to pull myself together for my social services interview.

Allowing myself a few more minutes to feel sorry for myself,

I dig deep and pull up my big girl panties. Releasing myself from Molly's grip I stand, smoothing out my fresh set of blue scrubs. "Where's Tyler?"

"He's in the waiting room with everybody else."

"Everybody else?"

"Harper, after the shock and loss of the day and with you and Huck both injured, there was no way we weren't all going to be here for you. Penny and the gang from the office are all waiting to make sure you're both okay and to see if you need anything. Besides, there are some really hot Marines in that waiting room, you'd have a hard time pulling most of us from the building without a security escort."

The moment my Chucks step into the waiting room, my big brother rushes me and hugs me harder than I can ever recall him hugging me. His anxiety evident by the scent of cigarettes and the tightness of his never-ending hold on me.

"Have you been smoking, Joshua Keaton?" I whisper to lighten the mood.

"Shut up. My sister was kidnapped and almost murdered. I think I'm allowed."

"Well, I'm fine. You can toss them out now."

He pulls back to look me in the eye. "Are you fine?"

"I will be," I answer honestly.

"Harper, I am so sorry about Liza. I really don't know what to say. I'm still trying to wrap my head around the fact that this was all done by a man we've known for years. Shit, we spend our holidays with him. It makes no sense."

All I can do is shrug. I have no answers for any of it. How can anyone explain something like this?

"My sweet girl."

Josh steps aside when my dad swoops in. "Hey, Dad."

"Harper, should you be out of bed? Should they have released you?"

"Dad, I'm fine. I've just got a minor concussion." I don't tell him I haven't *actually* been released yet.

"Sweet girl, you were knocked unconscious. That doesn't seem so small to me."

"Dad, I'm fine."

Sutton's face is full of compassion as she stands to my left rubbing circles on my back.

"Michael is damn lucky Huck got to him first. I wouldn't have taken it so easy on him."

And there it is. One of the many elephants in the room. Huck killed a man today. With his bare hands.

"Randall, not now. Can't you see Harper is still in shock over everything. Let's just be grateful she's standing here right now. Speaking of standing, why don't we find you a place to sit."

When my family steps aside, I see my little hero clinging to his mommy's leg looking scared and stressed. My heart expands in my chest at the sight of the sweetest boy I know.

I take a couple of steps and then kneel on the ground so I'm at his level and sign to him. "Thank you, Tyler. You saved my life." I open my arms to him, and he comes running. Throwing his tiny arms around me.

We stay like this for a minute before he pulls back so he can sign. "Is he okay?"

"Huck?" I sign back.

He nods.

"The doctors are fixing him up and he'll be good as new."

"You okay?"

"I am. Because of you. Thank you for telling Huck where I was."

"Welcome," he signs back shyly.

Thomas taps Tyler on the shoulder and when he turns around his spiky blonde head tips so far back, I hold my hands out in case he falls backward. Thomas is a herculean sized man but dressed in head to toe in camouflage you could say he's just a bit intimidating. Tyler steps back so he can feel me there for support.

"Harper, will you sign for me?"

Before I can answer, Molly steps in. "It's okay, Harper. I can do it."

Bending down to one knee, Thomas offers his hand to Tyler. A little shell-shocked, Tyler doesn't instantly react, so I gently touch his arm signaling him to shake hands.

Thomas' hand engulfs his tiny one. "On behalf of the men and women of the United States Army, we thank you. Because of your superb eyesight and tremendous memory, you were able to save two lives today and for that we are thankful."

Thomas stands back up and all four of the men salute him. His pudgy hand raises to his forehead and salutes them back.

Thomas gives Molly a nod of his head to let her know he's done and she picks Tyler up while his eyes never stop following the men in uniform. And even though I'm a little out of sorts I don't miss the look Ford gives Molly or the way she watches him walk away. Her cheeks pink and there's a sparkle in her eye.

Stiff and sore, I stand again, and Thomas takes his turn hugging me. "He knew. That stubborn asshole knew something wasn't right. From the moment you texted saying you were at Liza's he knew something was off and he couldn't function waiting for your next text."

"Really?"

"Really. He may be an idiot from time to time, but he sure is in love with you."

We shall see.

"Thanks Thomas, you're sweet but—"

"Enough of this mushy stuff," the tough Master Sergeant says, clearing his throat. "Now, let's find a place for you to sit."

"Thank you, but I have to find the woman from social services. They need to talk to me about Morgan."

A sweet older woman with a kind face stands holding files at her side. Even though she appears kind, her appearance fills me with dread. She looks like the kind of woman you want to have as a grandmother only in a business suit and unfortunately here for all the wrong reasons. I would soon learn the woman with the warm tawny complexion and ebony hair streaked with silver up in an adorable bun was actually as sweet as her first impression.

"Hello Miss Keaton, I'm Helen Kennedy with social services."

"Please, call me Harper."

"Harper, if you're up to it I'd like to find a private place for us to talk."

29

Huck ~ Now

I know before I open my eyes where I am. I've spent enough time in hospitals to recognize the feel of the scratchy sheets against my skin, thin blankets not really supplying any warmth, and the way my skin is being pulled underneath the tape holding my IVs in place. If I didn't know better, I would even think I could hear the incessant whirring and beeping of the machines in the room.

The room reeks of anti-bacterial cleaners. The ones that say they are fragrance free, but couldn't be further from odorless. Spend enough time here and you'll know what I mean. What I wouldn't give for the scent of mangos right about now.

Harper!

Peeling my eyes open I'd say there was gauze over them but again, I know better. It'll take a minute or two for my vision to clear and I'll feel queasy for a day or two. I keep my head back staring at the tile squares above my bed knowing once my eyes can see the little dots in the corrugated fiberglass I'll be good to go. I know without looking she isn't here, so there's no rush in regaining my eyesight. If only I could shut out the images rushing through my mind that even closing my eyes can't wipe away.

I can still feel the heat from the Cody's home burning in a raging inferno.

The taste of the vomit that threatened to spill at the sight of Harper bound and helpless hasn't gone anywhere.

The crushing of Michael's windpipe still radiates in my hands. The life leaving his body and his eyes falling void of existence will haunt me but only because of Harper.

I killed a man with my bare hands with her only feet away. She may not have witnessed the act, but she knows every detail. How will she ever look at me the same again? She must think of me as some sort of monster.

Sensing movement in the room, I muster up the courage to look somewhere other than at the ceiling. Finding it's just a nurse coming to check on me is defeating yet expected. She's talking to me, but I'm not focused on lip reading just yet. Whatever she has to tell me doesn't matter. I don't care about the state of my shoulder if Harper isn't okay or if I've lost her.

The feel of soft skin on my arm pulls me away from my pitiful musings. Her mocha skin and warm brown eyes are flawless and hard to miss no matter the state I'm in. She has a caring smile, adorable reading glasses precariously balancing on the end of her nose and her scrubs are covered in cartoon cats. You just know in an instant this woman is comfort and caring personified.

"How do you feel, Mr. Finnegan?"

She's speaking slowly so she must have gotten the memo that I can't hear.

"Fine thank you. Do you know how my girlfriend is doing? Her name is Harper Keaton."

Is she still my girlfriend?

"She's doing good," she says, leaning over to the little table on wheels next to the bed. She's still talking but not looking at me, so I don't catch everything, but I'm pretty sure she says she stopped by earlier. Then she holds an envelope with Harper's writing on the front up in front of me and leaves it on my chest.

Huck

She gives it a nice little pat pressing it against me as if she knows the same thing I do. It's a Dear John letter.

I think she says something about there being a room full of people waiting to see me which makes no sense.

"Is she one of them?" I say, holding up the envelope.

"I don't know, sweetie, but I can check. Anyone else you want to see?" There's no hiding the pity in her eyes.

"Nah, that's okay, thanks."

She squeezes my hand and points to her name on the dry erase board. The board also contains my name, information about my injury, the doctor's name, and the last time I was given my painkillers. She makes sure I know where the call button is and tells me to call if I need anything.

"Thank you, Ruth."

She helps me with some water and leaves me on my own.

A pick up the letter and stare at her writing. Maybe if I stare at it long enough, it will change what is inevitably going to be inside.

Bradford walks in still in his uniform and his face says it all. She's not coming.

He starts talking and signing right away, "You just had to be the hero, didn't you?"

"Is she okay?"

"She is."

He doesn't elaborate.

I hold up the letter letting him know what he isn't saying.

"What's that?" he asks, kind enough to feign confusion.

"My Dear John letter."

He shakes his head. "No way, dude."

"What else can it be?"

"So, you haven't read it?"

"Not yet."

"Asshole, she's been through a lot. She's got a lot on her plate. You should probably read the damn letter."

Bradford is interrupted when the doctor comes in. He shakes my hand and his and asks if Top can sign for him.

He tells me about the surgery. Something about blood vessels and needing to leave the bullet inside. That it wasn't safe to remove the bullet or something like that. I don't really know. I see Top signing and his lips moving, but the fifty-pound letter in my hand makes it hard to focus on little else.

The doctor asks if I have questions and I have only one. "When can I leave?"

He says something again about blood vessels and that I'll be here a couple of days. I've heard that before. The doc leaves and it's just me and Bradford.

Picking the letter up and holding it in front of my face he says, "Read it. Hear her out and see what she has to say."

"I killed a man with my bare hands with her a few feet away. Pretty sure I know what it says."

"Dude, you've both been through a lot. You need to give her some time to adjust to everything."

What the fuck is there to adjust to? It's not like I'm going to make a habit of this and she needs to get used to the fact that I'm a fucking serial killer.

"Gonna leave you alone for a few. I'll be back and you better have found your balls and read the damn letter."

I know he's right and there's no use prolonging things. Rip the band-aid off and face reality. With one index finger covered in what I know after months in the hospital to be a pulse oximeter, I pull open the letter gingerly, like it holds anthrax or something toxic in it.

I have a feeling it does, but I bite the bullet, no pun intended, and open the folded pages.

Huck,

I'm sorry I couldn't be there when you woke up. There's a lot to take care of with what happens next with Morgan. I have to be at a meeting with the social worker and won't be there when you wake.

I am so sorry about everything. I'm sorry you were injured because of me and I'm so sorry you had to step in with Michael and do what you had to do to protect us. I don't know what else to say other than, I'm sorry.

I need you to know how thankful I am for you. You saved our lives today and I'm not sure I can ever thank you enough, but I plan on spending the rest of my life trying. But before I assume I'll get that chance I need to be sure you have all the information because after the events of today my life is forever changed.

As you know, I'm Morgan's godmother. It is also in Michael and Liza's will that should something happen to the both of them she would go to me. This means I now have a six-month-old. I'm a mom, Huck.

I never mentioned this probability to you because nobody ever thinks these things will happen, but here we are.

I have a baby.

I have no idea how I'm going to do this, but I'll figure it out.

I don't really have a choice, but you do.

I know I just moved in and I get this is a lot more than you bargained for. I've already talked to Brian and I can go back to my old place so please don't feel obligated. Take all the time you need and think about things. If you don't want to become an instant family, I get it. It's a lot.
Please know I love you, Huck. I love you more than you could ever know and I'm so glad we found each other again. This is not me saying goodbye, but this is me saying I understand if you need to. It will break my heart to lose you again but also know that I will understand. No matter what happens or how little time we may have had together you are the love of my life and I will never stop loving you.
I'm here when you're ready to talk. I'll always be here.

Love,
Freckles

Whoa.

She doesn't think I'm a monster.

She isn't leaving me.

She's giving *me* the chance to leave *her*.

She's a mom and she thinks she's going to do it without me!

What the fuck?

Adrenaline and a need to get out of this godforsaken hospital bed light a flame under my ass and all I want to do is get shit done. There's a big white plastic bag sitting in the chair in the corner and I can see the camo of my uniform peeking out and pieces start coming together. I need that fucking bag.

Where the hell is the fucking call button?

Ruth floats into the room and glances at the machines showing my blood pressure numbers. "Mr. Finnegan, what are you up to?" she asks, slipping the pulse oximeter back on my index finger.

"Sorry 'bout that, Ruth. Hey, was she out there?"

She grimaces with a shake of her head.

"That's okay." God, I want out of this bed. I have shit to do, but I know Ruth isn't to be tested. Not sure how I know it, but I do. Using my hands to push myself up so I can sit up in the bed, blinding pain splices through my shoulder and reminds me why I'm here.

Ruth shakes her head and slaps the remote control for the bed in my hand. I know she's chastising me at the moment, but I don't even try to read her lips.

"Ruth, do you think you could bring me the bag over there holding my things?"

She narrows her eyes and looks leery.

"I promise not to make a run for it. I just need something out of my pants pocket and then you can take it back."

Speaking slowly so I can understand she says, "Let me guess? Phone?"

"Nope. Even smaller."

She brings me the bag and it's amazing the weight of my boots hasn't ripped through the bottom yet. I dig around until I find what I'm looking for while Ruth updates the information on the dry erase board on the wall to the left of my bed.

"I'm finished. Thank you."

She puts the bag back in its spot.

"You know the big guy that was in here a few minutes ago? Can you see if he's still here? Please?"

"Promise to take care of that shoulder?"

"Scout's honor."

She doesn't need to know I was never a Boy Scout.

"I'll be back."

While I wait for Bradford, I read the letter over and over

again. She loves me and I know that's what matters, but the fact that she thinks I would bail when things get hard doesn't sit well with me.

I'm on my third pass of the letter when Ruth returns with Bradford.

"You two stay out of trouble. Something tells me the two of you together could be dangerous."

Bradford smiles that smile of his that I know for a fact won over Annabelle the first night they met. The women love the tall dark and handsome bastard, but he only has eyes for his wife. I know exactly how he feels.

"Did you read it?"

"Sure did, and I need you to find her for me. I need to see her."

"What did it say?"

I know it's private, but I don't know how to tell him about Morgan when he and Annabelle have been struggling for so long to have another child. So, I hand him the letter.

He hands it back after finishing it.

"Will you find her for me?"

"She's still in the meeting, but I'll send her your way when she's done."

"Thanks, man."

"You up for this?"

"I have no fucking idea."

"This is big."

"It is."

"I'll send her in."

"Thanks."

~

The warmth of her breath on my cheek and the light touch of her lips to my forehead wake me gently.

I'm still gripping her letter tightly between my fingers when I open my eyes only to be dumbfounded by her beauty. Her jade eyes tired yet still vibrant. Her perfect button nose painted in freckles like stars in her very own solar system. Chestnut hair pulled up in a long ponytail and a little baby girl passed out on her shoulder.

"Freckles," I say, moving her letter to my other hand so I can reach up and touch her face.

She smiles though it doesn't meet her eyes. She's been through so much and she's trying with all her might to be strong. For me. For Morgan. I doubt she's even taken a moment to mourn Liza.

"Did you mean what you said about the rest of your life?"

Her eyes fill with tears and the corners of her mouth quiver when she tries to smile again only this time her efforts don't come to fruition. When she nods her reply the tears cascade down her cheeks and her chest bobs up and down with her sobs.

"Well, that's a good thing because I plan on loving you the rest of my life too."

She covers her mouth and cries even harder.

"Harper, do you remember that first night in Bali when I told you to remember the date?"

She moves her hand and stares at me wondering where I'm going with my question.

"I told you October nineteenth was a day you'd want to remember. Do you remember that?"

Another nod and a sniffle as her cries subside.

"Do you know what today is, Freckles?"

Her mouth falls open and her eyes light up when she puts it together.

"That's right, it's October nineteenth, baby." I try to dry her tears but to no avail. "Do you also remember me telling you that same night that I was going to marry you one day?"

More tears and another nod. How the baby is still asleep with the shaking of Harper's shoulders, I'll never know. Times like this I realize how lucky I am that I still have my voice. I can talk to Harper without signing allowing me the luxury of also holding her hand and attempting to dry the tears from her eyes. It also means I can slide one hand under the cheap hospital grade blanket to get the box I took out of my uniform pocket.

"This isn't how I planned it happening, but I did plan on asking you a question tonight. This morning I thought you might think it was too soon. But after everything that happened today, I don't want to wait another second." I let go of her hand to open the box.

She shakes her head back and forth. Not in the way that says she's turning me down but in a way that says she can't believe it's happening. Her perfect pink lips say, "Oh, my God. Oh, my God."

"I know today has been the worst day of your life and I'm sure every expert out there would say this is the wrong thing to do, but I need you to know I'm not going anywhere. I was planning to ask you to be my wife. To be my family. And I was going to ask you tonight on the beach. But here we are, Harper. Life happened today and everything has changed. The one thing that didn't change is that I want to be your husband and I want us to be a family. The addition of this sweet little girl just makes that family a little bit bigger, a little bit quicker. If you want time to think about it, I get it. Just know I'm here, Harper. I'm not going anywhere and I'm ready to take this journey with you. You're my home. My True North. You always have been."

Exhaling forcefully, her crying calms. Her delicate hand shakes in front of me and this time, thank God, her smile meets her eyes. I slip the solitaire on her ring finger. Nothing has ever looked so right. Lifting her hand, I kiss her palm and whisper the words I love you against her skin.

"I love you," she says, lost in my eyes. Looking for answers I don't have, yet finding the love that is all hers. Love that will help guide her through the pain of today that will undoubtedly last for years to come. Love that will help her raise and love the little girl in her arms. The little girl who lost both her parents in the last twenty-four hours.

Ignoring the pain, I make room in the bed for the two of them on my good side. Harper slips her shoes off, crawls in next to me carefully maneuvering around my IV. When she lays back, Morgan lifts her head. Her blue eyes connect with mine and I silently vow to take care of her for the rest of her life. To love her like my own. Because she is mine now. She and Harper are my family.

Her long-lashed eyes grow heavy again and Harper turns onto her side just enough that Morgan snuggles in tight between us.

With her hands unable to sign, Harper looks at me and the events of the day and the pain and anxiety in her heart are evident without a word. So is her love.

Her best friend was murdered at the hands of her own husband today.

That same husband kidnapped her and was moments from killing her too.

She became a mother and she has no idea where to even begin with this. Not to mention, all of Morgan's things were lost in the fire today and we'll be starting from scratch.

Becoming a fiancée today wasn't done in the most romantic fashion, but at least she knows she's not alone.

I'm here for her.

Always will be.

EPILOGUE

S*ix months later…*

The colors on the monitor in front of us begin to slow dance across the screen as Morgan's favorite song comes to an end.

"Blackbird," my namesake, is her go-to.

Shortly after she became ours, my visual tuner came into my life thanks to Harper. Using it along with the vibrations through the floor or the six-string against my chest I'm playing and singing again, and Morgan loves it. "Blackbird" is the song we use on those nights when she doesn't seem to be able to settle.

The first couple weeks were a hard adjustment for all three of us. Harper was shell-shocked from the events of October nineteenth. Finding the balance of mourning the loss of Liza yet being strong enough to care for Liza's daughter was a struggle.

Morgan may have only been six months old but she was still nursing and it was clear she had a close bond with her mother. She cried day and night and more times than I care to remember I would find Harper rocking a hysterical Morgan as she sobbed unstoppable tears all over herself and the baby.

For me, the healing from my wound was inconsequential compared to the twisting of my heart watching Harper in such a state. I did everything I could to help with the baby, but Harper found it hard to let anyone step in and help. Fiercely protective and subconsciously guilt-ridden she made it her life's mission to take care of Morgan.

One morning when Harper was taking a shower—one of the rare occasions she would let me watch the baby on my own—I started singing "Blackbird" to Morgan. Within seconds, the vibration from her crying into my shoulder changed to short stuttering breaths as her wailing turned to sniffles and before long, she calmed and fell asleep in my arms. Petrified to wake her, I kept singing the song on a loop. Harper's mouth fell open when she found us in the spare bedroom, now a make-shift nursery. After singing the song through a couple more times, the two of us tiptoed to the newly assembled crib, laid her down and left the room with her baby monitor in hand.

She slept for five hours. Five hours. We napped. It was a miracle.

Five hours later we packed her up in her brand-new baby seat and set out to purchase her a musical attachment for her crib. We ended up with a little fish tank that played, what Harper described as the song flower girls walked down the aisle to at a wedding, but not before having our asses handed to us by the supposed *easy to open* stroller. By the time we got the stroller put together and felt the baby was securely in place, we were both a sweaty mess and ready to throw in the towel and head back home. But, we stuck with it. We bought our musical fish tank and other baby provisions and proceeded to have our asses handed to us once again. I'm not quite sure the stroller was completely folded down when we threw up our hands and shoved it in the back seat of my king cab, but it was good enough.

Yep, those first couple weeks felt insurmountable, but here we are. Six months later, the day after celebrating Morgan's first birthday, Harper and I are singing "Blackbird" to our content little nugget, whose blonde hair has finally started coming in, as she sways back and forth to the rhythm of the song. The three of us are on the floor, where we spend a lot of our time these days. My back is against the couch while Harper sits between my legs resting her head against my healed shoulder.

When the song ends, I put Eleanor up on the couch behind me so my hands are free to rub Harper's growing belly. Morgan will be close to sixteen months old when her little brother gets here.

It's a lot.

It's fast.

I wouldn't want it any other way.

When Harper's nurse tracked her down in my room to make sure she had her follow up instructions, I was certain I had read her lips incorrectly when she congratulated her on her good news. At first, I thought she must have been referring to Morgan, but that would have been awfully insensitive given the circumstances. The look on Harper's face and the way her hands wrapped around her flat waist when she turned around to face me was all I needed to confirm my translation.

Holy shit.

"Did she just say…are you…Harper, what's happening?"

The news had her gobsmacked and when she spoke, she forgot to sign. I knew what she was saying, but I still looked for clarification. "Harper, are you pregnant?"

"We're pregnant," she signs.

We both look at Morgan asleep on the bed between my legs and then we look at each other and the exhaustion of the day catches up to us when we both burst out in hysterical laughter. We laugh until we cry and have to catch our breath and each other.

"I love you, Harper."

She starts laughing again but manages to sign, "I sure hope so!"

"Freckles, I told you October nineteenth would be a day we would remember forever. I'm just sorry all the good has to come with the sadness of the day."

She climbs back up into the bed and we lay there with Morgan taking it all in.

Now, here we are in our little two-bedroom house on the beach, our little girl playing with her toys and our little boy on the way. We've found our rhythm, that I'm sure will be disrupted once our peanut arrives and we move into our new place, but life is good. It's not the way I planned, and I may not be able to hear Harper's giggle, but I look at it every day.

Months ago, without her knowing it, I recorded my favorite sound and had the sound waves of her giggle tattooed onto my forearm.

Her giggle on my forearm, her compass on my heart and her in my arms.

My home.

My True North.

Blackbird Playlist

In My Blood ~ Shawn Mendes
No Brainer ~ DJ Khalid (feat. Justin Bieber & Chance the Rapper)
Hold Back the River ~ James Bay
I'm Yours ~ Jason Mraz
Happier ~ Marshmello & Bastille
Unforgettable ~ Thomas Rhett
Girls Like You ~ Maroon 5 (feat. Cardi B)
Nice for What ~ Drake
The Few Things ~ JP Saxe & Charlotte Lawrence
Miracle ~ CHVRCHES
Kamikaze – Walk The Moon
Blackbird ~ The Beatles
Sorry ~ Nothing But Thieves
I Like Me Better ~ Lauv
Ain't No Mountain High Enough ~ Marvin Gaye & Tammi Terrell
Be Good To Her ~ Bexar
Soldier ~ James TW
Let Me ~ Zayn
Best Shot ~ Jimmie Allen
Two High ~ Moon Taxi
Get Back ~ The Beatles
Falling ~ Mansionair
You Got Me ~ Olivia Lane

ACKNOWLEDGMENTS

Dreams. They say they don't always come true, but this one sure did. When I say this book is a dream come true, I actually mean this literally. You see, months back my amazing husband woke up and told me he had had a dream where I told him what my next book was about. He gave me one sentence. "A couple meets on a tropical vacation, and the next time they see each other he…" That was it. Let the journey begin! My husband is my best friend and partner in crime. In fact, he was so involved in this project that when we took a seventeen-hour road trip (each way), I read what I had already written to him out loud. On the way back, I read him the new chapters I had written on our vacation and he gave his input. I may have written this book, but I can't help but feel it's our book. I am one lucky girl, I know. I couldn't love him and our adorable son more.

There are so many people who make the life of an indie author possible and at the top of that list are the readers. Readers make this world go 'round, and I couldn't love and appreciate you more. Bloggers, what would I do without you? Thank you for sharing your love of books, for your reviews and all of your unending support.

Allison, the best BETA this girl could ask for. You dropped everything and plowed through the book, and I cannot thank you enough. So glad I have you to share my cake pops with. #BBC

Kristin, my sweet Kristen. Thanks for making it so easy. Thank you for all the pretty things but most of all for being my sounding board and my friend. You are a badass woman and I'm so glad to have you on my team. xoxo

To my TRIBE. Thank you for taking me in and being there when I need your sage advice, a good laugh, and more importantly your friendship. Love you ladies.

To my new little Private Party Book Club family. Love you guys. You are one talented group of crazy authors and I am honored to be in your presence. Thanks for all the laughs and here's to a fabulous 2019!

Ellie at My Brothers Editor, your chill, your guidance, and your flexibility are irreplaceable and I thank you so much!

Tandy, you are the best! Available at a moment's notice, and so good at what you do. Thank you, thank you, thank you!

Christina Manis Westrich, thank you for the inspiration! You're the bomb, lady!

WHAT TO READ NEXT…

The You & Me Series

(A series of Standalone Novels set in the You & Me world.)

Read this three-book series of sweet and sexy standalone novels filled with love, loss, secrets, and sass.

You & Me

More

Something Just Like This

The Gorgeous Duet

A steamy, suspenseful romance about breaking the rules and following your heart.

Gorgeous: Book One

Gorgeous: Book Two

ABOUT THE AUTHOR

Lisa Shelby is a contemporary romance author who calls the Pacific Northwest home where she resides with her husband, their son and two dogs. Reading has been an obsession and writing has been a secret passion of hers. It was that passion that led her on the journey to write a book for her husband. What began as a gift turned into an inspiration of love, and with the encouragement of family and friends the desire to share that love with everyone.

NEWSLETTER SIGN-UP

Don't miss a thing!
Stay up to date with Lisa Shelby news, appearances, sales, giveaways, and new releases when you sign up!

Sign-Up Here:

www.lisashelby.com